SILENT

DAVID MELLON

MeritPress

Published by
Merit Press
an Imprint of Simon & Schuster, Inc.
1230 Avenue of the Americas
New York, NY 10020
www.meritpressbooks.com

ISBN 10: 1-5072-0168-0
ISBN 13: 978-1-5072-0168-8
eISBN 10: 1-5072-0169-9
eISBN 13: 978-1-5072-0169-5

Printed in the United States of America.

10   9   8   7   6   5   4   3   2   1

This is a work of fiction. Names, characters, corporations, institutions, organizations, events, or locales in this novel are either the product of the author's imagination or, if real, used fictitiously. The resemblance of any character to actual persons (living or dead) is entirely coincidental.

Many of the designations used by manufacturers and sellers to distinguish their products are claimed as trademarks. Where those designations appear in this book and Simon & Schuster, Inc., was aware of a trademark claim, the designations have been printed with initial capital letters.

Cover design by Frank Rivera.
Cover images © Getty Images/MG_54.
Interior illustrations by David Mellon.

*For information about special discounts for bulk purchases, please contact Simon &
Schuster Special Sales at 1-866-506-1949 or business@simonandschuster.com.*

For Judith

Part 1

In a circle of oak not far from the river Aisne, in northern France, Coal sat and slept, leaning against a tree for twenty-two years. As the snowflakes changed to cowslips and crocuses, and falling leaves turned to snow once again, he must have dreamed. But when the boy woke him, scraping at the gold watch buried in the palm of his hand, the only dream Coal could remember was about the bottle of cognac. He could still hear it shatter as it fell to the marble floor of the restaurant.

Chapter 1

Restaurant Perséphone Reine
July 24, 1914

Coal gazed across the room at the table full of German officers and thought about starting a war.

Any damned fool could start one. The trick was doing it with subtlety and a little imagination. A war that would be talked about for ages. How passionately it had begun. How tragically it ended.

But of course, one had to make sure it didn't go on too long.

Pulling a worn leather satchel from beneath his chair, Coal opened the flap and removed a bottle from a nest of cotton rags. Pushing dishes aside, he placed it on the table.

No common bottle of brandy, this was a Cognac Grande Champagne, Château de Compiègne, from Napoleon's own cellars. The emperor's eagle, engraved on the label, black as a crow. Sealed ninety-six years ago, the bottle had been sitting on a bookshelf in Coal's house, waiting for this day.

The most extraordinary thing, though, was that in addition to the spirits, the bottle contained one hundred and thirty grams of cyanide. He'd added the poison himself, the day it was sealed.

Brushing at the dust on the bottle's shoulder, Coal looked around the room for his waitress.

• • •

Adi Dahl was hiding beside the hot water urn, tugging at the tight collar of her uniform, cursing Mozart.

"I think it's Mozart," said Adi. "Whatever it is, I hate it."

It was Schubert. The string quartet had been playing him most of the morning on the balcony above the table where the German officers were making so much noise.

"*They* probably like this music, whatever it is."

It wasn't the officers she was referring to, however, but her brothers. The more aggravating her day got, the more she wanted to blame it on the twins.

"The Little Princes," she muttered. "If not for them, I'd be— well, I'm not sure where I'd be, but it wouldn't be in this awful little restaurant, in this awful little country."

Stretching her neck, she yawned and looked up at the clouds painted across the ceiling. Some god or other, in a chariot, was carrying away a nearly naked woman as fat little cherubim showered them in rose petals. A Greek myth? Roman, maybe. She was never sure which was which, though the scene would easily fit any number of Hindu stories she'd heard growing up. The gods were always stealing someone away.

"I wish someone would steal me away. Somewhere, anywhere, other than this—"

"Ting, ting, ting."

"What now?" she said, peeking out of her hiding place. "The drunk young men? Or the—"

Of course. It was the man at table seven. He was tapping a fork against the side of his teacup. "Oh, well," said Adi. "It's not the worst birthday I've ever had. But it is getting higher on the list." She sighed and began making up a fresh pot.

• • •

As soon as the doors had opened that morning, she'd seen him come in. Thirties, early forties, maybe, tall, with a leather satchel tucked under the arm of his overcoat, he marched in and took the table in the corner. Not bothering to remove his coat, he slumped back in his chair and surveyed the room from under the cover of his neglected black curls.

When she presented herself, he started in on how he would like his eggs poached in wine.

"Pardon, *monsieur*," she said. "I only serve the tea and coffee."

"I don't like my waiter," said the man.

This was odd, as his waiter hadn't yet come over to the table.

The *maitre d'*, in his scarlet vest, scooted by. Adi held up a finger to the man at the table.

Chasing down the *maitre d'*, Adi explained her predicament.

"We're a man short," he said peering down his great nose at her. "Take his order." Just as he turned, Adi yawned, again.

"A little sleepy?" asked the *maitre d'*.

She was about to say she'd been up late reading, when she saw the look in his eye.

"Yawn again in front of the customers," he whispered, "and you'll have all the time to sleep you'd like." Dishes fell in the kitchen, rescuing her.

She returned to the table, muttering, "Oh, what I wouldn't give 'to sleep. Perhaps to dream.'"

The man at table seven looked up at her.

"Perchance," he said.

"Pardon?"

"The quote from Hamlet. 'To sleep, *perchance* to dream.'"

"Ah. Of course, *monsieur*."

He looked at her for a long moment and then continued. "Eggs poached in wine, a Riesling from Alsace should do."

Adi had been hired to serve tea; the menu was unfamiliar to her. To make matters worse, the man had bewildering instructions for every dish he ordered: the oysters should be salted and braised, the rabbit served with the head, etcetera. She scribbled it all down as best she could and ran off to the kitchen to deal with the chefs. They didn't like being told how to cook, least of all by a tea girl.

She had other tables to attend to. Most of them were little trouble. "Could you bring coffee after the cheese plate?" "Might the child have a candle on top of her cake?"

The table of women with great big birds on their hats was gabbling on about the trains colliding in Strasbourg the day before.

"Those poor children! *Can* you imagine!"

Happy to change the subject, however, the women were delighted to have a girl from a foreign land waiting on them. They were relentless with the questions.

"India, ma'am," said Adi, as she poured tea. "Two weeks ago, ma'am. Yes, my father also has hazel eyes. Yes, and the dark auburn hair. Thank you, ma'am, very kind of you. Delighted to be here. Such a beautiful country, ma'am."

She finally escaped. "People talk too much!"

Then there were the two young men sitting next to the window.

They might have been seventeen or eighteen. Hard to say as they were laughing like children. Bottles of yellow liqueur were scattered across the table, unaccompanied by any sign of food. One of the young men waved her over.

"*Monsieur?*" she said. They fell about laughing again.

The one with the spectacles—a liqueur stain ruining the front of his beautiful white shirt—held up his hand trying to regain his composure.

The second young man, not as handsome as the first but nearly as intoxicated, composed himself enough to ask, "What my friend, George"—he gestured to the young man in the glasses—"is wondering, *mademoiselle*, is if you might wish—to sail down the Amazon River with him?" This sent them into fits of laughter again.

"Augustin. Stop!" said George, lifting his glasses and wiping his eyes.

Adi's cheeks flushed. "If there's nothing else," she said, turning on her heel.

They called her back, but she pretended not to hear.

"Is this what the men are like here?" she said.

She passed a couple of the other tea girls, but they were no help. They whispered to each other, giggling. Not a surprise; Adi had hardly gotten a word from them in the four days since she'd arrived.

• • •

The German officers, an even twenty with their adjuncts and aides, had come in an hour or so after Coal, but they were more than keeping up. Their table groaned from the plates heaped with pig's knuckle, rabbit, blood sausages, steins of beer, and countless bottles of wine. A surprise, considering how many dishes and bottles the general at the head of the table had sent back. "Won't do!" he shouted, pulling at his extravagant mustache and stamping his perfectly shined boots on the marble floor.

It was past noon now; the restaurant was bustling with chatter and the clink of silver on china. The Schubert had turned to Rossini.

Adi stood next to Coal's table holding the last of the desserts he'd ordered: a chocolate soufflé, searing her fingertips.

He refused to have anyone take away his dishes, so there wasn't an open space on the table bigger than a pack of cigarettes. She noticed a dusty unopened bottle standing in among the mess. Where had that come from, she wondered?

Coal dragged his eyes away from the Germans, looked over at the girl and then at his wreck of a table. Putting his cigarette between his lips, he started pushing dishes aside.

"I could take those for you, *monsieur*," Adi offered, for the umpteenth time. He shook his head and watched the girl put the soufflé down next to the bottle of cognac.

"Not too close to the bottle, *mademoiselle*."

Coal knew the girl's name. Adi Dahl. Fifteen years old. Indian mother and British father, which explained her complexion, as lovely as the rest of her but conspicuous in this part of the world, where any skin color was acceptable as long as it fell between ivory and alabaster. He knew that she and her brothers had shown up in Italy fourteen days earlier to find their grandmother dead of a stroke. The girl was terrified of spiders and afraid of heights, and she often cried when no one was around. He knew this and much more. None of it mattered to him. He had chosen her for two reasons. She was quite pleasing to look upon. And she was foreign. Other than the brothers, whom she didn't seem to like much, she knew no one here. And no one knew her.

He leaned forward and picked up the bottle, tall and fine and black as death.

"*Mademoiselle*," he said. "Would you be so kind?"

"*Monsieur?*"

"You see the gentleman at the head of the officers' table? The one with the large mustache."

"Yes, *monsieur*."

"He's an old colleague of mine. I want to surprise him." Coal held the bottle out. "You have a corkscrew?"

"I should fetch a waiter, *monsieur*, I'm not—"

"No," said Coal. He pushed the bottle into the girl's hands, then leaned over to dig around in the satchel beneath his chair, emerging with a bottle opener. "He'll enjoy this much more from a beautiful young woman like yourself."

He dropped the corkscrew into her apron pocket.

"But—*monsieur*, who might I say it's from?"

"Tell him it's compliments of the restaurant. And, here—" Coal reached into a vest pocket and pulled out two enormous gold coins. "For your trouble."

The coins, thick and old, weren't like any others she'd seen in Europe. She spotted 1786 on the front as he slipped them into her pocket.

• • •

Holding the bottle tight in her arms, Adi crossed the room to the officers' table. The two drunken young men were watching her, the bird-hat ladies as well.

Near the kitchen doors, Adi spotted the *maitre d'* whispering to the waiter from the general's table. Wide-eyed, the man clutched a bottle of wine to his chest, waving the cork helplessly.

Oh, God, she thought, closing in on the officers. They've rejected another bottle.

Standing next to the general at the head of the table, a little colonel, with mean little eyes, was telling a story, something about the Devil's grandmother, talking in a shrill voice and making all sorts of dreadful faces. A few chuckles from the men, but the tale did not seem to be going over well. Limping to the end, the man spotted Adi.

"Did no one teach you not to spoil the end of a story, girl? In whatever little brown-skinned country you washed up from?"

The general glanced over at the girl. Seeing Adi, he turned and studied her more closely. With a bow of his head, he said, "You should have interrupted sooner, *fräulein*. My five-year-old tells a better joke than this man."

The colonel grumbled in response.

"Sit down, Blumbach," said the general. The men at the table laughed.

The colonel glared at Adi, but did as he was told.

Looking at the bottle in the girl's hands, the general asked, "Have you brought us some more sad wine, *fräulein?*"

"Not wine, *monsieur*." Adi held the bottle out. "Cognac, I believe."

He leaned forward and studied the label, an eyebrow rising; his finger brushed across the seal on the top of the bottle.

"N for Napoleon," he said. "And the seal appears to be tight. Where did this come from?"

Adi hesitated, then managed, "From the management, *monsieur*. Compliments of the house."

"Just as I was beginning to think they didn't care for German officers here. Unless," he said, scraping his thumbnail along the edge of the seal, "you're planning on poisoning us all?" He looked up at the girl again.

The men laughed.

Across the room, the *maitre d'* caught Adi's eye. He was holding his hands wide in bewilderment. The general looked over as well and gestured to the man. The *maitre d'* rushed to the table, his hands fixed in prayer.

"Thank you for the cognac, *mein herr*," said the general. "Are we to drink it from our teacups?"

Staring at the bottle, the *maitre d'* needed a second to recover from his confusion. He turned to the waiter at his heel. "Why have you not brought the brandy glasses?" Tears in the man's eyes, he took a look at the bottle and ran for the kitchen.

"I'll have the sommelier come and open this for you, *monsieur*," said the *maitre d'*.

"No," said the general, nodding at the girl. "I want her to do it."

"But—but of course, *monsieur*." He leaned and whispered to Adi, "You'll tell me later where you got this bottle. Can you open it?"

"I believe so, *monsieur*."

The *maitre d'* ground his teeth, but smiling to the general, he withdrew.

Adi had little affection for her father these days, but just then she thanked heaven that he had insisted she know how to open a bottle properly. Slicing through the seal, she peeled it aside and slid the corkscrew in. Popping the cork, she bowed and handed it to the general.

"A hundred years old," he said. "In one piece! Bravo, *fräulein*." The officers hooted and clapped. All but the colonel, who sat there sucking at his teeth.

The general picked up his water glass, splashed its contents into his plate and held it out to the girl. "Let's see what the emperor has left us."

• • •

"A shame about the general," muttered Coal, watching the girl pour. "He's played his part so well."

Coal broke off a piece of his soufflé and popped it in his mouth. He was tempted to stay and watch.

"But there's no sense being here when the police arrive."

He imagined the authorities, for a moment at least, would reckon that the Germans had stumbled upon a bad bottle of cognac. Before long, though, someone was bound to notice the foreign young lady who had opened the bottle. She'd tell a story about the man at the table in the corner. But that would be forgotten quickly enough when they found the vial of poison and the letter tucked away in her cabinet in the back of the servers' area.

He took a quick look at his pocket watch. Satisfied, he clicked it shut, dropped it into his vest pocket, and rose from the table.

• • •

Maybe things are not so bad, thought Adi.

The officers were happy. The *maitre d'* was doing a little dance over by the kitchen. Two gold coins lay heavy in her pocket. That could get new shoes for Xavier and fill the pantry with more than turnips and potatoes. She held the bottle tightly in her arms and thought about how Xander had pecked her on the cheek as he ran up the steps to school that morning.

The general swirled the amber liquid around in his glass, rhapsodizing upon the color. Inhaling the aroma once more, he raised it to his lips, just as the waiter charged over to the table, twenty crystal brandy glasses chiming on his tray.

But the general was unwilling to wait. Waving the man away, he raised his glass again, its golden poison a whisper away from his tongue.

From under the long tablecloth, the little colonel kicked hard against Adi's heel.

Protecting the bottle like a baby, she lost her balance and fell into the general's shoulder. His glass shattered against his teeth. A drop or two on his tongue, but the lion's share of the liquor and cyanide poured down on his medals and his perfect uniform.

Trying to recover her balance, Adi's elbow caught the edge of the waiter's tray. Twenty glasses tumbled, cracking like fireworks upon the table. With a wretched moan from the cello, the quartet stopped playing. The entire restaurant turned to look.

Across the room, Coal watched the girl's heel land on the broken stem of a glass. Her hands opened like wings as she fell, but it was only the bottle that flew away.

Even the cooks in the kitchen heard it shatter into a thousand pieces as it struck the marble floor.

Chapter 2

Adi stood in a puddle of cognac while the broken glass was swept up around her feet. The *maitre d'* reprimanded her, promising appropriate punishment. The little colonel banged on the table and shouted that a mere reprimand would not satisfy them. The general slumped in his chair saying nothing.

Taking Adi by the strap of her uniform, the *maitre d'* marched her through the kitchen doors and pushed her over to the girls' dressing room. "Hurry up," he said, shutting the door. "I've got a restaurant to run."

She leaned her head against the door, speechless at the pace at which her life had turned upside down. She pulled off her apron and uniform and dropped them on a hook. Taking her dress out of her cubicle, she noticed a little bottle and an envelope tucked in the back.

Where did that come from? she thought, pulling her dress over her head.

Before she could look closer, she remembered her tips in her apron pocket. She scooped up a fistful of little brown ones and the two beautiful gold coins: 1786, it read under the profile of, perhaps, a Spanish king.

At least there's this, she thought. The coins clinked in her fist.

"What've you got?" said the *maitre d'*, poking his head through the doorway. He snapped his fingers and held out his palm.

The change went into the tip jar for the tea girls. The gold went into the pocket of the *maitre d'*'s red vest. Xavier's new shoes and the shepherd's pie and pudding they might have had for supper vanished as quickly as they had appeared. The *maitre d'* handed her a paltry ten francs and held open the alley door.

• • •

Leaning against one of the great stone lions guarding the steps to the school, Adi noticed that the buttons on her dress were mixed up. She redid them, but they kept coming out wrong. She slid to the pavement, her eyes welling with tears.

What am I going to tell them? Dismissed. After four and a half days. All because of that stupid bottle of—

Stop it, she ordered herself, wiping her eyes. They're going to be here in a minute.

So what! Let them see me. If it weren't for them . . . I'd . . .

She looked over at the lion's face, staring at her with those big solemn eyes.

She wanted to yell at the boys. At the *maitre d'*. At her grandmother! Deep in her heart, though, she knew who she was mad at.

• • •

Three months earlier, five thousand miles to the east, in the city of Kanpur, India, Adi's father had arrived at her little house unannounced. Her servant, Gita, seated him in the drawing room and brought him his gin and quinine. He attempted small talk, but the woman would have none of it.

"Your daughter will be returning from school soon," she said and left the room.

Adi appeared, pretty and proper in her crisp white blouse, tie, and navy blue uniform. With no more greeting than an incline of her head, she seated herself before her father.

"I have a job for you," he said.

"A job?" asked Adi.

"The boys are nine now. Their mother and I think it's time they go abroad, to a proper school. You're fifteen. It's high time you went as well. I want you to take them."

"Me? Take them where?"

"To Europe, of course. To my mother's house in Alorainn. She's excited to see you. To have you stay with her for a while."

So it was arranged.

• • •

In 1914, the early summer trip from Bombay to Europe by ship could be uneventful, even pleasant. This was not the case for Adi and the twins.

A storm off Arabia. Their ship broke down halfway through the Suez Canal. Xander's trunk was stolen in Brindisi. She and the boys squabbled.

But the greatest blow of all was that instead of being greeted by their grandmother, Adi and the boys came down the ship's gangway to find the Italian polizia and the coroner. Their grandmother, Tillie, had taken the train from Alorainn to collect them, but she had a heart attack in the dining room of the charming little pension, two days before the ship docked.

The woman had come to India years before to visit, when the twins were toddlers and Adi just eight. The boys didn't remember, but Adi certainly did.

The woman had shown up one hot, dusty afternoon, depositing a pyramid of trunks on the steps of the little house in Kanpur, where Adi lived alone with the servants.

"I hope you don't mind," announced the woman, with her shock of white hair and rather terrifying overbite. "I'll be staying with you for a while."

The only explanation she gave Adi as to why she had left her son's home in Lucknow was that "children who can't hold up their side of the conversation are of no use to anyone."

Adi suspected there was more to it than the woman was telling her; she might have been only eight but she already knew better than to believe the stories adults told.

Whatever the reason, for the next four months, Adi had a grandmother. "You may call me Tillie," she said to the child. "I don't need to be reminded of my age every time I'm addressed."

She wore eccentric clothes—sometimes even trousers. And she seemed to take it as her mission to clear up any conventional notions that Adi might have acquired. She informed the eight-year-old, in no uncertain terms, that "nothing good in this world would ever come from men."

Often, she would swoop in and kidnap Adi from school and take her into shadowy parts of the city to search for the bronzes and little paintings of Indian deities she treasured. All the while, she enthralled Adi with stories of her adventures: how she had left her husband, scandalized her neighbors, and fled England to live in Alorainn, the tiny principality in eastern France.

If it sounded like something out of a romance novel, this was appropriate, as romance novels were pretty much the only thing the woman read. Of the many trunks with which she traveled, one was filled to the brim with books. She'd brought along Andrew Lang's "Coloured" Fairy Books for the children. But after Adi devoured those, Tillie began recommending Dickens and Robert Louis Stevenson. Soon it was *Red Pottage* and *Lady Audley's Secret*. When Tillie departed she left the trunk with Adi.

• • •

Adi had spent the first few years of her life with her father and mother, in a house on the banks of the Gomti River in Lucknow, a city in northeast India. That her father was a British soldier and her mother an Indian woman was of no consequence to the child. She remembered they were happy.

Adi's mother, a nurse in the employ of a maharaja in the Northern Territories, had (so the oft-repeated story went) saved the soldier's life after he was found at the gate with a broken arm and a bullet lodged in his left lung, the result of an ambush in the mountains. The doctor was away; the task of attending to the wounded soldier fell to her.

The beautiful, dark-eyed Priyanka Patel, schooled in medicine at the University of Madras, told the soldier he was most likely going to die. Happily, she was mistaken. Michael Stuart Whitachre Dahl recovered his health, but lost his heart. He and Priyanka were married. Adi was born—short for Aditi, meaning "boundless" in Sanskrit. She arrived at the end of June, along with the rains of the monsoon.

Years later, when Adi was seven, Lance Corporal Dahl was back with his regiment in the mountains east of Srinagar when cholera swept through the maharaja's kingdom. With the maharaja's wife and daughters in danger, Adi's mother returned to care for them. Adi stayed with the servants in the house, an arrangement she would become familiar with.

The maharaja's family survived the cholera. Priyanka did not.

By the time word reached Lance Corporal Dahl, he had already missed his wife's funeral. He stayed with Adi for a week, much of the time with a glass of gin in hand, before he told her he needed to get back to his regiment. The next morning, packed and ready to leave, he pulled his gold pocket watch from his tunic and handed it to her.

"But that's the watch Mother gave you."

"I want you to hold on to it for me," he said. "It's my promise to you that I will always return."

Adi hadn't been aware that a promise was required in this regard. She gripped the watch tight in her hands as he rode away.

The visits became less frequent, the excuses for his absence more slight, until for most of the next year, he didn't come at all.

• • •

The city of Lucknow was flooded, but no one was complaining. It was the end of June and after eight and a half months without a drop of rain, the monsoon had finally arrived. Adi woke in the middle of the night to a rapturous deluge; the air, ashen and foul for months, had been restored by an ocean breeze from a thousand miles to the south. Gita did a puja for Indra the god of storms and she and Adi danced in the yard in their nightgowns.

Three days later, Adi returned to find her father's horse hitched up inside the gate and her father sitting on the porch. Despite her umbrella, she was soaked through.

She ran up the steps through the water cascading off the roof. He told her to change into something dry, but seeing the present with a big bow next to him, she gave him a drenching kiss and dropped down beside him on the porch swing. He inquired about her day, letting her ramble on until he interrupted and informed her that he had a new wife.

That day, the captain (now no longer a lowly lance corporal) told Adi a new story. It was not the fairy tale that she had heard as a child.

The part about the beautiful nurse and the brave soldier was still there. She had saved his life. He was grateful. They fell in love and got married.

But as things often are in real life, he said, it's more complicated.

In a perfect world, everyone would have embraced them. A perfect couple. A beautiful child. But in the 1890s, neither India nor Britain was anyone's definition of perfect.

The captain's family opposed the marriage, vehemently. His father, the Bishop of Sodor and Man, took to claiming his son had been killed in action. Vehement was too mild an utterance to express how Priyanka's family felt about her choice. It was as if she had never been born. The British army was no more open-minded.

Tracing his finger around the rim of his glass, the captain said, "After your mother died, I was . . . well, I met a woman. The daughter of my commanding officer."

Feeling foolish now in her dripping clothes, Adi listened to the rain, her fingers wrapped tight around the watch she wore on a chain around her neck. Even with the downpour splashing upon the pavers, she could still hear her father.

"We married and we have twin boys, your brothers. You should see them. Of course you will see them. Soon. I promise."

Adi picked up the present, tore away the bow and paper, and lifted out a lovely cream-colored boater. She looked at the hat for a moment and then flung it through the curtain of rain out into the yard. Pulling the chain from around her neck, she dropped the watch at his feet and ran crying into the house.

The captain's new marriage was a disaster. The only thing he had in common with the general's daughter was white skin. She was as beautiful as a rose in winter and as arrogant and pretentious as her father. Neither of them was ever going to accept a child with brown skin, no matter how bright or beautiful she might be.

To get his family fortune back, to advance his career, there was only one thing Captain Dahl could do: renounce his youthful error and abandon Adi.

• • •

The children began pouring out of the front doors of the school before the second bell had tolled.

Among the multitude of kids, Xavier and Xander, with their wide-set eyes and burnt auburn locks, would have been easy enough to spot. That they were as alike as two sparrows, made it inescapable. Adi dressed them differently in hopes of telling them apart, though they often switched clothes to confound her.

They were surprised to see her.

Dropping his books to the pavement, Xavier clambered up onto the back of the stone lion.

"Sister Charlotte said we weren't to climb on the lions," said Xander.

"I thought you were going to meet us at the park?" Xavier said to Adi, ignoring his brother. "Why aren't you wearing your work clothes?"

"It was slow," she said, looking across the boulevard at the cathedral. "They let us go early."

The boys shared a look. Adi spotted scratches on Xavier's cheek and a bruise under his eye. "What's this?" she asked.

"Nothing."

"Xavier?"

"I told you. It's nothing."

Their father, in the brief time he'd spent preparing Adi for the journey, had let it be known that Xavier had had the "occasional rough patch." *Occasional* was the word he had used.

This was news to Adi: the Little Princes—not perfect?

But other than his fascination with American outlaws and his ability to pick the lock on the cabin door aboard ship, she had seen little evidence to support her apprehension.

"They don't want us here," said Xander.

"Of course they do. They're just—"

"No," he said. "We got kicked out."

"What do you mean, you—"

"I got into a fight," said Xavier.

"And they're expelling you? Did you hurt the other boy?"

"Wasn't a boy," said Xavier. "It was Sister Agnes."

"Xavier! What do you mean?"

He didn't respond. She turned to his brother.

"Sister Agnes," said Xander, "she saw you dropping us off this morning and said mean things about you. In Latin. But Xavier's good with Latin. Almost as good as you. He said things back. Sister Agnes got upset. She went after him with her ruler."

Adi didn't know what to say. She wasn't even sure if this was true. They made stories up constantly. He was all scraped up, though.

She looked over at the school. "You're going to have to go apologize."

Xander slid down off the lion. "She's the one that needs to apologize. Aren't we s'posed to be standing up for our sister?"

"Oh, for goodness sakes, Xavier. I hardly even count as your sister."

"Maybe. But you're the only one we've got."

Adi shook her head. "Get your books. We'll . . . worry about it tomorrow."

• • •

As they walked, Adi reached into her pocket and brought out chocolates wrapped in red foil, marked with the name of her former place of employment. She'd grabbed a fistful of them on her way out the door.

"You said school in the summer was going to be fun," said Xander, unwrapping his candy.

"I lied. It was the only way they'd let you start in the fall. It was hard enough to get them to agree to that."

Xavier looked at the wrapper from his chocolate. "You got fired, didn't you?"

Adi stopped. "I broke a bottle. It was old and expensive."

"Not our most brilliant day, I guess," said Xander.

"Doesn't seem like it," said Adi. "At least I wasn't fighting with a nun."

• • •

For most of her life, Adi had hated the boys, blaming them for taking her father away from her. She had pictured their perfect little lives, the chatty family meals, the birthdays and Christmases filled with presents and laughter. Someone always there, praising them for their accomplishments, drying their tears.

Looking at them now, it was dawning on her that the boys' lives weren't much more of a fairy tale than hers. They knew all too well what being raised by servants was like. Being sent to Europe wasn't a holiday, it was a banishment. Their mother had no more use for them than she did for Adi.

They stood on the sidewalk of the wide boulevard, marveling at the motorcars; in India, you'd be lucky to see two in a day.

Without thinking about it, Adi grabbed them by the hands, shouting, "Hold on!" They ran, hooting and laughing, across the street between fast-moving automobiles. Not until they were safe on the other side did it occur to her that she was holding hands with them. Clumsily, she pulled free.

• • •

At a dizzying height above the street, Coal sat next to a weathered gargoyle on the cupola of the cathedral. The great stone dragon, cracked and covered in lichen, had perched there for four hundred years. It was no surprise that it was loose from its mooring.

The sky had cleared, though more dark clouds were moving in from the north. For the moment, though, the sunlight forced Coal to squint to see the figures on the walkway below. He pushed his shoulder against the gargoyle; the brittle tiles beneath it splintered under the sudden weight.

He stopped.

"Is this the best you can manage?" he said. "She won't even know it happened."

For a moment he considered the idea that dropping a gargoyle upon the girl might be excessive, even for such an excellent bottle of cognac.

But more, it showed a troubling lack of invention for occupying himself for the few days he had before he headed south.

He wiped the dust off his hands. His plan had been wrecked, his bottle broken. But, as he was given to say, "If you don't have a backup plan, you don't have a plan." He'd heard a man say that right before the man jumped to his death. He always wondered if he was being ironic. Or did he simply know something that Coal didn't?

Chapter 3

Three days later

In the moonlight, the half-eaten fig rinds littering the ground were just visible beneath the old tree. A few yards out from the kitchen windows, its roots had buckled the foundation of the rundown little cottage, giving the house a topsy-turvy appearance. All the windows were dark now, the smoke gone from the chimney. The only sound was the crickets and frogs, still exuberant over the afternoon showers.

Coal had been sitting in the tree for so long that a cluster of jackdaws had taken up residence for the night. As he dropped from the bottom branch, the birds burst from the tree and flew away into the fields. A fox, with a mole clutched delicately in its teeth, looked up to watch the shadow crossing the yard to the front entrance.

Coal's hand, ghostly in the moonlight, reached for the door handle. Not locked. The door swung open. The shadow slid into the house.

As he stepped over the threshold, the moonlight through the door illuminated the tiger.

Coal paused, taking in the fearsome eyes and formidable teeth. Stretching out his hand, he tapped lightly upon the nose of the ceramic beast.

He closed the door behind him and looked around the room.

Every nook and cleft was crowded with all manner of curios and bric-a-brac. Animals and masks and sculptures. A porcelain queen on the back of a lion. Buddha, at the feet of Mary. Hindu gods everywhere, with the heads of elephants, a hundred arms, dancing on demons.

Though the only illumination in the room was the pale light coming through the curtained windows, Coal had little trouble seeing as he wandered about. The mantel and the walls surrounding the fireplace were crowded with pictures.

He found one of the girl, five or six years old, a formal studio portrait. She stood between a British officer and a dark-eyed Indian woman. Another, a few years on, showed the soldier with a different woman, this one fair-haired, polished, European. She was holding two matching infants in her lap. The Indian woman was gone, as was the girl.

The chirrup of a bird. Coal looked into a cage hanging beside the fireplace. "Still alive," he murmured.

There were photographs of the grandmother, a couple taken in this very room. There she was at the Egyptian pyramids, another, on safari in Africa. One from India with the girl. The woman appeared to favor men's trousers.

Just as he was reaching for his watch, the clock on the mantel chimed twice.

Coal turned and found his way down the hallway to the back part of the house. He stood between two adjacent doors, the one on his right a few feet farther down the hall. He leaned his head against the door to his left and stood that way, silently tapping his fingers on the doorknob as if he were making up his mind.

"'For the world's more full of weeping than you can understand,'" he whispered.

Then he noticed the small door at the end of the hall.

• • •

Adi awoke.

She was on top of the covers in a long nightgown, with a book open on her chest, a stub of a candle about to gutter out on a side table.

She sat up, looking out at the moonlight on the fields behind the house. She heard nothing but the frogs outside.

They'd come home a few days ago to find the front door wide open and a few things out of place. As far as they could tell, the only thing missing was a picture of the boys and their father that had been sitting on the mantlepiece.

"What's that?"

There it was, a banging and a cry. She looked at the clock.

"They can't be awake."

Something heavy being dragged on a wooden floor and a voice that didn't sound like the boys! She slipped out of the bed, her book of Italian folktales falling to the floor.

She tripped over packing crates scattered about the room. Grabbing the door handle, she pulled. It wouldn't open.

"That can't be. There's no lock on this door."

Then she heard the boys screaming.

She threw herself hard against the door. It was rickety, like the rest of the house. But Adi was small and slight of build—she couldn't break through. Looking around her in the candlelight, she picked up a wooden packing crate, held it to her chest and ran hard at the door. The panel in the middle cracked. With a second try, the door splintered, and Adi crashed through to the hallway. Pulling herself to her feet, she darted up the hall to her brothers' room. That handle wouldn't turn either.

More cries. She banged hard on the door with her fists.

"Xavier! Xander!" she screamed. "Open the door!"

No reply. Just the sound of a harsh low voice.

She ran to the front of the house and snatched up the iron poker beside the fireplace.

Back down the hall, she swung wildly at the boys' door, leaving long gashes in the wood, curlicues of paint flying—but to no effect.

She smashed at the door handle.

"Open! Damn! You!"

The handle shattered; the bolt and the other half of the doorknob fell to the floor inside. She pushed the door open with her shoulder.

The bed was jammed into the corner, the covers off, the bluebird lamp in pieces across the floor. Brushing bits aside, Adi knelt to look under the bed. Nothing but a sock.

The boys shouting. A scream. But from where?

In the hall, at the far end, the door was open. The cellar door, as far as they knew. It had never been open. They hadn't yet found a key.

The door creaked as she pushed it with the tip of her poker. She could just make out stairs disappearing into a faint light below.

"Why is there any light?" she whispered. "Are they down there?" There was a bump and a rattle from below. Down she went.

It wasn't easy. Each step was cluttered with the overflow of their grandmother's figurines and knickknacks from her travels. By the bottom of the stairs there was hardly a place to put her foot. It got worse.

It had been a mystery to Adi since they'd arrived—where Tillie's beloved novels might be. There was a cupboard full of cookbooks in the kitchen and a stack of fairy tales in the boys' bedroom. But she'd begun to think perhaps Tillie had simply discarded books at every stop, as she had with the trunkful that she gave Adi as a child. Now she knew.

Atop crates and boxes and teetering on old furniture, the books rose nearly to the ceiling on both sides of a narrow corridor going off to the left. She saw some art magazines and a few travel books, but mostly they looked to be novels.

Where the light was coming from around the corner, she heard a skittering and something falling to the floor. Raising her poker, she stepped along the corridor, turning sideways to squeeze through the stacks. A tap tap tap from inside the little room. She leaned forward and saw a lantern perched on a chair.

Wings in her face. Something popped her on the forehead. She spun about swinging the poker, and a pile of books taller than her head came down around her.

From the floor she saw a little bird—their tiny songbird. A thread was tied to its leg, a bobbin unspooling as it circled the room.

"You little mongrels!" cried Adi, pulling herself up out of the mess, banging the poker on the floor. "I am going to throttle you both!"

It took her a minute to reel the bird in, pull the thread loose, and get the little yellow thing back in its cage. In a fury she grabbed up the lantern and started up the stairs.

It wasn't until she was near the door that she smelled the smoke.

Chapter 4

Stumbling up the stairs into the hallway, Adi had to stoop to stay clear of the smoke.

"Xander! Xavier!" she screamed. "Where are you!" She looked into the bedrooms as she flew past.

Ahead of her in the front room, there were flames. Beside the sofa, she saw the kerosene canister from the porch, slashed open, on its side. Fire spread like a river amidst the tigers and gods, touching off everything in its path.

Shouting for the boys, Adi ran outside through the kitchen door, dropping her poker and tossing the birdcage into the hedge. Back and forth she ran, crying and shouting. She found a bucket and emptied the trough next to the old pear tree, but to no avail. The cottage was burning and it was not going to be put out by a girl with a bucket.

Adi stumbled and fell to the ground. Trying to get up, she fell back again, then sat like a child, her legs out before her in the high grass watching the flames consume Tillie's house.

Coal rapped his knuckles on the bench he was sitting on.

Adi scrambled to her feet looking around in a panic. She ran for her weapon. Brandishing the poker before her, she faced the man sitting a dozen feet back from the blaze on a weathered church pew next to a rusty table, lighting his cigarette.

He took a drag and stared at the girl, sodden and muddy, dirt streaked across her face.

"Help me," cried Adi, gesturing at the house. "Something's happened to my—"

Coal reached over to a box of items on the table and lifted out a coffeepot. The fire illuminated his face.

Adi stepped back, too surprised to even raise her weapon. "I—I know you!" she cried. "The restaurant. The bottle . . ."

He poured himself a cup of coffee, dug around in the box and pulled out a glass bottle of milk. He gave it a sniff and poured.

"Where are my brothers?" she yelled at him. Raising the poker again, she shouted, "You will leave me no choice but to use this." The trembling in her hands gave the lie to her words.

"The boys are safe—enough," said Coal. "If you want to hear any more about them, put that down." He pushed the hair out of his eyes with his long fingers and took a sip from his cup. He gestured to the end of the pew.

Adi looked at the house. Flames were coming through the roof tiles. What could she do? The nearest house was far away. She didn't even know who lived there. She sat down on the pew, as far away from the man as she could manage. She held on to the poker.

Coal motioned his cigarette toward the blaze. "I trust I have your attention?"

"*Monsieur!*" she shouted, stamping her foot. "Where are my brothers!"

"Coal."

"What?"

"You may call me Coal. *Monsieur* Coal, if you wish."

"I don't care what your name is!" cried Adi. "Where are my brothers?"

Coal began digging around in the box again. Folded over the side was a dress, a needle and thread sticking out; Adi was in the process of embroidering little flowers on the collar. He pulled the thread from the needle and carelessly balled it between his fingers as he watched the house burn.

"We don't have any money," Adi said. "My father is a soldier. We've only just—"

"Shush. I don't want your money." Coal took another drag on his cigarette and flicked it at the fire. As if on cue, a great flame erupted from the back windows of the house. Perhaps the books in the cellar had ignited.

"Why are you doing this?" Adi asked.

"Doesn't matter," said Coal, shaking off the spell cast by the flames. "I have them, so you're going to do as I say."

He turned to face her on the bench.

"I think we should play a game, you and I. Whoever wins the game"—he snapped his fingers—"gets the boys."

"What are you talking about?"

"So," he said, as if it were decided. "The boys! That's what you've got in the game. What am I wagering, you ask? It's only fair."

He began pulling things out of his pockets. A teaspoon. A wad of twine. A pair of women's earrings. He dropped them onto the table. "The earrings are not bad?" he said, peering down at them. "Little birds, with little diamond eyes. Though that one is missing."

Adi stared at him as if he were out of his mind.

Patting the front of his suit coat he pulled out a little cardboard box closed up with a red rubber band. "Not yet for that," he said. Leaning forward he placed the box carefully upon the table. He continued his search.

From his side coat pocket he pulled out a small jar. In the hard shadow it was difficult to tell what was in it, some dark shape.

"Oh, not you," he said. "Not after all the trouble you gave me." He held the jar right up to Adi's face. "See?" With a scream, Adi jerked back. Some sort of dreadful insect skittered and convulsed within the glass. Coal grinned and slipped the jar back into his pocket.

"Got to be something." His eyes lit up. "Ah. This could do."

From a vest pocket he pulled out his watch and chain.

"This is what you get. If you win." The timepiece glinted gold in the firelight.

"A mere watch for your brothers, you say?" He set the watch down on the table, squaring it just so. "But there's more here than meets the eye. Give me your hand."

Adi shook her head, but before she could pull away, Coal reached over and grabbed her wrist. With his other hand he plucked the needle from the dress on the table and jabbed it into the tip of the girl's index finger.

She shrieked, but Coal held her firm. Dragging her over, he squeezed a drop of blood from her finger and smeared it across the top of the watch.

Adi fell back on the pew, tears of rage stinging her eyes. She sucked at her finger.

"Now," he said, as if nothing had occurred. "Your given name is . . . Adi? Correct?"

Adi said nothing.

"I know more about you than your name, girl."

Holding the watch in his palm, he appeared to be scratching something into the surface with his fingernail. After working at it for a moment, he blew away tiny whorls of gold. Clutching the watch tight in his fist, he closed his eyes, concentrating, whispering.

"We'll start around sunrise. When the clock strikes six."

Coal opened his hand and hung the chain from his fingers, dangling the watch before the girl. He looked up at her.

"Are you sure you want them back? These brothers of yours?" he said, with a cheerless grin. "You don't seem to like them very much. I could drown them for you like a sack of kittens."

Adi glared at him.

"What I mean," he said, "is that there is no going back. Once you—"

"Tell me what you want!" cried Adi, banging her fists on the bench.

"All right then. Once you take it," he said, swinging the watch back and forth like a hypnotist. "It's yours. The game is on."

She thrust her hand at him.

"Until you win. Or lose." He dropped the watch into her palm.

Adi's stomach pitched, as if she'd gone over Joga Falls in a boat. She put her head down, her hand over her mouth. But, just as quickly the lightheadedness passed.

Strangely, when she looked up it seemed, for an instant, as if the man might be in discomfort as well. But he snapped his fingers dismissively and pointed at the watch.

"You'll need to wind it. Every morning."

There, in the pale light, she saw Adi, engraved in elaborate letters on the top of the watch, each letter stained red from her blood. She flipped it over. The back of the watch was decorated with a little bird, a swallow. Circling it were the words: *Tempus fugit.*

"Time flies," whispered Adi.

"So they say," said Coal. "Open it."

She slid her thumbnail under the lid and lifted it.

"But, how . . . ?" On the inside of the cover was a delicate portrait of the boys, with Xander and Xavier written beneath.

"Keep looking."

Adi turned the watch to the light.

It was splendid. Solid and balanced and beautifully made. Except that it wasn't running. The red second hand on the little subdial within the larger circle was fixed and still.

"Click the stem and push against the face. That's right." To Adi's surprise the face swiveled around. On the opposite side, amidst lots of florid engraving, a row of little squares ran across the middle, no larger than baby's teeth, each under a tiny domed crystal.

"This side of the watch," he said, "counts down the time, to the very last second. So what'll we say? How many seconds do you need, Adi? A day's worth? Ten days? A hundred days?"

"What?" Adi looked up at him.

"Surely, a clever girl like you will find them in no time. Doesn't matter." He leaned in and swiped at the watch face with his index finger. Numbers, clicking and whirring, appeared in each of the little squares.

"There. All the time you need. Ah—and lest we forget. Click the stem. Four times." He motioned with his thumb.

Adi complied. On the fourth click, with a little tink, the portrait of the boys popped open. Behind it, there were two gold disks—like pages of a tiny round book.

"I've left you riddles. As is, I believe, traditional in these circumstances."

He didn't elaborate.

Adi rubbed her fingertip against the lines of finely etched type on the discs. She would need better light to read them.

Coal sat back on the bench, scratching at the top of his head with his nails.

"Now that I think about it, though . . . You will be searching for twins. How hard could that be? Not as if I'm taking them to the moon. I think you need something a little more challenging.

"Ah. Here we go," he said, as if he had just thought of it. "While you're searching, you must be"—he leaned over the bench and whispered—"silent."

"Silent?" Adi shook her head. "What do you mean?"

"I'm saying, you'll be doing it—the searching for the boys—without talking. No writing either."

"What?" She stared at the man as if he were speaking gibberish.

"People talk too much, Adi. Don't you think?"

He leaned forward and put his thumb on the edge of the little box with the red rubber band, no larger than a pack of playing cards. He slid it slowly along the table until it sat right before the girl.

Pulling loose the rubber band, Adi lifted the top. With a scream she lurched back.

Cradled in a pool of crimson lay what seemed to be a little finger, like one belonging to a young boy. The light from the fire glistened off the nail.

"I'll hear you speak, Adi. Wherever you are. In a boat in the middle of the ocean. Standing alone in a field. I will hear. And every word you speak will bring you a gift like this. An ear, a toe, a finger. There are so many pieces to send."

"Oh, no no. But you can't . . . expect someone . . . Please, *monsieur*." Tears welled up in her eyes. "Let them go. They're just children." She reached out and clutched at the man's sleeve.

He pulled it away from her. "Ready to give up before you start?"

Adi shook her head, loosing tears down her cheeks.

"Why are you doing this to us?"

Coal looked up at the branches of the elm, his eyes grown dull and cold. "What do you care, Adi?"

He stood up. Straightening his coat, he started walking toward the front of the house. He yelled, "It's simple. Solve the riddles. Find the boys. Keep your mouth shut. You speak or write a word, I take them. If you want out, you have only to say the word. But you know the cost of every one."

Adi looked down at her hands which were clenched hard enough to leave blood where her nails dug in. *Do something!*

Grabbing her poker, she charged after him, shouting, "Stop! Will you—Stop!"

Coal put his hand on the front gate latch, without a glance in her direction.

"I warned you!" she cried as she swung with all her might, striking the man across the shoulder; the hook at the end of the poker ripped a hole in his coat.

Coal pulled the iron from Adi's hands and pitched it into the fire. He touched the gash in his coat and looked in wonder at the blood upon his fingertips, black in the firelight.

The girl struck at him with her fists and then her nails, trying to reach his face.

"Enough!" cried Coal.

He grabbed her wrists behind her and pulled till she was bent backward. His face loomed over hers.

"Don't you EVER do that again!" he cried.

The ground beneath their feet started to tremble, with a groaning of wood and stone, as if the house was rising up on its foundation and then falling back with a grinding thud. The windows exploded, showering the ground with glass.

His arms tight around her, Coal squeezed the girl's ribcage. Adi looked up at the man. Unable to breathe, she managed, "Give me back my brothers."

Staring into the girl's eyes, he shook his head.

"Too late."

Chapter 5

Adi woke up where she had fallen, in the tall grass next to the front gate. She'd been dreaming about . . . something. She couldn't remember now. She opened her eyes. There were larks circling in the sky high above her. The gray clouds were just beginning to blush crimson.

She sat bolt upright.

"Xander. Xavier!" She looked around her.

The man was gone.

So was the house.

In its place were a few charred timbers on a dark square. A slab of the foundation protruded from the ground; the air was stale with the stench of damp cinders.

She caught sight of her nightgown, hanging upon her, torn and filthy. She remembered the finger in the box.

Adi cried hard, heaving and sobbing, until the gold pocket watch in her hand reminded her that she had no time to be frightened or amazed.

She fumbled the thing open—but it was cold and still.

"But what if I wind it?"

She did. It made no difference. The thing sat in her hand like a stone.

She looked up again at the sky, trying to gauge the hour. If it had been an Indian sky she would have been able to tell to the minute what time it was, but this European light was still strange to her. "Don't think it's much after five, though."

Rubbing her arms against the morning chill, she tried to think what to do.

Riddles.

"He said there were riddles!"

Four clicks on the stem opened up the panel behind the portrait. There were the two thin disks.

Holding it close in the pale light, she could make out lines of tiny engraved letters. She read the first riddle out loud:

"Men with no fingers have no time to linger,
when the devil with four knees,
to be free of its own fleas,
must like a witch with no broom,
fall to its doom."

"What in the world?" muttered Adi. She glanced at the other three riddles. Madness. With every line they grew more incomprehensible.

Below the last one, she saw one single line of very small type. It read:

"Clues you can't ignore, you may find the fifth if you plot the four."

"Oh, well," she said. "That makes it all clear."

Much of what she remembered the man saying had to do with how much time she would have to search for the boys. She closed the portrait and remembered how to hold the stem in and turn the clock face around.

Beneath the little crystal squares, there was now a row of numbers—137980800. Like the watch face, the numbers weren't moving either.

"What did he say? That it would . . . count down to the last second. So if these are seconds, how many days does that add up to?" She blew out her cheeks. "I may be good at language. I can't say the same for numbers."

She took up a burned twig from the ground, dropped to her knees, and began doing figures on a paving stone.

She did the whole thing twice. She began to do it again, but stopped herself. She stared at the numbers. Unless she was mistaken, the watch was telling her she had four years, four months, and thirteen days.

She clicked the disks back in place and shut the lid.

"At six, I'm not allowed to speak. That's what he said." She put her head in her hands. "Oh, God! Please let that not be one of their fingers." She felt awful for saying it, though. It was someone's finger in that box. A child's, from the look of it. "But how could he expect me not to speak? Or write? It's mad!" she said, louder, as if to protest the dictate.

She looked around at the wreckage of Tillie's house. "It's not the only mad thing that's happened." She kicked at the ashes.

"Oh, Tillie. I'm so sorry." She looped the watch chain over her head and hung the infernal thing around her neck.

She looked out toward the road. To the right, maybe a quarter-mile distant, she could make out the dark silhouette of the city of Saint Clouet. She had no idea what was in the other direction.

"Where else to start, if not in town?"

There was a crow standing on what remained of the garden fence. He cawed loudly and flew across the road to the roof of an abandoned house. Right beside the gate, Adi saw, there was the birdcage. The little yellow bird began chirping inside.

If that was not confusing enough, neatly folded over the fence was the dress she'd been embroidering. She held it up by the arms and let it unfold. There were no buttons on the sleeves, but other than a few unfinished blossoms, it was presentable.

"Better than what I have," she said, looking down at the disaster that was her nightgown.

With the last bit of water in the trough around back, Adi bathed herself as quick as she could.

She put on the dress, thankful to have some clothes. Though, truly, this was as baffling as anything that had happened to her. This man, Coal. He kidnaps the boys, and burns down the house.

"And then he leaves me a dress."

Back at the front gate, Adi opened the birdcage. The little yellow bird just sat on his perch looking out.

"I know, sweetie. But I think we have to."

Lifting up the hem of her dress, Adi looked down at her bare feet. "Too bad you didn't leave me shoes, *monsieur*."

The bird hopped to the ledge, tweeted once, and flew away.

Closing the gate behind her, Adi ran.

• • •

Under the very same sky, to the east of the city, someone else was waking up.

George was lying in a field on his back, his ash brown locks laureled with thistle. He was still wearing the fine linen suit he'd had on in the restaurant the day before, but it was soiled with grass and covered in morning dew. The yellow liqueur was still staining the front of his shirt. An empty bottle of it was close at hand.

A few feet away, a cow mooed and swished its tail. The huge tulip-shaped bell around its neck clonked as it turned away.

"Yes, you too," George mumbled as he slowly pulled himself up into a sitting position. He groaned and removed his glasses, rubbing his face with his hands, waiting for the spinning to stop.

After a moment, he took a deep breath and climbed unsteadily to his feet.

He patted his pockets.

"Oh, wonderful." His wallet was missing. He didn't seem any more surprised by that than by waking up next to cows.

Across the field, the town was visible through the morning fog. He started walking.

• • •

There was a time, when she was young, that Adi's feet were so tough she could have walked on broken glass.

In Uttar Pradesh in northeast India, where her mother's people lived, paved roads were rare as hens' teeth, as was the wearing of shoes by children. She would spend from spring until well after the monsoon without ever putting on a pair.

After her mother died, however, and she began attending the British Raj school in Lucknow, shoes became mandatory.

She shuddered to think what her mother would say if she could see her running barefoot into a European city.

• • •

Adi dashed up the boulevard toward the center of town, trying to get a clear look at the clock tower. People had begun to appear, opening up shops, heading to work. The motorcars were making their way through the horse manure. As she rushed into the town square, the trolly stopped and discharged more people.

But what good would it do to approach them? What would she say?

Though there might be some sense in asking about twin boys. But who to ask? What had this man done with the boys? Where would he hide them? He said they were safe. God only knows what that meant. But it wasn't likely they would be getting off the trolly.

She could finally see the clock tower, the crown of it, catching the morning light. It was only minutes before six.

She spun around, scanning the square, with only a vague notion of what might be in this part of town.

"The restaurant is, I think—up that way?"

On a side street she spotted a round green sign with white letters: Police.

Charging through the traffic of carriages and autos, she dashed up the block, ran up the steps, and banged through the doors into a quaint station house.

"Is there anyone here! Hello!"

No one was at the desk. She slammed the bell.

"What is it?" said a voice from the back. Adi heard the creaking of a chair.

A plump, sleepy officer pushed through the door from a back room, trying not to spill his coffee. "How can anyone be in such a hurry, so early in the—"

"Please . . . help me? I—"

Trying to catch her breath, Adi thought, How can I put this? That won't make me sound mad?

"*Monsieur*, a man came into our house . . . he took my . . . he set the house on fire and—"

"What?" said the officer. "What are you saying?"

But the only thing Adi could hear was Coal, whispering, "Wherever you are. In a boat in the middle of the ocean. Standing alone in a field. I will hear." Her head filled with images of fingers in boxes and terrible dark things writhing in jars.

The bell in the tower started to toll. "No, no! Not yet!" A sound behind her—Adi looked over her shoulder.

When she turned back, the officer was leaning over the counter staring at her feet.

"What is it? What are you on about, girl?"

She opened her mouth to speak; she tried, but she couldn't get a word out. It was as if her tongue had turned to wood.

The bell sounded: four, five, six.

The officer stared at the dark-skinned girl with no shoes and no voice. "Get out of here, girl. Before I put you in a cell for vagrancy."

Coal's Tale

Beneath the signpost on the road to Regensburg, Germany, Coal stood staring down at the old thief lying in the road amidst shards of broken glass. Though he was dead as a stone, the man's eyes were wide in astonishment. After most of a lifetime preying upon travelers on deserted byways, he had finally picked the wrong man to rob.

A dark drop splashed down into the dust between pieces of glass. Reaching up, Coal found a cut on his forehead where the thief had struck him with his pistol. His fingers came away black and shiny.

As he did every few years, Coal had come to the town of Frauenau, deep in the forest in eastern Bavaria, to visit the glassworks there.

For ages, he'd kept what he called his "bug collection" in little wooden boxes. But he'd never been satisfied with the containers. Eventually, the hinges rusted. And even a hardwood, like an Indian Ebony or African Blackwood, over time, could be clawed through—if the thing inside wanted out badly enough.

But glass, with a good solid stopper or a hinged lid, might last, if not forever, for at least a very long time.

That was what Coal had been carrying under his arm that day. Little jars, a whole crate full, with a brand new design for the seal. He thought them wonderful. The man who'd been waiting at the crossroads all day was not so enamored of them. When he found that Coal—in his fine suit and bespoke shoes—was carrying no gold or wallet, just empty bottles, he struck him across the brow. The box slipped from Coal's arm and crashed to the ground.

• • •

"Damn it."

Wooden hangers clattered as Coal shoved them aside to peer into the back of his wardrobe.

Not one suit remained. He could've sworn at least one was left.

When Coal found a suit he liked he usually ordered a half dozen or so. Going through them all was one of the ways he reminded himself of the passing of time. Though running out of them always seemed to happen at the wrong time.

He pulled off his coat.

"Ow!"

He stuck a finger through the rip in the cloth where the girl had struck him the night before. He'd thought his shoulder merely scraped. But as he removed his shirt he felt cotton threads tear out of a deep gouge. Looking around at his reflection in the wardrobe mirror, he poked at the spot with a finger. "Ow," he said again. The hook of the poker had sliced into the top part of his back. He stared at it for a moment, disconcerted when he saw that it wasn't healing.

Kneeling down, he pulled out the bottom drawer of the cabinet. "At least there are shirts." Taking one, he stood up, and found himself leaning against the cabinet as the room spun around. He pushed his thumb up under his eyebrow.

Teetering around a pile of shoes and stacks of dirty dishes, Coal maneuvered toward his makeshift desk spread on top of a concert grand shoved into the corner of the room. He sat down on his high stool and leaned his head on the piano, waiting for it all to stop spinning.

Recovering, he began to rifle through stacks of documents searching for the name of that tailor in . . . Paris? Luxembourg, maybe? A shoe, serving as a paperweight, fell off the edge, scattering papers and correspondence across the rug. Picking through the remaining pile, he flicked them away across the room one after another, until he spotted a letter with a Zurich return address.

"I should open my mail more often," he said, tearing the end off the envelope. He pulled out the letter.

"August 1911. I reckon Dr. Bleuler thinks I need to open my mail more often, too."

He skimmed the first few lines and then skipped to the end. Dr. Bleuler was suggesting he return to the clinic.

"I like Bleuler." Coal slipped the letter back into the envelope. "He's the only one who ever understood the notion that if you don't have a lot of little wars, you end up with an unmanageably large one. Not to mention, the turtle doves outside my window every morning. So soothing."

Trying to stow the letter somewhere, he looked around, as if only now noticing the clutter. The piano was covered with dishes and ashtrays, piled on top of papers and history textbooks. There was a bucket on the piano bench; a leak in the ceiling had filled it near to overflowing. The rest of the room was no better—random furniture and boxes, fused together with dust and cobwebs. In a birdcage perched on the edge of the piano, Coal saw the remains of two tiny birds nestled together on yellowed newspaper.

Coal reached for his watch, but found it missing, reminding him, again, that this digression was the girl's fault.

He ran the back of his fingers down the keyboard and then played a little melody from something. "Why didn't you drop her dead? Like that thief on the forest road, all those years ago. When was that? On the way to Leipzig, when Napoleon's Grande Armée had been getting itself blown up on the bridges."

He stopped playing and banged shut the fallboard. He couldn't imagine why he'd thought he had enough time for this foolishness. Feeling a bit steadier, he got up.

"Doesn't matter. She—and this idiotic game—will be over and done in a day or two."

He looked out the window at the dawn light gilding the tops of the trees. "I'm late."

Chapter 6

When Adi was a child her family lived for a time near the city of Mathura, where Lord Krishna was said to have resided. Her favorite holiday was Holi, wherein everyone would throw the most wonderful colors of powdered pigments at one another. The tradition was said to have begun when Krishna worried to his mother that he was darker-skinned than Radha, his beauteous goatherd soul mate. Krishna's mother rectified this by painting Radha's face with pigments.

It was the one day of the year when Adi didn't feel as if she stood out so much, darker than the British but lighter than the Indians. At sunset, after all the powder had been thrown, the rainbow-colored children would run screaming into the Yamuna River. Adi liked to walk in slowly to watch the color swirl off of her and fade into the dark water.

• • •

The front door of the house slammed hard in Adi's face. Through it she heard, "I don't know. Some mute girl, peddling a watch."

She opened her mouth to retort, but again, her pulse raced. Her breath caught in her throat. The color drained from her sight as if she might faint.

She had knocked on several doors with the same result. What else could she do? Her head ached with fatigue, but she kept moving.

As soon as the bell tower had struck six, the watch started to whir almost imperceptibly on the chain around her neck. Opening it, she saw the tiny blood red second hand tracing its course. On the other side, the numbers in the little squares across the face, at least the rightmost of them, began ticking off the seconds and the minutes. "What is it, girl?" the desk officer had barked. "I don't have all morning for your nonsense." Unable to contrive the simplest response, she had fled.

• • •

The bell tinkled above the door as Adi entered a bakery. She nearly swooned from the smell of fresh bread.

The shop girl looked up. "Morning, miss. May I help you?"

Adi tore her eyes away from the warm loaves stacked before her and held her watch out.

The shop girl took one look at Adi's bare feet. "Oh, miss!" she cried. "The owner is very strict about beggars. You'll have to leave."

She pushed the silently protesting girl out of the shop. Adi stood outside the door, her cheeks burning with frustration.

• • •

A few blocks to the west, George, having made it into town, was leaning his aching head against a cobbler's window, watching the little man inside doing something to the sole of a boot.

"Now that would be a good way to make a living," George said to himself. "Sit in that chair all day and make shoes. People would drop in. You could talk about stitching or grommets or something. End of the day you could point and say 'this is what I made today.' And there would be a pair of shoes."

Turning back to the street, he looked around at the buildings and tried to get his bearings.

". . . pretty sure it was by the . . ." He started in one direction, then changed his mind and headed in another.

"Damn it, Augustin. You couldn't have gone home tomorrow?"

As he crossed the street he avoided the truck, but nearly collided with a bicyclist.

"Sorry, my fault," he said after.

• • •

Adi stood outside the back door of a little red brick church. She had been politely but firmly escorted out by a no doubt well-meaning, but confused, choir director.

She sat down on the steps and leaned her head in her hand. The watch dangled before her on its chain.

Though Adi knew it was worse than pointless, she was about to break down and go back to her former place of employment when someone cleared their throat nearby.

"Excuse me, miss," said a nicely dressed man, tipping his bowler. "Might I be of some assistance."

She could hardly believe her ears.

Fumbling open the watch, she held it up for the man, pointing out the image of the boys. He stepped closer into the alley and looked at it with keen interest.

"Why, yes!" he said. "I think I have seen these boys!"

Adi looked up at him brightly, but then noticed his shirt collar was soiled.

"Let me get a closer look at that," he said, attempting to take the watch from her hand.

Adi pulled back, perceiving suddenly that his suit was garish and worn. She tried to push past him.

"Give us the watch," he hissed.

In a second he had it, shoving Adi to the pavement.

She scrambled to her feet; the thief was already turning the corner at the end of the street.

Half a block away, George turned a corner only to come upon an alley stacked with wooden pallets and trash. Above him there was a huge, faded perfume advertisement on the side of the building. He looked at the woman's face as if she might tell him which way to go.

He heard the sound of running. He turned. A seedy-looking chap in a bowler was rushing toward him. Farther back was a young lady, coming fast through the traffic in his direction.

With surprising agility, considering his condition, George stuck his leg out as the man passed. Down went the thief, dropping the watch onto the pavement. His hat rolled into the gutter. Cursing at George, he scrambled to his feet and ran away up the block.

George leaned over and picked up the watch.

Adi pushed past pedestrians, and seeing only a man holding her watch, launched herself at him, knocking him down onto the sidewalk. She dropped right on top of George and cocked her fist back in the way someone might if they'd never used their fists.

She caught sight of the thief running away up the street. She looked down in astonishment at the young man holding up her watch.

"—believe this is what you're looking for," mumbled George.

Adi opened her mouth to apologize and then slapped her hands over her lips. George looked even more confused.

She stood up, and with both hands helped the young man to his feet. George handed her the watch.

Adi attempted, through a series of remarkably inadequate pantomimes, to explain herself. The expression on the young man's face told her she wasn't having much success. Though upon closer examination she noticed that he appeared, perhaps, to be unwell.

Still catching his breath, George rubbed his head and said, "Don't mean to be uncooperative, miss. It's just that, it's early and—"

It suddenly occurred to Adi that the young man had been drinking! There was grass in his hair. And his fine clothes—she now could see clearly—had been slept in. For heaven's sake! Were there only thieves and drunkards in this city?

Close to tears, she put the watch chain around her neck, and with a wave of her hand she turned to leave. Another disappointment had taken what little wind she had in her sails.

"I know you," said George.

Adi stopped and looked back at the young man, surprised.

"You were at the . . . Perséphone Reine . . . at the restaurant, yesterday. Was it yesterday?"

She remembered! Him and his dreadful friend. Sailing down the Amazon! There was the yellow liqueur stain on his shirt.

She stumbled and sat down upon a step, her head spinning.

George, brushing his coat off, looked at the young woman.

"Are you all right?"

Staring down at her feet, she studied the scratches and dirt. She began to laugh a little, which turned helplessly to tears.

George rubbed the back of his neck.

"Good work, George," he muttered. Thinking about it for a second, he sat down on the step next to the girl. She flinched and tried to get up, but settled for moving over a few inches.

They sat. Adi wiped at her face with her sleeve, looking thoroughly miserable. George went through his pockets, found a rumpled bill and several coins.

"I've got no idea," George said, "what's going on with you and your—" He gestured at the watch. "And I seem to have misplaced my wallet. But I think"—holding out the coins in his hand—"I've got enough to get us some coffee and bread. And then maybe you could explain how a young woman who can't talk could be so terrible at charades."

Adi, her arms folded, leaned upon her legs and weighed her alternatives.

When she was growing up her father would say, "Use what you have." What did she have? A drunk who slept in his clothes and not a thing else.

She looked over at the young man in his damp suit.

George pushed the glasses up his nose, brushed the hair from his eyes, and climbed to his feet. He held out a hand.

"My name is George."

He didn't volunteer a last name. Adi was hardly in a position to complain.

She reached out a delicate hand, a bit darker than his. He took it and pulled her to her feet. He looked around and spotted a cafe down the block.

"After you," he said. They started walking. The sun was finally burning through the morning mist.

Chapter 7

June 28, 1914

In the city of Sarajevo, thirteen hundred kilometers to the southeast (as the crow flies), one bomb had already been thrown at the automobile that morning. Deflected by the archduke's arm, the grenade bounced off the folded top, and ended up under the car following behind. Several dignitaries were wounded in the explosion. But not the archduke, nor his wife. They were very fortunate. The archduke gave a short speech at city hall, and then changing his plans, headed to the hospital to visit the men who'd been wounded.

• • •

The open car carrying the royal couple backed up in order to turn around, stalling briefly in the process. The crowd scurried out of the way.

"Forgive me, Your Excellency," said the driver. "I should have turned back at the—"

"Damned idiot," mumbled the archduke. "Doesn't even know the way around his own damned city."

The archduke's wife patted him on the arm and continued to wave at the people lining the city street.

"Stop fretting, dear," she said, not minding this at all. Not sufficiently royal for her husband's family, she was rarely allowed to appear at his side for public events. She was also feeling elated because of the child she was carrying.

She stopped waving when she saw the little man with the feverish eyes pull the pistol from his coat. He stepped up to the car that had so conveniently stalled where he stood.

He fired two shots. One struck the archduke's wife in the abdomen, the other sliced through the archduke's jugular vein.

"It's nothing," murmured the archduke, as they died.

• • •

In the days to come when Coal pored, obsessively, over the newspaper stories, he wondered that not one of the reporters had made mention of a man standing across the street, leaning against one of the big windows of Moritz Schiller's Delicatessen, a cup of coffee in his hand.

Well, thought Coal, why should they? That's the whole point. Job done. And no more broken bottles of cognac to cry over.

Chapter 8

The waiter in the cafe was reluctant to seat a young woman with no shoes and a young man who had clearly slept in his clothes. But it was the morning rush; there was no time to argue. He hid them behind a column.

• • •

Perched on the edge of her chair at the little table, Adi practically inhaled her breakfast. Surely, she'd never tasted anything so wonderful in her life as this bread and coffee.

Across the table, George, bleary-eyed, stirred cream into his coffee as he examined the watch. Adi slathered butter on her bread and studied George.

She pointed to her name inscribed on the top of the watch.

"'Adi,'" he said. She nodded. He bowed his head. "Pleasure to make your acquaintance." He sat back and took another sip from his cup and looked at her anew—now that she had a name.

Opening up the watch, he looked at the portrait of the boys with the names below. "And who are these? Xander and Xavier." He glanced up at the girl. "Your eyes. Same tapered chin. Your brothers? Half brothers?"

She nodded.

George signaled to the waiter. When he came over George whispered, "Do you have a little brandy or something you could—?"

Adi almost concealed her look of disapproval.

"Maybe not," George said. "Can I borrow your pen?" The waiter surrendered it, reluctantly.

"As we've established that pantomime isn't your strong suit," said George, "why don't you simply—"

Adi looked at the pen with an expression close to horror and shook her head in distress—which turned to a humiliated blush when she realized the effect she was making. *He thinks I can't write!*

George withdrew the pen. "Well, lots of people can't, umm . . ."

Adi's jaw tightened. George fiddled with his spoon.

"I guess we've whittled it down to Twenty Questions then." George opened the watch up to the boys' pictures.

"All right. We'll start here. Your brothers."

Adi took a breath and nodded.

"Something has happened to them? Your brothers—ran away?"

Adi shook her head.

"Somebody—took your brothers?"

She nodded vigorously.

"What?" he said. "What do you mean, like, kidnapped?"

She nodded again.

"Really? I mean, are you sure they didn't just run off somewhere? When I was kid, it was a weekly occurance."

Adi looked as if she found this entirely credible.

"Okay," he said. "Do you know who kidnapped them? It wasn't that fellow you were chasing?"

No, no. Adi waved her hand dismissively. Pantomimed snatching the watch.

"A thief," said George. "This is . . . quite a morning you're having. But do you know the man who did take them?" She shook her head. "I'm assuming it was a man? One man?"

Adi nodded.

"You've seen him? But you don't know him?"

Yes.

"And this happened when? Today? Yesterday? Day before?"

Adi indicated yesterday.

"And they could be, where? Anywhere?"

She nodded.

"But where are your parents in all this?"

Adi shook her head.

"No parents. You . . . have no parents?" Adi hesitated, unsure how to respond. She waved her hand, indicating, far, far away.

"Relatives? Grandparents, aunts, uncles?"

Adi shook her head.

"Good Lord. Take some of mine. I've got more than enough." He spread some jam on his bread.

"And where is this, far away? Not hearing you speak, it could be any number of places. You might be Italian. Though I wouldn't call Italy far away. From the look of you, I'd guess Indian? Half British, maybe?"

Adi nodded. At least he'd not thrown in Spanish or American Indian. Or Hawaiian. She'd heard all of these since she'd arrived.

"So has this man asked for some kind of . . . ransom?"

Frustrated, Adi chewed on a piece of bread, trying to think of some way to explain.

She couldn't believe it herself. A madman followed them home, took her brothers and burned down their house, then presented her with something that very well might be one of their fingers. And if she speaks a word—more pieces of them will be brought to her, in little boxes!

It wasn't supposed to be like this! This was not the plan! She was going to deliver the boys to Tillie. Thank you very much. She'd catch her breath, make her apologies. And then make her break. To London. To Paris. She'd be a writer. A painter! And she would live a fabulous life, ecstatically alone—for the rest of her life! Far from this heartbreaking, tragic family of hers and these damned damned boys! But here . . . here she was, sitting across the table from this man, his hair full of leaves, holding this accursed contraption in his hand.

Adi, stop.

She put her hands over her mouth as if she'd been shouting out loud. Tears were streaming down her cheeks. What was she doing? Did she have anyone to turn to but this young man?

George sat, watching the storm rage in the girl's eyes.

"Why?" said George. "Why has this man picked you and your brothers?"

She took a deep breath and tried to pull herself together. Why? thought Adi. Because I broke his bottle of cognac?

She smiled sadly and shook her head.

"Are they . . . do you know whether or not they might be in immediate danger?"

She shook her head again.

"No—you don't know? Or no—you don't think they're in immediate danger?

Adi bit her lip, thinking about it. She shook her head again. She just didn't know.

"All right," he said. "Anything else to work with?"

She debated whether or not to flip the face around and show him the countdown clock. It made her head hurt to think about trying to explain that.

Instead she clicked the stem four times. The portrait popped open, revealing the riddles. She handed it to him.

George read one to himself, "'Were there a hundred sons of Alcmene, each one wielding an olive tree—'"

"Oh," he said, "riddles!"

Adi pointed out the three others. He flipped through, read one out loud.

Adi listened. It made no more sense than it had before.

"That's the thing about riddles," George said. "Gibberish till you . . . figure it out." A troubled look crossed his face.

"But what is all this about?" he said. "What is this doing in your—" George stopped suddenly, struck by a preposterous notion. "Did the—did the kidnapper give you this watch?"

Adi stared unblinking into his eyes and nodded. Yes.

George blinked.

"This is"—sounding much more sober—"getting a little complicated for yes or no questions, isn't it?"

He sat back in his chair, studying the young woman.

The bells from the clock tower began to ring. George clicked the riddles shut and looked at the clock. "Oh, hell! Is that what time it is?"

He got to his feet and took the bill and the coins from his pocket and dumped them on the table. Looking uncomfortable, he pulled on his earlobe. "I—I need to be somewhere, so—"

She stared up at the young man. What did she expect? He barely had enough money for coffee, and he seemed to be some kind of drunkard. He didn't even remember her speaking in the restaurant yesterday.

"I'm getting the impression," he said, "that you don't have any place to stay."

Adi stared. Shook her head.

"Well, under the circumstances"—he glanced at the young woman's bare feet—"I think we might have to disregard some formalities here. I'm not as disreputable as I look." He brushed grass out of his hair. "And," he said with a distracted look, "I do, actually, have an automobile around here somewhere. We don't have to walk."

Adi looked a little skeptical.

A bit impatient, George said, "*Mademoiselle.* I hate to be rational so early in the morning, but what were you planning here? You think this man's going to drop your brothers down on someone's front stoop for you to stumble across?"

The look on the girl's face told him this thought had occurred to her.

"All you're going to do is get yourself killed, or worse. Particularly seeing as how you're at something of a disadvantage as far as communication skills are concerned."

Adi looked around, as if some other more suitable alternative might present itself. But there was only this young man.

She reached out her hand. George pulled her to her feet.

Chapter 9

The girl hadn't spent much time in a motorcar. Even operating the door handle had mystified her.

On the other hand, despite how frightened she had seemed when they first got up to speed (they were traveling at over thirty miles per hour) it had taken her no time at all to fall asleep in her seat. Quite a feat considering the wind and noise produced by the open-top vehicle, George's beautiful silver and blue 1913 Vauxhall Prince Henry.

Well, he didn't suppose she got a lot of sleep lately, with all these goings on.

Assuming there was any truth to this crazy story of hers. George adjusted his driving goggles and glanced over at the girl.

Her feet were pulled up onto the seat, her head curled into her shoulder. Though she had tied her hair into a loose knot, it swirled about her face, more auburn than black in the bright sun. She slept like a child, her lips parted, her hands about her face. For the first time George got to see the girl without an expression of anguish or suspicion. She was really rather . . .

He jerked the wheels back onto the road, nearly swerving into the ditch.

Dammit, George! You want to kill the girl?

He kept his eyes on the road, shook his head.

Well, what else was I supposed to do? Just leave her sitting at the table, staring up at me with those big green eyes?

He slowed over a bumpy patch in the road.

Yeah. Well, I probably should have.

George was not entirely unaware of his penchant for getting tangled up in other people's troubles, especially women. Especially when he was bored. And he certainly had been that.

This is all your fault, Augustin! "One more drink before the train." Ha!

He rubbed the heel of his hand into his temple, wondering again how exactly he'd ended up in that field.

I'm just assuming Augustin made it to the station. Might be in a ditch somewhere.

At a milepost rendered unreadable by moss and ivy, George downshifted and turned off the main road.

Thomas will have a fit! Thomas is going to have a fit anyway, I might as well give him something to chew on. As a matter of fact, this might work out pretty well. Something to make lunch tolerable. Maybe.

The car proceeded along a curving road lined with gnarled beech trees and summer green wheat fields.

"Alcmene!" cried George out of the blue. Adi woke, pulled herself up in her seat.

"Sorry," he said, over the sound of the car. "Just remembered something! Greek mythology. Alcmene. She got tricked by Zeus. One of many. Someone's mother. Someone—Heracles! Heracles' mother! Almost positive. I think."

George held his fist to his lips, thinking furiously, gripping the wheel with his other hand. Adi just held on.

"Read me the rest of the riddle," he said. Adi opened her mouth. And then shut it again.

"Right. Forgot."

George, slamming on the brakes, came to a stop right in the middle of the road, startling a drove of sheep dozing beneath a nearby tree.

Adi handed him the watch.

"All right," he said, "I guess we're doing this here." He slid his goggles down and pulled his glasses out of his coat pocket. Opening the watch, he found the riddle and read aloud,

"'Were there a hundred sons of Alcmene,'

"Alcmene!" said George, "Heracles' mother!"

'each one wielding an olive tree,
seeking weeds to be worn,
as naked as a baby born,
t'would not be enough
no matter how tough,
to quarry the beast of stone in the east.'"

Adi looked over at him hopefully.

"If there were a hundred Heracles . . . each one with an olive tree. As a club? He's always carrying a big club. Made from an olive branch? Maybe? Whatever. It wouldn't 'be enough, no matter how tough' to—what? 'To quarry the beast of stone in the east?'"

He tapped his fingers against the steering wheel.

"No wait. The middle part. About 'naked as a baby.'" He moved his glasses down a little to squint at the watch. "'Seeking weeds to be worn.' Weeds?"

Adi pulled at the sleeve of her dress.

"Clothes! Right. Like . . . *Midsummer Night's Dream*. Oberon says, 'weeds of Athens he doth wear.'"

Adi didn't care, just then, if the young man was a drunkard. Or that they were stopped in the middle of the road. It was the first time in two days that she'd not felt as if she were falling down a well. She could have kissed him. She blushed at the thought.

Reaching over, she tapped on the watch with her finger.

"Right," he continued, collecting his thoughts. "Clothes. Seeking clothes. But what did Heracles ever wear but a lion skin?"

Adi nodded.

"So. Even if there were a hundred Heracles, looking for lion skins," he said, "it wouldn't be enough to . . . quarry the beast of stone? How do you quarry a beast? Why is it in the east? East of what?"

Adi watched the sheep all settle back into a lazy slumber beneath the tree. The lion will lie down with the lamb. She recalled the marble lion in front of the boys' school.

She raised her hand, like a schoolgirl.

"Yes?" he said.

Adi considered for a moment, and then held up two fingers.

"Two, what?" asked George. Then he caught on. "Charades. Right. Okay. Two words."

Adi nodded. One finger up.

"First word. How many syllables?"

One finger. She pantomimed a heavy thing in her palm. Threw it. Pointed to the thing.

"Rock?"

Adi indicated close. Almost.

"Stone?" he said.

Adi touched her nose. Right. Two fingers up, twice.

"Second word," George said. "Two syllables."

Adi mimed lying down, hands together on the side of her face.

"Sleep."

No.

"Lie."

Right.

She indicated a surface.

"Lie. Upon . . . ?"

She pushed her hands together.

"Lie. On? Lie-on? Lion!" said George. "First word. Stone. Stone lion! Stone lion?"

Adi pointed to the watch.

"A stone lion," he mused. "Quarry the beast. A big stone lion. In the east. Too big even for a hundred—

"Ha!" he hooted. "Belfort!" he yelled, the sheep scattering again. "The Lion of Belfort!"

Adi held her hands out, questioningly.

"Fifty miles away, north of here," said George, pointing off. "A great stone lion. Like, twenty meters high. Carved into the cliffside. It's huge! The French made it, after the Franco-Prussian War. Belfort," said George, settling down a little.

"So, what does that get us?" he said. "Unless! The answers to the riddles are all places?"

Adi turned to the last disk, pointed to the tiny line at the bottom.

George adjusted his glasses and recited, "'Clues you can't ignore, you may find the fifth, if you plot the four.'"

He pulled at his bottom lip. "'Plot the four.' So if you have four points, on the map, say." He poked at the air, "One, two, three, four. And then draw a cross between them. You get—" he placed his finger in the center—"the fifth."

Chapter 10

After George had started the motor going again and they'd left the sheep far behind, the excitement of solving one of the riddles evaporated. The conversation, what there was of it, faltered.

"Not much farther," George offered. They smiled at each other. Adi pretended to be more interested in the scenery than she was. George picked up the pace.

Past farm and field they flew. Barley and corn and oats, rapeseed and sunflower, still turned out in summer green. Across the valley they were headed toward a mountain range, serrated like a row of teeth, with one great fang rising in the center.

Winding through a small village, they scattered the churchgoers coming out of the front doors. "Sorry, sorry," George said, after, though it only slowed him down for a moment. Adi, by turns terrified and distraught, tried to find something to hold on to.

Where were they going, anyway?

Young women picking cherries, in wide-brimmed straw hats, turned atop their tall ladders and waved as the automobile sped through the orchard.

George finally slowed down, turning onto an arching stone bridge. On the far side, an old sign, nearly covered in morning glory, appeared to read La Maison Chinoise. The Chinese House. What does that mean? she thought.

To their left, she spotted a gated driveway leading to a large, beautiful house with several outbuildings and a verdant lawn. She pointed.

"That's the head gardener's cottage," George said. "We're, umm, going over here." As they came through the trees, he directed Adi's attention to the other side of the road.

Built above the river, leading all the way up to the cliffs, was an amazing assemblage of structures. A huge central house with turrets and domes, elegant steep-pitched roofs, and windows beyond count. This branched off in all directions around cloisters and a campanile to a row of a dozen or so identical residences, the backs of which were right up against the sheer wall of the mountain. It was all surrounded by gardens and vast lawns. And that was only the part she could see; the whole of it, like a small city, was circled by an enormous, high stone wall.

She turned and looked at George. He just grinned.

They sped across the bridge and through towering wrought-iron gates, black with elaborate gold-painted adornments. They zoomed past horses and stables and an ancient, beautiful round brick chapel. Through another archway they pulled onto a cobblestone courtyard backed by an open garage large enough to hold a half dozen automobiles, which it did.

A man in overalls looked up from a shiny orange motorbike with which he was occupied.

"Samuel," said George, killing the engine. "Tell me you haven't been working on that since I saw you?"

"No, Your Grace," he replied, wiping his hands on a rag. "Though it feels like it." He pointed to the light mounted on the front. "The bike is perfect. But I would be grateful to you if you would run this thing over with your car."

"I'm sure you'll fix it, Sam." Samuel didn't look so sure.

Adi turned to George. What had that man called him?

But George was looking up toward the house, at a young man making a beeline toward them down the vast steps.

Slight, in a charcoal suit, with nearly white-blond hair, he looked pleasant enough, though as he got closer Adi could see there was a storm brewing under his brow. It darkened when he noticed that George was not alone.

George held the car door open for Adi. The young man planted himself before the couple.

"Your Grace. *Mademoiselle*," he said, with a small bow in Adi's direction.

"Thomas," replied George.

"Your Grace."

"Thomas."

They stared at each other; Adi looked confused, though that had been her expression since they arrived.

Reaching an impasse, George folded first.

"Oh, for God's sake, Thomas. I'm sorry, all right?"

"You promised, George!" said Thomas. "You only had to make it through the rest of the day!"

"I know, I know!" cried George, "I just couldn't bring myself to face another hour of those pompous, condescending—uh, they have left, haven't they?"

"Yes. Just. After I assured them that they would be informed in the event of your body being found."

"That's funny, Thomas." He leaned to Adi. "Portuguese ambassador. Very unpleasant man."

Back to Thomas, "Anyway, sorry. I know I put you in a bad spot. Augustin suggested we have a drink, to steel ourselves for the afternoon. It ended up being a drink in town."

Thomas looked as though he had no trouble believing this. "And where has *Monsieur* Canclaux disappeared to?"

"No idea," said George, vaguely. "There may have been a train station at some point."

Utterly baffled, Adi looked back and forth between the two men, wondering what could possibly explain the seesawing nature of their relationship.

Evidently having resolved the issue, Thomas turned to Adi.

"Oh," said George. "Thomas, Adi. Adi, Thomas Hast."

Thomas bowed. "A pleasure, *mademoiselle*. Welcome to La Maison Chinoise."

Adi managed a wan smile and waited for George to explain her lack of response.

"Oh, right. The young woman can't talk. Well, at any rate, she isn't talking."

Thomas took this in, along with the young woman's lack of footwear, with remarkable equanimity.

"And, unless I'm mistaken," George continued, "it's Sunday. It is Sunday, isn't it?"

"I'm afraid so, sir."

George said to Adi, "By the way. You're having lunch with everyone. My, um, stepmother and such."

Adi looked appropriately alarmed. Thomas appeared slightly pained, but said nothing.

"Don't worry, she'll do fine," said George.

Suddenly he remembered more important things that needed considering. He said to Thomas, "I'll fill you in on the particulars, but we're going to need to get hold of—what's his name? Lendt, to talk about a missing persons matter. Soon as you can get him here. In the meantime, Adi will be staying with us. For—?"

He looked to Adi. She was at a loss. "For a few days at least, perhaps longer. And, she'll be needing—"

"Of course, Your Grace."

They looked over to see two figures approaching.

"Speak of the devil," said George.

A woman with a tiny dog on a leash and a strapping young man of about twenty in a swimming costume, a single rowing scull balanced on his shoulder, were coming up the stairs from the garden. Spotting George and a visitor, they changed direction and headed toward them.

"I'll take care of it," said Thomas. "If you'll come with me, *mademoiselle*." Adi looked back at George as Thomas led her away. Where was she going now?

"George," said his stepmother as she approached. "Who is that young woman?"

"Hello, Mother. Halick."

George's stepbrother, Halick, wiped the sweat from his short cropped hair and watched as Thomas led the girl up the walk toward the house. The weight of his boat and oars didn't appear to bother him in the slightest.

"Her name is Adi," said George, turning to the duchess. "She's a . . . cousin of Augustin."

"But it appeared she had no shoes?"

"Yes. She has no shoes," said George. Then reconsidering, he said, "Actually, I've no idea who she is."

The duchess studied George from under her shadowed brow.

"She's from India. I met her in town," he said. "She'll be staying for a few days. And joining us for lunch, if that's all right."

The duchess pulled up hard on the leash to keep the dog from wandering into the roses. "Bouton! Stop that!"

"She can't speak, by the way," said George.

"What? What are you talking about?"

"Sweetheart," she said, turning to Halick. "Put that thing away. It's dripping all over the walk."

"Yes, Mother," said Halick. He watched as Thomas and the girl disappeared into the house and then he headed off.

The duchess leaned over to pick up the dog. "Come on, Bouton. Time for your bath," she murmured as she walked away.

Chapter II

Thomas and Adi passed through a seemingly endless number of rooms and passageways on the way to her quarters. The whole time, Thomas kept up a steady monologue about the history of the house and its occupants. He began with the curious name.

In the 1790s, during the Reign of Terror in the French Revolution, when most of the family resided in Paris, the decision was made to flee east to a recently purchased property in Alorainn: a medieval castle that had been reconstructed after the Thirty Years' War. It was referred to in secret as "the house in the east," translated as "La Maison de l'Orient." In time it became La Maison Chinoise, the Chinese House.

This was rather ironic, as over the years, having escaped the Revolution, the family grew less inclined to engage in any sort of risky activities. Not only had none of them been to China, some of them scarcely traveled outside the walls of the estate.

Up a grand staircase they went, through enormous rooms, their footsteps muffled by carpets or tapping upon elaborate wood and marble floors. There were elegant furnishings high and low, and fireplaces large enough for a man to stand in. Everywhere she looked, the walls were covered with paintings, of men and horses and ships and Madonnas in blue.

Somehow, as they moved through the house, Thomas managed, with only the occasional gesture, to organize things. When they arrived at Adi's room, spacious and airy with a huge canopied bed and doors opening onto a balcony, there were maidservants waiting for them. Thomas made introductions, gave instructions, and, with a bow to Adi, left her to their care.

• • •

She sat in her bath drinking tea and eating toast. She looked at her little cup. It was impossibly thin and fine, with delicate pink rosebuds, its tiny porcelain handle in the shape of a braided vine. It might have been the most beautiful thing she had ever seen and it made her feel terrible.

She couldn't stop hearing the boys crying out to her. Coal said they were safe, that they would be fine. What did that mean coming from this man? She clung to the words nonetheless. It was the only thing keeping her from climbing out of her skin.

Listening to the soap bubbles popping about her head, she considered her options.

It wasn't doing her any good to keep knocking on doors, accosting strangers. Much as she hated to admit it, she knew George was right about that.

George.

Those men called him "Your Grace."

What did that mean exactly? This hung-over young man with stains on his shirt. Royalty. It made her realize how little she knew about this place she and her brothers had come to.

Alorainn. It had just been another one of those names on a map, different only in that it was where their grandmother had lived. And in that it was very small—this was endlessly fascinating to Xander and Xavier.

"You could walk across the whole place in a day," Xavier had said. "We've got cities back home larger than this whole country!"

A principality, a man on the ship had called it. Adi was not even sure what that meant. Something to do with a prince? Had she somehow managed to stumble onto the Royal Family of Alorainn? Her eyes opened wide.

Was she having lunch with the Royal Family of Alorainn?

A maid stuck her head in and asked if she was ready to have her hair washed. Adi looked at her helplessly and continued to do what she had been doing for the past hour. She simply nodded, yes.

She'd tried to tell them she was capable of doing these things herself, but they either did not understand her clumsy gesturing or simply chose not to.

No one had washed Adi's hair or dried her after a bath or anything like that since she was a child. Since Mother, most likely. Gita would have just pointed to the towel and told her to do it herself. Adi sighed, missing the little tyrant and her unsmiling steadfastness. She wouldn't lose her head in all this.

After they'd dried her (with towels the size of bedsheets), there were lotions and unguents and clouds of lovely powder.

And the undergarments, the corsets, and the camisoles. She'd no idea they could be so beautiful, so delicate and light. Nothing like the commonplace stuff she was accustomed to.

And they were nothing compared to the dress.

A seamstress came in and made adjustments to the fit. The woman was most kind, and very effusive about Adi's appearance. This only added to her growing concern.

Who was she fooling?! It was all well and good playing dress-up in this room, but she couldn't possibly go outside wearing something like this.

As one of the maids dressed her hair, Adi gazed out of the balcony doors. Beyond the great wall, the countryside, in its endless perfect detail, stretched on forever. It only made her more aware of the absurdity of her task. Two boys, in that—endlessness.

She looked around her room. The Chinese House. Wouldn't they be amazed. Oh, how she wished they were here being amazed. Instead of . . . wherever they might be. Her eyes teared up again.

Stop it! she thought, surprised at herself. You don't even *like* them. All the trouble they've caused. And now look what they've gotten you into.

It doesn't matter. Not like you have any choice. This is your best chance. Do what you have to do.

She caught herself in the mirror, hair piled extravagantly upon her head. Yes, this is torture.

• • •

George sat at the huge round table under the wisteria arbor. He was on time for a change—early, really; only a few cousins were midway around the circle. They waved. George smiled back.

He was considering, as he often had lately, the merits of trying to chase away a hangover with more drink.

"Hair of the dog," as his British friends would say. Though George never knew exactly what the dog had to do with it. He wasn't sure if it worked either, though he kept trying. He'd gotten to be something of a connoisseur of headache remedies.

"Perhaps a small beer." He looked about for a servant, but they were all busy setting up.

George was, despite the dark circles under his eyes, now looking resplendent in a suit of azure—Thomas's idea, to pick up the blue of the wisteria. George sighed, thinking how ridiculous his life was; he would have gone with the gray, picking up what the inside of his head felt like.

The table sparkled in the afternoon sunshine as the family began to take their places, coming in twos and threes, swarms of children being herded away by governesses. They took their seats, chattering away amidst the glasses and the silverware and spectacular vases of flowers.

Cousin Cecil looked as if he might be considering a chair next to George. He took one a few seats down instead, adjacent to an attractive cousin his age, a head taller. One of Uncle Audie's girls, I think, thought George.

• • •

The family (Adi would make it an even forty at the table) loved it when the season and weather permitted them to eat outdoors. This was a recent development; something George's mother's had initiated before she died. Previously, luncheon had been held in a cold, depressing dining room in a section of the house that dated to the twelfth century.

The Sunday gatherings had been happening since April 27th, 1856, to be precise. This was the day that George's father was born, and coincidentally also the day of the funeral of George's grandfather, George I, who had, to everyone's dismay, been reported killed in the siege of the Mamelon, one of the last battles of the Crimean War.

Happily, the funeral turned to celebration when George I walked in the back of the church (at 4:15) just in time to hear his own eulogy and then to hold his newborn son in his arms. Since then, the family had (with the exception of a few weeks in the spring of 1882 when the Audet overflowed) dined together on Sundays.

George complained about the luncheons but, if pressed, he had to admit that he enjoyed the tradition. As much as he had loved being in school in Paris before his father died, he'd ached with homesickness on Sunday afternoons.

Uncle Lionell and his new young wife Cici greeted George with kisses on the cheeks and took seats nearby. Following close behind, his stepmother (with Halick trailing) glanced over at him as she took her place on the opposite side of the table. Looking for the girl, no doubt.

He knew his stepmother wasn't the only one looking. Talk of the young woman he'd brought home would have spread like wildfire through the house. (What? No shoes, no voice!) He knew as well as anyone here that nothing stayed private for long in this place.

Seemed a good idea at the time, thought George, leaning his face into his hands. Something else for them to talk about, other than me ditching the ambassador.

He winced, imagining what his mother would say. ("You know, you're only making it worse, Georgie.") He knew he would never be behaving this way were she still alive. It wasn't the criticism he minded; he would have preferred someone yelling at him for his misbehavior. It was the quiet disappointment that he dreaded. The kindness of people who loved him even when he let them down.

Chapter 12

As Thomas led Adi down the stone steps through the garden, she was wondering if she might get out of all this luncheon business by fainting. She wouldn't have to fake it—her head felt as light and empty as air. It was one thing to sit in a cafe or motorcar and do twenty questions with someone, but with . . . She could see through the greenery into the arbor to the huge round table.

Oh, dear God! There were dozens of them!

Thomas presented Adi under a canopy of the bluest wisteria that, in addition to matching George's suit, also complemented the sash on the delicately pleated white linen summer tea gown she wore. It was high-collared, with long elegant sleeves and fitted to her slender waist; she was grace itself. Her only adornment was the watch and chain around her neck. One might have thought she looked a little nervous and not entirely sure what to do with her hands, but it was barely arguable that 1914 could have seen someone more beautiful.

She balanced on her heels beneath the blossoms. Never in her life had she had so many people staring at her. Definitely not so many in fine clothes and huge hats. Peering around the hedge, she saw several teenage girls, only a little younger than herself, whispering about her. She glanced behind to see if someone had come along after.

She felt rooted to the spot, like the ancient wisterias twining above her head. Might she be allowed to simply stay there like Daphne escaping from Apollo, her arms, branches, growing up into the canopy?

George turned from the conversation he was having on the other side of the table. Adi thought he appeared dumbfounded.

Rising from his chair, he came around the table to her. He gave Thomas a look as he took her by the arm. Thomas inclined his head ever so slightly and looked pleased with himself.

George leaned over to her, as if he were about to say something clever, but hesitated when Adi looked up into his eyes.

"You look . . . lovely," he said.

"George," said the duchess in a clear voice from the other side of the table, "I think it's high time we met your mysterious little friend."

A number of the family members chimed in.

Adi looked pleadingly at George.

"I apologize in advance," he said as he escorted her to the table. "Don't worry, they don't bite," he whispered to her. "Most of them, anyway."

Adi caught a look on the duchess's face. The woman was leaning over, making a comment to her son. The handsome young man didn't appear to respond; he was looking at Adi.

Most of those gathered seemed to have heard that she didn't speak and went out of their way to not ask questions she wouldn't be able to answer with a simple nod or shake of her head. The rest were considerate enough to think her merely shy, as one certainly might be, faced with this many strangers. Mostly, they just welcomed her and told her how lovely she was and how delightful to have guests for luncheon.

The two of them worked their way around the circle, through the endless aunts and uncles, nephews and nieces, grandparents and in-laws until they arrived at the head of the table, and the duchess.

George's stepmother reclined in her chair in a dress the color of an overripe plum, examining Adi from under heavy-lidded eyes.

"And finally," said George, catching his breath, "may I introduce you to my stepmother, Johanna, duchess of Alorainn, and her son Halick."

Adi tried something between a bow and a curtsy, having little idea what was proper in these circumstances. She didn't quite succeed at either. The duchess nodded as if Adi had confirmed something to her. She then proceeded to greet the girl—in nearly perfect Hindi.

When it was clear from Adi's expression that she comprehended the shift in language, the duchess smiled and continued.

"I'm afraid my Indian languages are not what they used to be," she said. "I don't get to use them much in this part of the world, as you might imagine."

Adi could see from the puzzled expressions around the table that she and the duchess were the only ones who understood what was being said. She smiled, unsure how she might respond.

The duchess gave a little trilling laugh. "Trust me, my dear, none of these bumpkins has the slightest clue as to even what language we're speaking. Just keep smiling," she said, as Adi's eyes grew wide.

"I don't know what you're up to, my dear, with your silence and your pretty little dress. I don't care. I simply want to keep our friend," she gestured to George, "from shaming this family any more than he already has. Not that I care what he does, as long as he does it unobtrusively."

"Mother!" said Halick in the irritated tone of a child not being paid attention. "What are you on about? No one has a clue what you're saying."

The duchess turned to the table. "Isn't it wonderful!" she said with a bright smile. "Someone with whom I can practice my Hindi! It was just a guess, of course, but there was something about that lovely brown skin. I knew at least one of her parents is Indian!"

Adi watched in amazement as everyone laughed and looked pleased with the explanation. Everyone except for George, she noticed. Maybe he knew some Hindi, or maybe he just knew his stepmother.

Halick looked at the girl and fiddled with the stem of his glass as if he were considering raising it. He stood up from his chair instead, a thin smile on his face.

"As no one bothers themselves with introducing me, I shall . . ."

The duchess interrupted him, "Darling, you were introduced and now you're keeping all these people from their lunch." Halick sat back down, his cheeks reddening.

Adi reached a hand to the young man. He glanced to his mother and half stood from his chair. A bit awkwardly, he kissed her hand. Adi blushed and took it back.

"Now," said the duchess, looking around the table, "let's find a place for our guest and we can start. How about next to—Albert! He does enough talking for two, my dear," she said to Adi, as if they were old friends. "Albert, would you be a dear and—"

"That's all right, Mother," George said, taking Adi by the arm. "She can sit over here with us."

"Whatever you wish, George," said the duchess, signaling to the servants to start the meal. "Hurry along then. They're pouring the wine. I imagine you're quite thirsty with all this."

Adi could hear George muttering something under his breath. As they made their way around the table she glanced over at him but he wouldn't return her gaze. She looked through the wisteria up at the clouds drifting away in the afternoon sun. Oh, how she envied them.

Chapter 13

Though the crow had been flying a great distance for several hours, it displayed no sign of fatigue. Nor did it show, despite the beauty and variety of the passing landscape, the slightest interest in what was beneath it. At least not until in the distance there appeared a huge estate circled by an equally impressive wall.

As it arrived over the gardens, the crow swung down, attracted perhaps by the shimmer of the silver and crystal on the round table below the arbor. It circled for a time and then fell like a shadow upon the house.

• • •

Turned out, it wasn't only Uncle Albert that did enough talking for two. Even if Adi had been able, she would hardly have gotten a word in edgewise.

Not that she minded. They were odd, this family. But they were all so funny and bright and they seemed to know something about everything. Accompanying the most remarkable feast, the conversation rolled and tumbled across topics with the greatest of ease.

One of George's aunts delivered a scathing critique of Mark Twain's book about Joan of Arc. This led to a disagreement about women's rights, which grew heated upon the subject of Mary Richardson, a British suffragette who had several months earlier taken a meat cleaver to a painting of a naked woman in the National Gallery. This turned into a discussion of hemlines and women's hats for a time, but came full circle back to the Maid of Orleans and the surprising revelation that there were scores of women who had disguised themselves as men to fight in the American Civil War.

As all this was proceeding, Adi couldn't help but notice that the weather appeared quite different on the other side of the table. The duchess conversed only perfunctorily with those around her and seemed to be doing her best to ignore the laughter and cheer coming from the other side. Mostly she fed scraps to the little dog sitting in her lap. The only person over there who appeared interested in her side of the table was Halick. It seemed that every time Adi glanced over, he was staring at her.

• • •

George sat back in his chair and watched the girl. She had her hands to her mouth trying not to laugh out loud at some story of Aunt Elodie's, about her luggage falling into a canal in Venice.

I'd have brought a girl to lunch sooner if I'd have known it would go over so well, he thought. Nobody here seems to mind her not talking.

Though the longer George watched her bright smile and sparkling green eyes, the more he had the feeling that it was unlikely this would work so well with just anyone.

I wonder what her voice would sound like if she were to talk?

Everyone was looking at him.

"What's that?" he said.

"Tell Adi the story about Klimt and your father," said Uncle Henri.

George laughed and scratched at the back of his head and said to Adi, "Just a funny thing, a few years ago in Vienna, at the coronation. Do you know this painter, Gustav Klimt?"

Adi shook her head.

"Austrian man. Always mixed up in some controversy. But he's really great! Amazingly talented." George popped a grape into his mouth and continued. "Well, my father had seen something or heard something about this man that he didn't like. And at the ball after the coronation he got into an argument with someone and yelled out, very loudly: 'Gustav Klimt! The man is nothing but a damned pornographer!'" George did this bit, presumably imitating his father's bearish roar.

Everyone laughed, including George.

"Then my father turned around and there was Gustav Klimt, standing right behind him, having a conversation with the archduke and his wife."

Everyone laughed and groaned.

• • •

Adi watched George as he told his story. This was a far cry from the hung-over young man at breakfast, with the sleepy eyes and the grass in his hair.

She took another bite of some delicious pie with meat and vegetables. Pastetli, they called it. She repeated it to herself a few times so she wouldn't forget.

Glancing about at the faces of George's family, it was obvious. They all adored him. She shook her head in wonder. What must that be like?

Great Aunt Jacquelyn leaned over to Adi and said too loudly, "We have a Klimt drawing in the library! It's quite risqué."

"Guests, Aunt Jackie," said George, loud enough for her to hear. "Behave yourself."

"I'll show it to you later," Aunt Jackie whispered.

"Father had Klimt up to the house a few times," George said to Adi. "Klimt gave him a drawing."

Adi looked confused.

"Oh," said George. "The 'damned pornographer' comment. Well, Father always came around, eventually."

Everyone laughed again.

"Only for you, Georgie," Aunt Elodie said. "You were the only one who could ever get the old man to change his mind about anything."

"He always spoke well of you, though, Elodie," said the duchess from the other side of the table.

"Oh, no," said Aunt Elodie. "I was only saying—"

"I guess I'm just not one of those people," said the duchess, "who can make sport of someone who isn't around to defend themselves. I'm old-fashioned that way."

She tapped at her teacup with her long nails.

"And I'm sure that our guest has not the slightest interest in these sorts of stories. Do you, my dear? Whomever your people might be, I'm certain they have more discretion than to gossip about the departed."

In dismay, Adi looked to George. George inclined his head ever so slightly toward the garden gate. Adi nodded.

"I couldn't agree with you more, Johanna," said George. "I think we've exposed Adi to quite enough for one evening."

George took a last drink of wine and stood.

"Thank you, everyone. A lovely time. On behalf of myself and Adi—"

"George," said his stepmother, "don't you think you could at least—"

He held his hand out to Adi. "Sorry, everyone, afraid we must be going. It's been grand."

• • •

Under the wisteria, they ran up the steps two at a time, giddy in their escape, detouring only to waylay one of the footman carrying a large tray. George snatched up a couple of pastries in his hands and veered toward the great hedge on their left.

"Get the gate," he said as they came to the gap. She pulled an ivy-covered gate open and stepped through, George right behind.

She was surrounded by the shapes of animals: elephants and camels, foxes and bears. Adi looked around in amazement at the splendid topiary garden; the trees and shrubs were a shadow menagerie in the early twilight. A half moon was reflecting in the long pool running before them into the garden.

They leaned against the great hedge and caught their breath. They could still hear, faintly, the sound coming up from the table. Talking about them, no doubt.

After a moment, George said, "I'm sorry about that, my stepmother and all." He looked up at the elephant before them.

"I don't know when she got so—whatever she is." He glanced over at Adi. "She used to be pretty nice, really." He shook his head. "I guess I used to be nicer myself."

Adi smiled to see him there, leaning into the foliage, holding the two pastries in his hands, slightly damaged but still beautiful confections. He reminded her, his hands before him like that, of a statue of the god Vishnu, in a temple by the river where she grew up.

"Here," he said, holding out a dessert. "Sorry, it's a little squished." Their fingers touched as he handed it over. They dropped down on the seat alongside the pool, the marble still warm from the summer sun.

Adi couldn't bring herself to take a bite of her pastry. So beautiful. Everything here was so beautiful.

George wasted no time stuffing half of the dessert into his mouth. He looked over at the girl, just as tears began to spill down her cheeks.

"Oh," he said, trying to talk with his mouth full. "I should not have made you do that."

Adi looked at him through her tears; trying to wipe them away, she only managed to smear chocolate across her cheeks. Then the dam burst. She broke down and began to sob, her shoulders heaving with each breath.

George looked off into the valley. The twinkling lights of houses were coming on one by one, just as the stars were above. He took the last couple of bites of his dessert.

When the crying let up, George pulled out a large handkerchief from his pocket and slid over next to her.

"Here. Give me." He took the dessert from her hands and chucked it into the bushes. "I'll get you another." He dipped the corner of the cloth into the pool and began to clean her hands, first one, then the other. Then he turned her toward him, cupped her face in his hand and began to wipe away the tears and streaks of chocolate.

"You look like a six-year-old."

Adi stared up into his eyes, the chirrup of a thrush and the splashing of the fountain the only sounds. George tucked a stray curl behind her ear and brushed her cheek with his fingers.

Automobile lights flashed up the drive.

"That could be our man," said George. "Come on." He stood and pulled Adi to her feet next to him. Taking her by the hand, they ran for the house.

•   •   •

Coal waited. Inconspicuous in the dusk, he lay on his back, high up on top of the manicured hedge. He watched a bat catching its supper in the evening sky and wished it were so simple.

A rustling below and a figure emerged from behind the bank of gardenia, only a few yards away from where George and the girl had been sitting. It was Halick.

Coal studied the young man as he peered around the foliage, watching his stepbrother and the girl running up to the house.

There was a large man climbing out of his car pulled up under the porte-cochère.

"Who, who might this be, said the owl," Halick whispered. "Who else has George invited to our home today?"

Coal was wondering the same thing. He saw the girl curtsy to the new arrival. He glanced back down at Halick.

The young man was plucking blossoms from the gardenia bush, flicking them to the ground one after another, muttering gibberish to himself. "As the lion lies with the monkey, the dog does the same with the donkey. Bethinks, I think, I think, I do believe, in another moment," he said, more seriously now, "he was going to kiss that girl."

Coal looked back up to the house.

George and Adi were leading the man inside. Halick scraped flowers into the flagstones with the tip of his shoe, devising doggerel rhymes to amuse himself. Satisfied, he wandered back down in the direction of the family table.

Coal dropped from the hedge and hit the ground with a yelp and a curse. It was as if the girl had struck him again. He looked around to make sure no one had heard, leaning on the hedge for a moment until the pain receded.

He found it hard to believe what he was seeing here, what the girl had managed. "She should be lying in the weeds weeping, but here she is—belle of the ball."

He wished he had another finger to send her. He'd gotten that one from a child in the morgue, after the train collision in Strasbourg a few days earlier. He should have taken another. Or an ear!

The girl's fireplace poker, he'd fancied for a moment, it had been poisoned, like a Bushman's spear or a Borgia's ring, sending venom coursing through his bloodstream.

But he knew it was not so. The girl was as artless as a child. There was another cause for his affliction. He rolled his shoulder to ease the ache and went off to find supper.

Halick's Tale

The tiny black salamander with the yellow spots looked up at the boy with large trusting eyes.

"Such a pretty little thing," thought the boy, as he shut the lid on the tobacco box.

He'd attached a bit of rubber tubing to a hole he'd pierced in the end of the box, to let in air. Didn't want the thing to suffocate. What would be the point of that?

The boy walked around all week with his secret hidden away where no one else could find it; in a box, under the ground in the garden, there was a little animal starving to death.

• • •

Since he could remember, Halick had collected secrets, the way children collected stamps or someone like, say, Thomas Hast, collected books of British fairy tales.

Halick knew Thomas's secrets too, of course. Knew he had kissed a boy when he was at school, up at the abbey.

Thomas Hast wrote this down in his diary, which was a foolish thing to do. What's the point of having a secret if other people could find out about it? And people were so careless. They left their private things lying about for anyone with half a brain to stumble across.

He knew all about Cook having been in Clairvaux Prison for five years. Knew about Uncle Marcel and the very young woman he kept in Strasbourg. He knew everything about anyone in the household worth knowing.

Halick would have liked to know his mother's secrets, but she was very good at keeping them. He could learn a lot from his mother. She lied better than anyone he knew.

Particularly, he would have liked to have known about his father.

Halick couldn't remember when he'd realized that his mother was making up all those stories about the man. It would have helped if she'd been foolhardy enough to have a diary or keep letters. But there was nothing like that. She just told the stories, over and over again; how handsome and kind he was; how he had died saving those children in the burning house. Saving children. A nice touch.

Though honestly, he wasn't sure that his mother didn't actually believe the stories she told. It might well be he would never know how his father had died. Not that it mattered. Not that he cared.

Halick never wrote anything down or told anyone his secrets. No one knew about the animals. Or the girls.

In his fourteenth year, as Halick changed from a boy to a strapping young man, it didn't take him long to turn his attention from small creatures to larger ones.

I mean, who could tell if a lizard or a mouse was really suffering? Could you be sure what any dumb animal was feeling?

A couple of years ago, on his mother's birthday, he'd talked the daughter of one of the hired maids into going to play in the old groundskeeper's house. He didn't have a plan; it all just fell into place.

Now, she was frightened. One didn't have to imagine it. It was right there in her eyes. She would have told him anything. Not that she had anything to tell.

The beautiful part was that they'd still not found the body. Hers or the little gypsy girl that he'd picked up on the road and given a ride. He had discovered the perfect place to put them.

He came to know about the lake in the mountains from a teacher, a man, who filled in briefly for his history professor who had taken ill. He didn't remember the man's name but he still had the old picture postcard from Lake Kore that the man had taken from his pocket and given him. He didn't give any of the other students postcards. Only Halick. Clearly, he didn't think less of him for not having a father.

So now, almost his mother's birthday again, here was this girl, this Adi. No shoes and no voice. It was hard not to wonder what secrets she might be keeping behind those pretty pretty eyes of green. He didn't believe for a second that she couldn't talk. She just needed the proper motivation.

Chapter 14

They sat in the library, George and the policeman on the sofa, Adi before them in a chair, her fingers worrying a tassel on the corner of the pillow in her lap.

The only sound was the scratching of Detective Lendt's pencil in his little notebook as he laboriously copied the riddles from the inside of the watch. He kept leaning forward to peer down at the device balanced on his knee. He was uncomfortable sitting in George's presence, but George had insisted on it, and on the cup of tea as well.

Aside from the library in Benares, Adi had never seen so many books in one place, certainly not in European languages. There were rolling ladders to reach the higher shelves and spiral staircases at both ends of the room to get to a second floor.

The space was also a museum of sorts. Along the walls, glass-top cases and beautiful cabinets were filled with all manner of treasures: sculptures, coins, and historical artifacts. The walls between the shelves were hung with strange and marvelous objects: masks and weapons and paintings.

She looked at the detective. In his overcoat, with his head down, he seemed like a great bear. He stopped writing for a second and took a surprisingly colorful handkerchief from his coat and wiped his brow. It was the only color on the man.

Between George talking and Adi nodding yes or no (and the strange gold watch with its picture and riddles), they had imparted as much information as they could to the detective.

He closed his notebook with a snap of the rubber band around it, and clicked the watch shut, shaking his head in consternation at the thing. "*Tempus fugit*, indeed," he said, handing it back to her. She put the chain around her neck.

Finishing his tea, the detective leaned over and replaced the tiny cup and saucer onto the side table. He looked at Adi and George; tugging at his wilted mustache, he puffed his cheeks out.

"Well," he said as he pulled himself to his feet. "It wouldn't hurt if we had more to go on. A last name for a start." He raised a bushy eyebrow at Adi. "Not to mention, addresses, schools . . ." Adi looked contrite.

"But the world is never a perfect place. At least we're looking for twins. That should give us some advantage.

"Good evening, miss," the officer said as he bowed and took Adi's tiny hand in his. "We'll do our best." She squeezed his hand tightly and gave him a hopeful smile.

"But," he said inclining his head to George, "if any additional information should arise—"

George led him to the door.

"I'll let you know immediately, Detective. And thank you for coming all this way. You see why it would have been difficult over the telephone. Now, are you sure I can't get you something before you head back? It's a long drive."

"No, thank you, milord, the tea will carry me. There are some things I want to check on tonight."

"Be right back," George said to Adi as he lead the detective out.

Dropping her head back in her chair, she looked up at the coral clouds painted upon the ceiling, her shoulders dropping a little in relief. Honestly, she could hardly believe these men were taking her seriously; she wasn't sure she would if she were in their place. She slid down and lifted her feet up, examining her marvelous shoes.

Thomas charged through the library doorway, out of breath and clearly agitated. He stopped when he saw that it was only Adi in the room.

"Oh, miss. Sorry to . . . have you seen his lordship . . . seen George?"

"Seen George do what?" said George, coming back in. "Where the devil have you been?"

Suddenly there were voices in the hallway; Uncle Henri and a couple of cousins were running past the library. They spotted George.

"George! Have you heard?"

"Heard what? What's going on around here?"

"Trouble," said Thomas.

Chapter 15

In ten minutes, it seemed that the entire household was in the library: family, servants, staff, many straight from the dinner table, a few already in nightshirts and robes. Adi didn't see the duchess and her son anywhere, though it was difficult to be sure. Everyone was talking at once, and it was impossible to say what they were on about. It was as if she were sitting in the middle of a train station.

"Would everybody be quiet for—everyone, QUIET!"

Adi looked around. There was George standing up on the sofa, yelling above the din.

It took a moment, but the noise settled.

"What is going on here, George?" cried several people.

"Okay, Thomas." George gestured for Thomas to climb up on the sofa next to him. Thomas stayed put on the floor and cleared his throat.

"All right, this is what—"

"Louder!" someone in the back yelled. Thomas continued a bit more forcefully.

"What I've heard—from Uncle Herbert, who's just returned from Basel, and via telephone, from George's cousin, Augustin Canclaux, who is in Paris; around midday today, in Sarajevo, Archduke Ferdinand and his wife were shot. And killed."

The room went dead silent. A large woman next to Adi (Aunt Effie, perhaps), gasped and grabbed the arm of Adi's chair to steady herself. People began murmuring all over the room.

"There are reports," Thomas continued, "of a hand grenade being thrown. But Augustin's understanding is that a young Serbian man fired a handgun, killing the royal couple. Not sure when they died; there are differing reports on that."

"It's 1870 all over again!" someone said.

A pair of sisters, faces covered in lotion, their eyes huge, collapsed onto the sofa. A little man with a tiny dog in his arms reassured the animal that everything would be fine, but tears were spilling down the man's cheeks.

Adi looked around. What was happening? What happened in 1870?

The woman holding on to Adi's chair began to moan and sway. Adi rose to give the woman her seat—the aunt fainted right into her arms.

About to topple under the weight, Adi heard, "Come on, Effie, not just here." George grabbed the woman and danced her over to the sofa, dropping her into a gaggle of other aunts.

The noise level was rising. Arguments were breaking out all over the room. A man in his pajamas started shouting that he had dreamed that this was going to happen. People started weeping.

"Come on," George said to Adi. They elbowed their way through the crowd toward the door.

George tapped Thomas on the shoulder and pointed to Uncle Henri. Thomas grabbed Henri by the arm. The four of them piled out into the hallway, pulling the door shut behind them.

"Good lord!" said Uncle Henri, catching his breath, "Hardly hear myself think in there."

"But, Uncle Henri," said George, "this won't go that far, will it? They're all first cousins, after all."

Who are first cousins? thought Adi. What in heaven's name was going on here? She looked to George and Thomas, pointing to the door.

"You might want to explain to the young lady why everyone is losing their heads in there," said Uncle Henri, his formidable mustache and eyebrows making up for being the only hair on his head.

Adi nodded.

George looked over to Adi. "How much do you know about European politics?"

Adi held her fingers apart, just a little.

"Well—the archduke—the man who got shot—he's the heir to the Austrian throne. Did you know he was the heir? Well, he was in the city of Sarajevo. Which is down south."

"Capital of Bosnia and Herzegovina," added Thomas. "Across the water from Italy. You should start with the Franco-Prussian War," he said to George. "Bismarck, unifying the German states and all that."

"She's confused enough. And that was forty years ago. She wants to know why the archduke—"

"The late archduke," Thomas added.

"—was visiting Sarajevo when he was—" George held his finger to his temple and made a bang sound.

Uncle Henri slapped him on the head.

"I said, explain it—not put on a farce! Some respect, please! Even if the man was a swine."

"You do it then," said George. "It's complicated."

"I suppose it is," said Henri, stroking his mustache. "All right. Somebody get me a drink and I'll try to explain. Come with me, young lady."

He offered Adi his arm and led the way down the hall. The two young men followed.

"Treaties," said Uncle Henri. "It's all about the treaties. All these countries in Europe have agreements to support one another, in case someone declares war on them. That is what's going to cause the trouble!"

"But no one's declared war yet, have they?" asked George.

"Not as far as I know," said Uncle Henri. "But the Germans, and, honestly, everyone else has been talking about it for years."

They came to some stairs.

"Is anybody else hungry?" said George. "I'm starving."

"Didn't you just eat?" said Thomas.

"I guess. I was kind of distracted."

"All right. I'll get the drink for Henri," said Thomas. "But quit it with the garlic. No one wants all that garlic in an omelet."

George looked to Adi. "You didn't eat much at dinner. And I threw away your dessert."

Adi shook her head no, then realized she was hungry. Ravenous, really.

She made a sign with her fingers, a circle and then a cracking motion.

"Good. How do you want them?" George said. "Scrambled? Poached? Henri. How 'bout you?"

They went down the stairs until they came to the kitchen and passed through what must have been an acre of stoves, pitch-black, cast-iron, under a low ceiling.

• • •

While George cooked, Uncle Henri carried on with his discourse, stopping only to take a nip from his cognac. (Adi had hardly been able to look at the bottle.) He'd sat himself down upon one of the stoves, indifferent to the soot on his trousers.

"So you see, young lady, the reason that this business with the archduke is so bad is that because of all the trouble they've been having for the last few years in the south of their empire, Austria is looking for any excuse to go down there and regain control."

George handed her a piece of red pepper. "And the assassination of the heir to the Austrian throne is a pretty good excuse."

"So." Uncle Henri held his palms out. "In this hand, you've got Austria, Germany, and the Ottoman Empire. Maybe Bulgaria. Who knows what Italy will do. Right? In the other hand, you have Russia and France and the British and us, of course. They all"—he made fists with both hands—"have treaties with one another. If Austria declares war with Serbia, everyone will line up on one side or another." He slammed his fists together. "Bam!"

Adi loved this, though she knew terribly little about European politics and history. She remembered when her father used to say "Politics is not a fitting subject for women to discuss." Which made Mother laugh, seeing as she was the one who had taught him everything he knew of Indian politics.

Henri let out a heavy sigh. "The irony, as George was saying, is that the monarchs of all these countries are related—every one! First cousins, most of them." He nodded to their "chef." "Georgie here as well." George flipped an omelet and grinned.

"But why won't that keep them from fighting?" asked Thomas.

Henri took Adi's hand and gave it a kiss and hopped down from the stove.

"Well, that was the idea, marrying all these families together." He swatted at the soot on his pants. "Unfortunately, these days the generals are in charge. They don't care that Queen Victoria was everyone's grandmother."

Uncle Henri took a sip from his glass and shook his head as if, in the saying of it, these things had become all too real to him. With a little bow to Adi, Henri said, "Now, my dear, that's enough of doom and gloom." She smiled and bowed in reply.

George slid the last omelet onto a plate.

• • •

They took their late supper at a long, well-worn table off the kitchen, joining several of the scullery crew. One of them offered to get George a glass of whatever dark ale they were having. George leaned his face against his hand and smiled. "Another time, lads."

He took a bite of his eggs and looked at Uncle Henri. "So, what is going to happen?"

Uncle Henri shrugged. "I'd like to say everyone is going to sit down and work out their differences like adults, but you may have noticed there are precious few of them about. However, I'm betting you and I and a few others are going to need to be off to Paris—tomorrow, next day at the latest."

Adi was sleepy but not so much that she missed this. She looked to George. He was studying his plate.

"We have one too, don't we, Henri? A treaty, I mean."

"That's right, Georgie," he said with little enthusiasm. "Made by your father, with France, when he wasn't all that much older than you are now." Henri nodded to Adi, not noticing the look of alarm in her eyes. "Not that anyone much cares what we do, we are but a flyspeck on the map. Unfortunately, we're a flyspeck just south of Alsace and Lorraine—two territories the French lost to Germany in 1871. The French want them back very badly."

George looked over to Adi. She was trying to be brave, trying not to look as if she thought her problems were comparable to a European war.

But they were—to her.

Somewhere out there, who knows where, the boys were counting on her.

She clutched her watch tightly to her mouth. It was all she could do not to scream and yell. She should be doing something! Anything!

Pushing away from the table, wiping tears from her face, she ran through the kitchen and up the stairs. These ridiculous shoes! She kicked them off. Down the corridor she went, until she found a door leading out into a garden and an orchard beside the house.

She ran through the trees. The moon had long set; the only light was from the fireflies that had come out in force. The leaves and branches whipped past her, until the cool grass and the night air began to calm her.

Coming to the high wall at the edge of the trees, she put out her hands to touch the moss-covered stone. Leaning her forehead against the wall, she heard steps through the grass behind her, slowing to a walk.

George stood for a moment and then came over and leaned a shoulder against the wall next to her.

Adi studied him in the faint light. He lifted his glasses up and brushed the hair out of his eyes. They stood quiet, listening to a cricket fiddle its tune. George reached out his hand and pulled at a loose curl along the side of Adi's neck.

"Bad timing," he said.

She wasn't sure what timing he was talking about. Meeting each other when she couldn't speak? A war starting when she was trying to find her brothers? It didn't really matter. It was all pretty terrible.

She was about to start crying again, though she really didn't want to. George leaned in—Adi saw fireflies reflected in his glasses. He kissed her lightly on the lips, once, and again.

For just a second it all stopped, there was peace and silence, there was nowhere to go, nothing to do, no riddle, no war, no tomorrow.

They looked at each other a few inches apart, sharing the same atoms of air. He was about to kiss her again when they heard Thomas calling through the trees. She put her hand against his chest.

George took her by the hand. They walked back through the apple trees to the house.

Chapter 16

Adi took one more look at the map of France and slammed the atlas shut on the library table. Tiny flecks of dust from the old book drifted up into the last beams of afternoon sunlight.

Damn. Damn.

She'd been sitting here by herself since George left, with nothing to show for it. She tried to concentrate on the riddles but managed only to fall into daydreams of gardens and driving fast through the countryside.

What a fool she was. Thinking that she was anything but an evening's amusement to this young man. Had she forgotten all of Tillie's advice? She could only imagine what her grandmother would say if she could see.

But no matter how forcefully Adi upbraided herself, she went right back to thinking of the night before, her fingers brushing against the moss on the orchard wall.

• • •

When she came down from her room that morning, everything was different.

George and three of his uncles were leaving on the 2:30 train to Paris. They were to meet the following morning with the French and Belgium prime ministers.

The household was buzzing with activity, packing and preparation everywhere she looked. It took her a while to even find George amidst the trunks and paraphernalia.

Something had shifted. What had been delightful and easy between them was now awkward. Nothing was said about the night before. Adi, of course, couldn't say anything anyway, and most everything that George said seemed nervous and nonsensical. There were a million things to do and endless questions to be answered, so any opportunity to recover kept getting interrupted by details.

And then, all of a sudden, it was time for him to leave.

Adi watched as George and his uncles—Henri, Michel, and Andre—said their goodbyes to the family.

What had she been thinking? When did she ever get so cheeky? Kissing a man! A man she had met the day before. To whom she had not even been properly introduced. Adi buried her head in the curtains.

Truth was, she knew little about what real people did, and nothing at all about men. She'd certainly never kissed one before now. Most of her life had been spent in that little house with Gita and Amrit, Indian women from rural villages. Neither ever married. And they were old.

At the British Raj school she'd attended, there were only girls; and being half Indian meant that Adi was left out of the important conversations. There was little for her to go on but the plots and characters of the Victorian novels left her by Tillie. The woman had done her best to fill Adi's head with the notion that the made-up men in those books were the only ones worth bothering about.

• • •

They were all there, gathered on the front drive, George's step-mother and Halick in the fore.

The duchess made a dramatic show of delivering a toast, something about "a farewell to our gallant warriors." Halick leaned up against the railing on the stairs and looked blank, except for the times when he would glance over in the direction of Adi's balcony, as if he guessed she was behind the drapes.

They were all toasting now, raising their glasses. Adi could see George, surrounded by everyone, looking through the crowd for her.

At least, that's what she imagined he was doing.

How could she go out now? Everyone would be looking at her, expecting . . . something.

She shook with exasperation. Yes! Everyone will look. Is that worse than being this much of a coward?

There was a knock on her door. She was considering whether to burrow further into the drapes when the door opened. It was Thomas.

She could tell he had taken in the situation with a glance, the blush in her cheeks telling him all he needed to know.

He inclined his head to the doorway, to inquire with his eyes what she wished to do. It was a language Adi was becoming familiar with. She looked at him imploringly. He crossed the room and leaned in to take a discreet look through the curtains, down at the people on the drive.

"If we go now," he said, "we could make it before they leave." Adi just stared and clung to the curtain.

It occurred to her that he'd said "before they leave." Not Thomas? She pointed to him questioningly. He continued to study the crowd.

"I'm remaining at the house," was all he said.

They could hear the duchess calling, "You're going to miss your train!"

It was too late. George took one last look at the house and then climbed into the back of one of the cars with Henri. Off they went, the gentlemen, with their valets. All except for Thomas.

● ● ●

She tried to stay clear of her preposterously comfortable bed. The library was a better place to work, but it, of course, contained within it a matchless collection of British authors—just the kind with which she most loved to soothe herself. Before she knew it, she was halfway through *Little Dorrit*, every chapter of wasted time weighing on her conscience like a brick.

She took to wandering about the house and the grounds, hoping that movement might help her focus. Or that she might see someone—George or perhaps Detective Lendt—coming up the drive. It was very concerning that nothing had been heard from the detective.

Most everyone she came upon was kind to her.

Cook, the great, burly head of the kitchen, gave her lovely snacks and told her about the time he'd spent as a sailor in India and Ceylon.

Aunt Elodie and her companion, Adelaide, had Adi for tea in their lovely apartments in a great turret on the south wing.

Uncle Lionell's wife, Cici, took her out riding one morning. Not speaking was a little awkward, until Adi realized the woman was more than happy to ride in silence as long as they rode hard and fast. As the child of a cavalry officer, Adi did not disappoint her.

But inevitably it would become too difficult to keep the smile on her face and anxiety would overwhelm her once again. So as courteous and kind as they all were, she didn't remain in anyone's company for long.

Except for Thomas. He checked up on her as often as he could without it seeming as if that was what he was doing. No doubt, George had left instructions, along with all the bits of information he had learned from Adi about the boys and the watch and the riddles.

Though her participation was necessarily limited, Thomas would sit with her in the library and speculate upon the motivations of the kidnapper and ponder the meaning of the riddles: Why would "Jeremiah be quite blind?" How could the "devil have four knees?" Round and round they went.

They did manage to figure out the correct date that the seconds on the watch added up to. Examining a Catholic liturgical calendar, Adi realized that 1916 would be a leap year. This altered her calculations by a day (or 86,400 seconds). The time would run out on the eleventh of November, 1918—not the twelfth. They were excited to get the figures right until they considered the horrifying idea that it might require four and a half years to find the boys.

After a time, Thomas would have to go and Adi would be on her own again. A wave of fatigue would wash over her and draw her back to her room and pull her down into that damnable bed.

She would then wake hours later to find she'd, again, done nothing, which just made her more despondent and want to sleep more.

• • •

This came to an abrupt end, when, on the third day after George's departure, Adi woke late in the morning to find Duchess Johanna sitting in a chair at the side of her bed. The little terrier, in her lap, was eyeing Adi suspiciously.

As always upon awakening, Adi had that instant of panic that she would speak before she could stop herself, so it must have appeared as if she were waking from a nightmare.

The duchess murmured at seeing the girl awake, but didn't say anything for several minutes. Adi sat up in bed, trying her best to straighten her nightgown and brush the hair out of her face.

"I've always been good at languages," said the duchess, apropos of nothing. As if they had been in the middle of a conversation. She scratched her dog's forehead.

"Good at languages, even for someone from Holland. Everyone in Holland speaks four or five. Surrounded by all those countries, you rather have to, you see. By the time I was your age, I was fluent in a dozen different languages. I had a knack, as they say."

Adi nodded, waiting to see where this was going. The duchess seemed lethargic, almost as if she'd been drinking. Though her speech wasn't slurred. She seemed more dreamy than drunk.

"That's how I met the duke," she continued.

"I was a translator for the Danish ambassador at the court of . . . somewhere. Doesn't matter." She didn't bother to finish the thought.

"The ambassador used a great deal of, shall we say, colorful language." The duchess smiled. "George always said he fell in love with me as I struggled to translate." She looked up at Adi.

"Of course, I mean the duke. I'm certain your George could never be accused of . . . well."

She straightened the rings on her hand, appearing to get lost for a moment in the facets of a huge dark ruby.

"I met a man when I was just about your age. Just about . . ."

She put her head back in her chair and gave a little shiver, her eyes nearly closed.

"The one . . ." she murmured, "the one you fall in love with . . . with his eyes, blue as the sea . . . that is the one . . . you end up hating. He'll reach inside and take a piece of you . . . that you'll never get back. And every day you . . . look into the eyes of your child . . . and are reminded of that part. The part of you that's gone . . . and is never . . . never coming back again."

Adi could only stare.

"So you see," the woman said, raising her head and continuing, as if nothing had happened, "I wasn't always a duchess." She said the word as if it seemed preposterous. "There was a time I was a young woman with an occupation, and a child."

The duchess petted her dog and looked over at a little painting of a horse on the wall near Adi's bed.

"I don't know why I'm telling you this. I suppose just to say—I understand how difficult it is in this world for a woman."

For once, Adi was glad to be without a voice. She wouldn't have known what to say. She smiled tentatively.

The duchess didn't smile back.

"That's why I want to give you this." She pulled an envelope from beneath the dog and placed it on the side table.

"I'm sure it's not as much as you'd hoped, but it is . . . substantial, for a young woman such as yourself." She tapped the table with her fingernails and stood. The terrier hopped down.

"I will need you to be gone before they return from Paris." She turned to leave. "Talk to one of your maids when you're ready. I will arrange transportation."

A hundred things crossed Adi's mind. She jumped out of bed, snatched up the envelope and dashed over to the duchess as she was reaching the door. The dog bared its teeth and growled.

The duchess turned and looked at the girl and at the envelope she held out. Adi shook her head.

The older woman's eyes grew hard. She pulled the envelope from Adi's hand. "Have it your way."

"Come, Bouton. Time to go." She left without another glance at the girl.

Adi leaned against the doorway and rubbed her face with her hands. How much trouble was she in now?

Two more days would pass before she was to find out.

The Duchess's Tale

After the funeral was done, after all the heads of state had departed, when she thought she would scream if she had to listen to one more heartfelt condolence, the Duchess Johanna wandered off to find her son.

Passing through the rooms of the obscenely large house—her house now, she thought—she threw aside pieces of her costume, littering the hallway with gloves, cape, hairpins.

She found her son curled up, fast asleep (or pretending to be) in the back of one of his closets where he often built himself a nest.

For a moment she considered joining him; it seemed like a sensible idea to curl up into a ball and hide in a pile of blankets. But she knew he would be distressed by her presence. She couldn't remember the last time he had allowed her to touch him.

She was hardly in a position to complain. When her husband had his rendezvous with a bullet the week before, dying on a pile of leaves in the forest, he did so without any recent memory of her touch.

• • •

Johanna was acting as translator for the Danish ambassador when she first met the duke of Alorainn.

It was not lost on him how deftly she navigated the rocky shoals of the man's use of language, nor how fetching was her figure.

When she was approached by the duke's people to work as translator for a private luncheon, she thought little of it other than that she was pleased to be hired—her finances were, as usual, tenuous.

It didn't take long to notice that no one at the party spoke anything other than French, German, or Italian, all languages in which the duke was perfectly fluent. He took every opportunity to interact with her. It was no time at all before he began to court her more conventionally.

But what was the point—other than the obvious one. She could hardly be seriously considered, being in only the most glancing way of any royal lineage. There are rules, after all.

But the duke was—like this queer little province of Alorainn— an unusual mixture of the traditional and unorthodox. The people of Alorainn did things the way they'd done them for generations, but what they did was as likely as not to be unconventional. The royal family, and the inhabitants as well, thought all this quaint. Johanna considered it undisciplined.

But she was tired of polishing the worn spots on her shoes. She longed for once, not to have money be the last thing on her mind as she fell asleep at night.

And, of course, there was Halick, her strange child, with his dark blue eyes and too-full lips. His father's features, but combining to entirely different effect. A face impossible to read, and hard to trust.

She knew the boy would not be keen on a large family; she herself thought most of them fools. But a father and a brother might pull him out of himself, if it was not already too late.

• • •

But here she was instead, wearing widow's black. Johanna leaned against the window frame and looked out to the twilit garden, fiddling with the glass stopper on a bottle of paregoric that sat atop the cabinet. She pulled it open, gave it a sniff and carelessly took a drink of the opium tincture. The bitter taste of it took her back to her childhood when it was often given to her for an upset stomach.

Johanna finished off the bottle and watched as the light faded to black.

Chapter 17

Thomas charged in through the library doors and found Adi in her usual spot.

"Ypres!" he said.

Adi shut her book and looked up at Thomas. He held up a hand while he caught his breath. Just as he was about to open his mouth, servants began to pile through the doors with big trays, laden with silver serving dishes.

She had been reading about Moses in a big old dusty Bible, trying to figure out the first riddle with the bit about the "wanderers' Father" and the "forty years of thirst." They agreed that it must be something about Moses, but couldn't make heads or tails of the "Jeremiah" reference.

Thomas directed the servants to put the covered dishes on the table before the girl. Adi was thoroughly confused.

"Hold that thought about Ypres for a second," he said.

This was not difficult, as Adi hadn't the slightest clue as to what an "e-pray" might be.

Thomas took a piece of paper from his vest pocket.

"Cook," he said, "sends his apologies for not having any fresh cardamom. And"—Thomas reviewed his notes—"that the . . . paneer is basically ricotta cheese. Am I saying that right? Paneer?"

Adi nodded, and lifted a lid. The scent was ambrosial and took her home in an instant. She picked up a fork and took out a little cube of cheese from the creamy red sauce with the peas and potatoes.

Matar paneer! Not bad. She certainly wasn't going to be fussy about it. Bless Cook for trying. It was the first Indian food she'd had since she got on the boat. She looked under several other silver lids. Rice, raita, and a bread sort of like naan. It's a feast! She gave Thomas a big smile.

"But, hold on," he said. "Before you get started, I've had a brainstorm—about the second riddle."

Adi was all ears. She put the lid down.

"Okay, here," he said, folding his hands together, like a schoolboy reciting.

"Men with no fingers have no time to linger,
when the devil with four knees,
to be free of its own fleas,
must like a witch with no broom,
fall to its doom."

He looked quite pleased with himself.

"All right, now," he said excitedly. "There's a city in Belgium called Ypres."

Adi nodded. All right.

"I remembered," he said. "They have this strange tradition, I don't recall why, they've been doing it forever. Every few years they throw cats off of this great tower in the middle of town."

Adi gasped.

"No, no," said Thomas. "They don't throw real cats anymore—just stuffed cats or something."

Adi spread her hands, questioningly.

"Right. What's this got to do with the riddle? Well, here's the thing." Thomas held up a finger.

"The reason they started to throw the cats off the tower—some time in the Middle Ages, I'd imagine—is, it represented casting out the Devil. And witches and such. So it hit me—'the devil with four knees.'"

Adi clapped her hands to her mouth, then gestured for Thomas to go on.

"'To be free of its own fleas,'—Right?

"'Must, like a witch with no broom'—"

Adi held on to the edge of the table.

"—'fall,'" Thomas said, "'to its doom.'"

Her mouth wide in wonder, Adi sat back in her chair.

"There is one more piece, though," said Thomas snatching up a pen and paper off the desk. "This part is a little odd."

Adi gave him a look as if to say, What about this isn't odd?

Thomas laughed. "Okay, the first line, 'Men with no fingers have no time to linger.'

"The name of the town is Ypres. Or in English . . ." He wrote in big letters on the paper—Ieper! "A capital 'I' looks like a lower case 'l,' which makes the name look like 'leper.' As in 'men with no fingers.'"

Adi sat thinking it through, looking for flaws in the logic. The bit with the capital and lower case was devious, but that seemed perfectly appropriate given its source.

Clapping her hands, she gestured for Thomas to join her. There was enough food on the table for ten.

"I'm afraid you're going to have to have it all to yourself, *mademoiselle*," said Thomas, looking dubiously at the foreign dishes. "I'm—I've got to—"

She heard something in his tone other than reluctance to try strange food.

"I didn't want to worry you," he said. " But I've got a meeting in town with the chief of police."

Adi snapped to attention.

"Not about the boys," Thomas said. "Well, not exactly. It's Detective Lendt. No one has seen or heard from him since he left here."

Adi sat back, a chill, sick feeling wrapping around her stomach, replacing her momentary sense of victory.

She looked to Thomas, questioningly.

"I don't know," he said. "But it is troubling."

Adi got to her feet and gestured that she was coming with him.

Thomas looked down at the table. "You will break Cook's heart if you don't eat this while it's hot. The instant I get back, I'll let you know!"

With reluctance, she let herself be convinced.

After Thomas left, she pondered this new turn of events. Too excited to eat, she found her thoughts turning to the detective.

He hadn't struck her as the irresponsible sort. It was hard to picture him running off with a mistress, or holed up in an opium den. He could have crashed his motorcar, but wouldn't someone have seen it by now?

But what's the alternative? Adi had a horrible feeling that she knew.

She looked at the silver dishes on the table. Not so hungry anymore. But she must eat some of it, so she might praise the meal to Cook later on.

A knock on the door. A maid came in carrying a tray with a single dish.

"Begging your pardon, *mademoiselle*," said the maid as she placed the small silver-topped bowl before Adi. "Dessert."

Adi nodded in thanks as the maid gave a little curtsy and departed with a glance back over her shoulder.

Adi lifted the lid. Oh! Gulab jamun! She took a bite.

She might as well start with dessert.

Carrying the dish and a spoon, she wandered about the room.

She took another bite. The consistency of the little fried spheres was quite good, but there was an odd aftertaste to the syrup.

Not too surprising. Where did Cook even get a recipe for gulab jamun in this part of the world?

She came to the great framed map of Europe hung between the shelves. It was twice her height. In eastern France was the town of Belfort; there was even a little illustration of a lion carved into the mountain next to the name. Looking upward to the north, in Belgium, nearly to the English Channel—there was the city of Ypres. She drew a line in her mind between the two cities. Two more to go.

She reached out her hand to the map and touched the glass, tracing the shape of Alorainn tucked so neatly into northeastern France. She wondered, as she had many times in the last few days, how she'd come to be in such a place.

She imagined herself floating high up in the sky looking down upon the earth, passing over the rivers and mountains.

She tilted her head a little and watched, as first the silver spoon and then her dish slipped from her hand and fell so slowly to the carpet.

Adi followed, but was out before she hit the floor.

Chapter 18

Paris

"Where the hell have you been?" George asked.

George's cousin Augustin stood for a moment in the doorway, grinning. Though wearing clothes from the night before, he was still, as always, impeccably attired. He turned immediately to George's breakfast table.

"Talking with a one-armed man, in front of the hotel," said Augustin, as he looked under lids. He piled a few sausages and sliced tomatoes on a plate and proceeded to open the bottle of champagne languishing in the bucket.

"What happened to what's-his-name's daughter?" George asked, as he tried to figure out how to get one of the hangers out of his traveling wardrobe. "I thought you were bringing her to the—?"

"These little sausages are good, aren't they?" said Augustin.

"But weren't you going to—?"

Augustin looked around at George's accommodations. "Your rooms are nicer than mine. Why is that?"

"All right," said George, taking the hint. He gave up and shoved the suit and hanger into the overfull trunk. "I didn't like her anyway." He attempted to wrestle the suitcase closed.

"Aren't we late for the meeting?" said Augustin. He plopped himself onto George's unmade bed without tipping his plate and champagne flute. Augustin was not a handsome man in any ordinary sense; he had a flat face with close-set eyes, atop a great long nose. And yet somehow with the element of his grin thrown in, the face managed to be more than the sum of it parts. He sat up against the pillows and watched his friend fight with his suitcase.

"Why are you doing that? Where's Thomas?" Augustin looked around, noticing for the first time that Thomas wasn't there.

"I told you, I left him with . . . he's still at home."

"You never go anywhere without Thomas," said Augustin, suddenly suspicious. "You left him with . . . you left him with that girl. The girl who can't talk!"

George said nothing.

"I remember!" said Augustin. "No, actually I don't. Tell me again. I wasn't paying the slightest attention last night. Something about a watch—and a pastry."

"Gus. You're like a sieve. Help me with this damned suitcase. Do you have your car?"

"Of course," he said. "Where are we going?"

• • •

The luggage was dumped into the back of the brand-new red Minerva. George talked as Augustin drove them east across the open French countryside.

"You see, it doesn't make sense," said George over the sound of the engine. "She's reading Charles Dickens? Doesn't it follow that she would be able to write?"

"Maybe," said Augustin.

"I know people who can't talk," said George. "Roman's boys, for instance. They sign. They write notes. They seem . . . more used to not being able. Adi acts as if this condition just happened last week."

"You really need to stop drinking so much," said Augustin, passing underneath a great arching stone aqueduct.

"What? I drink as well as you do."

"I don't think so," said Augustin. "You don't remember, do you?"

"Remember what?"

"You've heard this girl talk."

"What?"

"Not a lot. '*Monsieur*' might have been the size of it."

"The only thing I remember was her walking away."

"We asked her to join us in South America."

George looked pained.

"You don't know," said Augustin, "if anything she's told you is true. Probably after your money; some sort of weird confidence game. It is pretty far-fetched, the not talking, the twin brothers, this watch thing." He looked over. "I do recall her being attractive."

George raised his eyebrows. "Like you wouldn't believe."

"Well, there's that. But, God's sakes. What are you, twelve? You're with this girl for a couple days and you already sound like you did with—what was her name? When you were twelve."

"The worst part is, I hardly said goodbye to her before I left. I don't know what happened to me. I kissed her, the night before, then I sort of . . . panicked."

"Just a kiss?"

"Yeah."

They drove in silence until rain started to come down on their heads. Augustin pulled over as the road widened near a train depot.

They got out of the car and started pulling up the top.

"The generals aren't wasting any time, are they?" Augustin said, looking over at the depot. It was not lost on them that most of the men waiting on the platform for the train were in soldier's garb, carrying their kits.

"That's what we should be doing," said George.

Wiping rain from the end of his great aquiline nose, Augustin looked over at the men on the platform.

"What? That? Ha. You couldn't if you wanted to. The family's not going to let their precious heir go off and get himself shot. Anyhow. A war? Not going to happen."

George looked as if he weren't so sure.

"You heard Petain, the other generals too. They all think we can win a war. 'Done before Christmas,' he said."

"Aren't we supposed to be in that boat going up the Amazon by Christmas?" said Augustin. "You can bring your girlfriend."

They climbed back in, just ahead of the downpour. Augustin pulled out onto the road, skidding as he sped away.

George lifted his glasses up on his forehead and rubbed his eyes, moaning.

"I've run out on my uncles. Again! What is wrong with me?"

"Yeah. Henri's never going to let you forget it."

"I know, I know! You're right. I know you're right. About everything. About being played. About behaving like a schoolboy. The whole thing's preposterous. The riddles, the kidnapper, the not talking—all of it."

He leaned over and slugged Augustin hard on the shoulder.

"Ow! What d'you do that for?"

"'Cause you're supposed to be talking me out of this!" said George. He put his feet up on the dash and slumped down in the seat. "You know, I've never brought a girl home."

"Oh, no kidding," said Augustin. "Anyway, why would I talk you out of it?"

"Because we have a deal."

"Yes, well. I don't know if that's such a good idea for you anymore. Of course, it's bound to end badly. But maybe there's no sense in both of us being cynical and bitter about women, all the time."

George looked over at his friend. "What's happened to you?"

Augustin shrugged and grinned. He downshifted and stepped hard on the accelerator. "I can't wait to meet her."

Chapter 19

It took the glacier a million years to come and go. In its wake it left behind a valley with sheer cliffs, a half-mile deep, and at the bottom a small lake with water so dark and cold that it often had ice until the dog days of summer. Not that one could often see through the constant fog.

Not much had changed here since, other than that someone had been brave and foolish enough to build a road on the cliff-edge high above the water.

The lone gull circling overhead didn't seem to notice the long black motorcar passing below; any sound that came from the engine was swept away by the rising wind. The clear sky, so bright and hopeful that morning, had been overtaken by a summer storm. There'd been another car earlier, but the black one now had the road all to itself.

• • •

Halick drove as someone who was more accustomed to riding in the back. He hunched up close to the windscreen, his hands gripping tight about the wheel, his dark eyes checking the mirrors.

"She's a gentle person, my mother," said Halick. "Most people don't appreciate that about her. How many times have I seen her come upon a dead bird or a rabbit caught in a snare. Her eyes fill with tears. Days later she'll still be going on about it. Of course, she can't afford to show that side of herself. She is a duchess, after all."

Halick glanced into the rearview mirror. Adi, unconscious, was stretched out across the back seat.

He swerved a little as his attention was drawn back to the road. There was a stone bulwark along some of the more dangerous sections, but it was unlikely that it would stop a car of this size.

"Which is why . . . by the bye, firefly," he continued, "I told her not to worry her pretty head about you."

"'I'll put her on the train,' I said to Mother. 'With a suitcase full of dresses and a generous wad of cash in her pocket. She'll forget all about this little adventure of hers and start a new life far, far away.'"

Halick slowed down as he spotted a number of standing stones along the cliffside. Pulling the car into an open patch across the road, he stopped the engine and sat listening to the car's cloth top thrum in the wind. He looked over the back seat at Adi. She murmured, as in a dream.

"Anyway," he said, climbing out of the car, "That's the great thing about my mother. She'll believe any crap I tell her."

Halick removed his suit coat and hung it neatly over the steering wheel.

"You see, Mother's got plans for me. I've got plans for me, too."

Pulling open the back door, Halick hoisted Adi from the seat with no more trouble than picking up a child.

"The thing is, the plans all work better with George drunk and bored. Really," he said, shaking his head, "you weren't helping there. He's hardly had a drink since you arrived. I was watching."

He carried her in his arms across the road, and stood on the cliff's edge next to the circle of standing stones looking out over the fogged-in chasm.

Balancing on one foot, he kicked a rock. It flew high and far before it disappeared into the cloud. "Listen . . . five, six, seven, eight." There was a distant crack.

He sat the girl up against one of the stones and straightened her dress.

The mist was turning to a drizzle. He did his best to pull her hair back from blowing loose in the wind.

"Doesn't matter." He got up, brushing his pants off as he walked back to the car. "Idle chatter, pitter patter, growing fatter . . ."

The seagull landed on the rocks nearby.

As soon as Halick turned his back, Adi's eyes fluttered open. She stared down at her lap, at her hands open upon the rocks. She'd been dreaming about the syrup from the gulab jamun staining the carpet in the library.

She was still half asleep; her stomach felt as if it might tip over. Lifting her head, she saw before her stone and mist.

Hearing a sound, she turned her head. There was a black motorcar across a road and some man leaning in to take something from the glove box.

Halick? Why would Halick be here?

He came back across the road toward her, removing a large knife from a leather scabbard. He turned the knife about as he walked, studying the gleaming blade with a curve at the tip.

Adi's heart heaved.

She didn't know if she could get up or stand once she had risen, but she knew she couldn't outrun this man.

In another second he would see that she was awake.

Lowering her head, she shut her eyes and tried to quiet her breathing.

She heard the whisper of Halick's footsteps across the grass and then upon the rocks. Through her downcast eyes she made out the tips of his shoes standing before her. Halick dropped the empty leather scabbard on the rocks. It had long fringe and beads decorating the side, as something made by American Indians.

"Come to watch, stupid seagull?" said Halick. "You do know that's not a sea down there, don't you? Come here. We'll see how well you fly with your wings cut off." He swished the blade through the air.

He leaned over to Adi. She was sure he must be able to see her heart pound in her chest.

"It's called a Bowie knife. It was given to me by an American friend. Well, someone my mother knew. Named after some American who liked to cut people up with his big knife."

He reached around the back of Adi's neck and pulled her forward, fine rain beading upon her face. His breath upon her cheek. "I know you're awake," he whispered. "How stupid do you think I am?"

The fist-sized rock in Adi's hand slammed against his head. Dropping the blade, he fell to his knees, howling.

Adi scrambled to pick up the knife; her fingers closed around the handle. He pushed her hard onto her side and grabbed her wrist to wrench the knife away. Adi scratched at his face with her nails and raised up the blade, shimmering against the dark sky.

Hard as she could, she slammed the butt of the knife into Halick's temple. He dropped like a sack of flour on top of her. Unable to move the big man, she lay there gasping.

"If you use the pointed end," said a voice from behind her, "you won't have to keep doing that." Adi strained to look past Halick's shoulder.

Sitting upon the boulder where the seagull had been was Coal.

Pulling his overcoat tight, he slid down off the rock. He put a couple of fingers to the lad's neck and checked his pulse.

"Fortunately for you, you didn't kill him," he said.

Sticking the tip of his black boot in between them, he shoved the young man off of her. The body came perilously close to the edge. Before she could move, Coal leaned down and snatched the knife from her hand. Her eyes grew large.

"What? You think it's me you need to be worrying about, with the people you've gotten mixed up with?"

Coal admired the blade for a second, and then tossed it far out over the edge. He grimaced a little as if the motion hurt him.

Adi sat up, her head spinning, as much from the turn of events as from whatever had rendered her unconscious. She groaned as her stomach pitched.

Remembering her watch, she felt for it around her neck. Not there! Searching through the grass and rocks she reached the edge of the cliff—and scuttled back from the precipice. There was a break in the fog. She'd had no idea what she had been lying inches away from.

"Looking for this?" said Coal. Leaning down, he flipped open Halick's coat and plucked out the watch and chain from a vest pocket.

But, as if he'd picked up something hot from the stove, he dropped the watch back onto Halick's chest. He tried to hide his reaction, but it was clear that something about the watch had startled him. Adi grabbed it and looped the chain around her neck. Pulling herself to her feet, she held on to one of the stones and tried not to look at the abyss stretching out before her.

The rain was coming down harder, darkening the face of the standing stones. Coal reached out his hand and ran a finger around a large circle carved, ages ago, into one of them.

"An ouroboros," he said. "That's what this is called. A serpent, eating its tail. Time without end. You figure you've got so much 'time without end' that you can play dress-up? And go to parties as if you were on holiday?" He pushed a thumb up under his eyebrow. His face was haggard, his eyes bloodshot. He kicked at Halick. "I should have let him cut you open. I'd be done with you now."

Reaching forward, he put his hand around Adi's neck. She tried to pull free but backed into one of the stones. He tightened his grip and lifted her from the ground.

"Maybe I didn't make myself clear. Those tiresome little brothers, no one is going to find them for you." Adi clawed at his sleeve, fighting to catch a breath. "But, what difference does it make? You don't care about them. And nobody in the world cares about you. Your handsome prince. He kissed you and ran away as fast as he could. What about your detective? Surely, he will help? But he's not going to, Adi. His car went into a ravine and smashed against a rock. He couldn't even save himself."

Coal turned to his right—Adi's feet swung out over the gorge. The fog coiled up around her as if it might devour her. She'd have cried out if she had been able.

"Let's try this again," said Coal. "This time, with a lesson in gravity."

He opened his hand.

Part 2

Chapter 20

Coal looked around the room from his seat at the piano as he played a drowsy version of a ragtime tune called "Breeze from Alabama."

The ladies and what was left of the clientele at this hour of the morning were sitting on the plush sofas in the main room of the brothel. Some were dozing, others watched as a tall woman dressed in a man's suit sketched a portrait of two of the girls, their arms draped about one another.

A general, not looking well, was leaning on the piano.

"It's nothing to brag about," he boasted. "At Rossignol, Joffre had thirty thousand wounded in one day. Twenty thousand dead. And that was just on our side. One day! Can you imagine?"

Coal said nothing.

The general had whiled away half the evening eating and boozing; the rest had been spent here at the brothel. Except for his bloodshot eyes and great ruddy nose, his coloring was startlingly gray. For the last hour or so, he had been hanging on the piano, holding forth on everything from the art of French sausage-making to the different gauges of railroad tracks being the reason Germany hadn't invaded Russia sooner. But mostly he talked of casualty figures in the war, and his not immodest contribution to them.

Coal didn't look much healthier than the general. Yellowish around the eyes, his skin was ashen. In a vest and trousers with a fine white shirt, he played with long graceful fingers, though he seemed to be favoring his left side. His shirt, just at the edge of his vest, showed a wet spot above what was clearly a leaking bandage.

The general, looking a little dizzy, plopped down next to Coal on the bench.

"Move over, boy. I'll show you how it's done." He began to play an old-fashioned waltz. Fumbling it badly, he stopped after a few bars, looking around the room.

"Where's that whore with my drink?" he said.

Coal glanced over at him from under heavy-lidded eyes and resumed the jazz tune.

"I don't think anyone has ever gone through so many men in one day," continued the general. "Ever. Napoleon, maybe, coming out of Russia. But that was weather and Cossacks. Not real combat. Not like—"

"Not like we have these days," suggested Coal.

"No. Not like these days."

The general stared into space, gave a little cough.

"Not that you have anything to be ashamed of, General," said Coal. "For a man who has spent almost no time in real combat, you have managed to kill thousands."

The general was drunk but not enough to miss the veiled insult. He looked at the piano player for the first time.

"What the hell do you know about combat?" he said, his speech slurring.

Coal played a little trill. "Not a thing, General. I'm only the piano player."

"Damn right," he muttered, pressing into his chest with the palm of his hand, his breath growing more labored.

"I have heard," said Coal, "that you managed to shell your own men. An attempt, perhaps, to raise your casualty figures?"

The general stared hard at the man. "I don't need to listen to this," he groaned, pushing his knuckles into his chest. Attempting to stand, he fumbled his fingers along the keyboard; discordant notes soured the tune. He dropped back onto the bench, his hands falling to his sides. Coal caught him as he pitched forward.

"Come on, General." He slapped the man's face a couple of times. "Not just here."

Pulling the big man to his feet, Coal walked him over to a wing-back chair in the corner behind a potted ficus and dropped him down into the seat. The general, his eyes bulging, struggled to speak.

Coal sat on the footstool in front of him and, like a doctor, examined his eyes, first one and then the next.

"Not looking so good, Ducky."

The general choked, "How . . . could you know . . . ?"

Coal unbuttoned the top of the man's tunic.

"That that's what your sister Colette called you? Oh, I know more than that, Ducky. Poor little Colette."

The general shook his head back and forth, struggling to rise.

"Don't bother, General. You're all done with that."

The big man gave one last cough. His head fell to the side. Coal checked for a pulse.

Back over on the couches, the artist was making a great show of applying color to her drawing, slashing at the paper with seeming nonchalance but to great effect. Powder from the pastels cascaded down the front of her vest onto her trousers. No one noticed the piano player and the general in the corner. No one saw Coal push back the man's head, drop open his jaw, or pull something out of his mouth. They most likely wouldn't have believed what they were seeing. The poor light. Too many drinks.

• • •

Though it was far too long ago to remember the where and when, Coal could still bring to mind his astonishment at seeing the event occur for the first time.

A woman, not old, he recalled. She'd done something—poisoned her children? Her husband? Along those lines. Careless with the thallium or the potassium cyanide, she followed them sooner than she'd planned. Coal had been about to leave the house when he saw the thing creeping up out of the woman's mouth: soot black, spider-like, but with too many pairs of legs. It stood straddled over the woman's open eyes for a few seconds before scurrying away into the dark.

It was some time before he witnessed this again and longer still before he could understand the type of people, the dark, damaged souls, who were likely to beget such progeny. Before long, he was collecting the things. Every one different, like snowflakes. As the creatures did poorly in company, he began separating them—hence the jars. In what seemed like no time at all, he'd collected so many of them that he was forced to have shelves made and soon entire rooms in his house dedicated to them.

• • •

Coal studied the thing he'd extracted from the general's throat, a centipede with wriggling legs and a pair of dreadful mandibles. It curled and bit at his fingers, crazed at having been exposed to the light.

Producing a small glass jar from a pocket, he unfastened the lid and coaxed the bug into it. Nearly too large to fit, it coiled like roots in an overgrown pot. Coal fastened the lid.

Arranging the dead man in the chair to look as if he were sleeping, Coal stepped back over to the piano.

A young woman in a camisole was there, looking around the room.

"What happened to the general?" she asked Coal. "I've got his drink."

Coal sat down. "He's taking a nap in the corner. He asked not to be disturbed."

"Well, what am I supposed to do with—?"

"Here," said Coal. "Give it to me, and I'll play your favorite song for you."

Coal took a sip of the drink, put it down on the piano, and started to play a sad melody.

"That is my favorite song," she said, marveling at the trick.

She sat down on the edge of the bench next to Coal and watched his fingers for a moment. She looked up at him.

"I'm all done for the night, if you wanted—if you felt like . . ." She stopped, noticing the bit of blood leaking through his shirt. She asked if he was all right.

"It's nothing," said Coal. He glanced over at the girl, all huge eyes and sad little mouth. He gathered she was offering herself to him, though he wasn't sure why; seemed something of a busman's holiday for her, didn't it? Who could know what women were about? God knows, not him.

Coal searched in his mind for the girl. The one he'd lost. He sensed nothing. Not a surprise. In the year and a half since he'd parted company with her, she had been entirely hidden from him. Her and the damned watch. She might've died. But he didn't think so.

He had been foolish. He knew that if one wasn't careful in the mist, instead of dropping someone a dozen feet, they would fall all the way down to the bottom.

He'd gone back later in the day, after he'd attended to Halick. But other than what might have been a spot of blood, he found nothing.

• • •

The artist was done with her drawing, packing up her gear. Most of the clientele had gone home. Coal looked over at the girl beside him.

She smiled sadly and shrugged. He finished the song with a little flourish. It was time to go.

Chapter 21

On a day trip to Uttar Pradesh, Adi and her grandmother had come across a young sadhu, a holy man. Sitting under a tree by the river, he wore only a loincloth of saffron and a smear of sandalwood paste across his forehead.

For Adi, growning up in India, this was a common sight. But for Tillie, on her first trip to northern India, this was mysterious and romantic.

Motivated by the promise of sweets, Adi had acted as translator. Unclear of the distinction, Tillie had Adi ask questions of the sadhu as if he were a palm reader in a gypsy camp: Would she have a long life? Would she find love and fortune?

The response was unsatisfactory, as one might expect. Her grandmother, disconcerted but fair-minded, passed a few rupees into the man's palm for his trouble.

As Adi bowed and turned to leave, the holy man reached into the cold ash from the fire next to him. Rubbing his fingers together before her, he appeared to produce a tiny gold ring from the dust. He placed it in his palm and held it out to the girl. "How about you, *sundarra ladaki* (beautiful girl)? Have you no question for me? Or do you already know everything about creation?"

Adi knew from the servants that many of the sadhus were not to be trusted. "No better than beggars," Gita would say.

"Well," said Adi. "I certainly know more than a . . . person who owns nothing but a bowl and a stick!" Blushing, she took her grandmother's hand and marched her away. Tillie kept asking, "What was it? What did he say?"

For years after, Adi thought about the young man. The look in his eyes. The gold ring in his hand.

She knew she'd behaved badly. Truth was, Gita would have spanked her if she heard her talk to anyone that way. And she thought about every tale, told to her in the cradle, about Shiva walking in disguise among men. She should have asked the man something. Perhaps he did know all of the dark and mysterious secrets of the universe.

Because lately she wasn't sure she knew anything at all about this creation.

• • •

The first time Adi woke, she heard the sound of rain on a roof. A cough, a groan, voices conversing. A pillow beneath her head. Cotton sheet under her fingertips. Her ribs ached on the right and there was a pain in the back of her head like a rusty nail. She tried to open her eyes, but drifted off again before she managed it.

The next time she woke, she heard distant thunder accompanied by the sound of a woman screaming. She worked hard to open her eyes. When she did, she saw a nurse with a fresh-born babe in her arms. The woman glanced over at Adi as she went past. "The Indian girl's awake."

Sometime later—an hour? a week?—Adi opened her eyes in a fright. Where was the watch? She tried to move her arms; it was as if she was under water. A cool hand touched her forehead. "Shush. It's right here." She picked up Adi's hand and placed it on the watch tethered to its chain around her neck. "It's wound every morning," the woman said. "Not that that keeps you from yelling about it at night."

This was distressing to Adi, though she couldn't remember why. Drifting off, she dreamed of boxes containing thumbs and toes and children's ears.

• • •

In the long, high-ceilinged room, the days passed one after another, for the most part quiet and gray.

Madame Bernard, their captain and queen, who snipped the babies' cords and closed the eyes of the departed, read to them in the evenings, medieval romances and eighteenth-century French authors. Or she would have one of the women play the piano or the cello, or recite verse. There was squabbling among the women about whether the windows should be opened at night, but before long, the rain turned to sleet and it got too cold to have them open at all.

• • •

The first time she climbed out of bed, Adi wobbled for a moment and then fell to the floor like a rag doll. Madame Bernard picked her up and put her back under the covers. The next morning the woman appeared at Adi's bedside carrying two canes. She asked Adi to go to the window at the end of the long room and let her know how many sailboats there were on the lake today. It took two hours and many bruises for Adi to find Madame and tell her that there was no lake, only a wheat field rolling away over the hill.

She used both canes for a time, then one, then none. The chores she could accomplish progressed accordingly.

• • •

She'd been brought to the hospital by a paleontologist nephew of Madame Bernard. He had found the girl wandering the ring road above Lake Kore with no voice and a ghastly amount of blood running down the back of her head. With a war looming, it might have been safer to take her somewhere to the south. But where? He knew she would be welcomed and cared for by his aunt.

In Madame Bernard's hospital, talk of the war was kept to a minimum. There were only women here, and many of them were elderly or with child or damaged in some way. Her doctors had all been taken by the war, as had much of her equipment and supplies. Were it not for her devoted and resourceful nephews and her dwindling cache of seventeenth-century Dutch paintings, she would have had to cease. But the "discord," as she called it, was still beyond the village of Sampigny to the north and as long as it was, Madame intended to keep it outside of these doors. When the sound of shelling got too strident she played Italian opera on the phonograph in the middle of the room.

None of this mattered much to Adi. After her long sleep, she climbed out of her bed, but still spent most of her days in some small space in the back of her mind. She did her chores, whatever needed to be done: sweeping and sewing, brushing hair, washing pots, mashing turnips.

Now and again, when the curtains were open and the shadows from the clouds drifted over the fields, Adi would remember herself and think that there were things she should be doing. Soon, she would go. But there was always a new baby or another gray-haired woman who needed care, another bed to be made, a potato to be peeled. So, as long as the watch was wound and the bedpans were shining, Adi wandered the quiet rooms like a beautiful ghost.

• • •

Then one day, it began to snow.

• • •

Crown Prince Wilhelm, the eldest son of the German emperor, was put in command of the 5th Army. Only thirty-two, he had never commanded anything larger than a regiment. He determined that the only thing keeping the 5th Army from enlarging the salient, southeast of Verdun, was the river Meuse and the French soldiers in the village of Sampigny. Though not a superstitious man, he took the uncommon snowfall in the first week of November as a sign from God. Before sunrise, the attack began.

• • •

As the bombs fell, Madame Bernard curled up on the floor between the beds with the old women. She told them everything was going to be fine. *The Marriage of Figaro* played as loud as it could on the Victrola in the middle of the room.

But when Mozart could no longer be heard above the artillery and the great windows in the front of the chateau began to explode in the morning sun, Madame called to Adi, "Take the duvet from your bed and run!" Adi, in her nightgown, turned to get clothes. "No, girl! Run, now! To the other end of the lake!"

Chapter 22

Bright white. Burning cold.

Adi pulled herself up out of a snowdrift only to be dusted in powder by a man on a horse leaping over her head. There was shouting and the crack of gunfire, though most of the sound was swallowed by the snow.

A soldier stopped in his tracks at the sight of the young woman in a nightgown, sitting waist deep in the snow. He stared for half a second, before a bullet left a nick on his forehead and dropped him beside her.

She tried to stand, only to be slammed back into the snowdrift by another horse and rider, oblivious to the girl beneath them. With steam billowing from the horses' nostrils, the men, spikes on their helmets and great fur collars on their coats, swept the other soldiers before them over the crest of the hill.

Then it was quiet, with just the sound of her teeth chattering and her heart beating, like a mouse shivering in its hollow. She lay buried, too cold to weep, for Madame Bernard or for the old women. She had seen the chateau and the village of Sampigny burning against the white landscape. There would be no more sweeping, no more bedpans. She'd be frozen and gone in the time it would take her to recite her favorite poem all the way through.

I'm afraid of a kiss
Like the kiss of a bee.
I suffer like this
And wake endlessly.
I'm afraid of a—

She heard a sigh. Without thinking about it any more, she woke from her long dream and lifted her head.

In front of her, staring calmly up into the sky, the soldier was lying on his back, his helmet cradled in the snow.

Adi climbed out of her hollow.

He was small, and didn't look much older than Adi. Hardly old enough to have a proper beard. A piece of the back of his head was gone. He said something about Paulette, then died.

She watched him for a moment, rubbing her arms, the thin cotton gown worthless against the wind. She may as well have been naked. She put her hands on the young man's chest. He was still warm.

Pushing him up onto his side, she managed to pull the pack from his shoulders. With stiff fingers, she undid the buckles.

There were a few useful items in the pack: biscuits, chocolate, a sewing kit. But with the exception of a handkerchief and a sock, there wasn't a single article of clothing.

A gust of wind swirled snow into her eyes. She had the boy's coat halfway off of him. She stopped and touched the buttons on his tunic, the knife on his belt. The sky to the north started drumming with artillery again. Madness, madness.

• • •

There was likely no one else coming up this hill today. The Germans had killed more French soldiers than the French had killed Germans. The hornets' nest would swarm for a while and then they'd dig in once again.

But if you were coming over the rise a half hour on, you would have seen what appeared to be a young soldier pulling on his greatcoat. If you were observant you might notice that his belt was cinched tighter than usual and his leggings wrapped high up the knee, to disguise trousers that were too large.

If you were quick, you might see what seemed to be long locks of fresh-cut auburn hair blowing away over the hill.

• • •

Adi, in the young soldier's uniform—a humble second lieutenant, as far as she could decipher the French insignia on her sleeve—ran her hand up the back of her raggedly shorn head and put the knife back in its scabbard on her belt.

She was not quite as cold as she had been. But just as important, she no longer appeared to be a young woman in the middle of a war. At least, so she hoped. In addition to hacking off her beautiful hair, she'd torn strips of her nightgown and wrapped them tightly around her chest, grateful that she was as small-breasted as she was.

She was still in great danger, and not sure where it might be safe to go. Living in Madame's world, she'd had only the vaguest notion of where she was and what was going on outside the walls. She assumed the Germans were on French territory, but it was just a guess. If she tried to get away, would she be considered a deserter? She knew they would not look kindly upon that.

His name was Jean Joseph Goux, number 3233.

Adi stood beside the grave—nothing more than a pile of rocks covering the young man, the best that could be done with the frozen ground. Silently, she repeated a prayer her father had taught her as a child. She felt terrible about taking the boy's clothes and leaving him alone in this cold place. But there was nothing else to do.

She hung his little aluminium identification tag on a branch of the tree next to the grave. She had considered holding on to the ID tag, but had decided it would be safer to say she'd lost it than to risk running into someone who knew the young man. It would have been safer still to simply bury the tag; sooner or later someone would find him and that could cause complications. But she couldn't bear the idea of leaving him here in an unmarked grave.

Didn't matter. She would be out of this uniform and away long before that could happen. She put on her helmet and pulled the strap tight under her chin.

Chapter 23

My God! How do they do it?

Adi trudged down the side of the hill. She'd had no idea soldiers' packs were so heavy.

She'd tried to get rid of anything in the backpack that seemed unnecessary. She threw away the shaving kit. The extra pair of boots. A small shovel. But it didn't seem prudent to lose things such as the cooking pot or the lice powder or the "housewife" containing needle and thread, buttons and soap and such.

She didn't know what to make of the strange mask device, with the tube dangling from the front, like an elephant's trunk. She reckoned she'd keep it, though, until she could figure out what it was.

The young man had a book, *Le Mystère de la Chambre Jaune* by a Gaston Leroux. Adi held it in her hands, feeling the most terrible craving. More than anything, she longed to curl up somewhere and fall into a book. She put it next to the boots. No more time for stories.

She was about to do the same with a dog-eared copy of a magazine called *Union Jack* (which was odd, as the young man was French). Then Adi spotted the date on the cover: August 1915. She sat back on her heels, her hands over her mouth.

It's not even a new magazine! she thought. Could she have been there so long in Madame Bernard's? Sweeping and dreaming?

She popped the lid on the watch and flipped the face around to the row of tiny numerals. There were millions of seconds gone! She fumbled again and again with the sum in her head. Almost a year and a half! The faces of the boys stared at her.

Were they still alive? She shuddered at the possibility of missing pieces.

You will quit whining about your pack, and crying over your hair! She stomped her new boot heel. There's a war on.

After some consideration, she also left behind the young man's rifle. She could hear her father yelling at her all the way from India. But it was heavy and she felt, right or wrong, that it was more likely somebody would try to shoot her if she was holding a rifle than if she was not. As a concession, she kept the clever little pistol on her hip, so she was not without protection.

With all that, it still seemed as if she were carrying a load of bricks. The first time she tried to stand with it she tottered in circles and ended up on her back like a hapless turtle.

• • •

She stumbled down the hill through what must have been a small woods, nothing left of it now but shattered, blackened tree trunks. Even under the blanket of snow, she could make out the ground torn and pitted with huge craters. Growing up, her father had told her a thousand battle stories. There was nothing like this. After seeing Sampigny, though, she was beginning to grasp what could cause this much ruin.

She was down the road about ten yards past the trees when she heard the sound of the engine behind her. A motorcar! She turned to run back for the trifling cover of what was left of the trees. Never going to make it, she threw off her pack and dropped herself into the snow filling the shallow ditch. Praying they hadn't seen her, she closed her eyes and dug in as the vehicle careened past.

She heard a shout. With a spray of ice and gravel, the car's brakes locked up and the thing skidded to a halt. Gears grinding, it lurched into reverse and came to a stop—right in front of her. She peeked up to see a wreck of an ambulance, boggy green with a red cross fresh-painted on the side.

She was about to make a run for it, when a voice shouted, "God's sakes, boy! Do you want to walk? Get your ass in here!"

She raised her head a bit more, snow sliding off the front edge of her helmet.

He wasn't speaking German. Seemed like a good sign.

Scrambling to her feet, she managed to get her pack up onto her shoulder and start toward the front of the car. The driver, a little man with huge ears, was looking anxiously up at the skies. As if on cue a high-pitched whistling came from the northeast.

"Not up there!" the voice croaked from the back.

Hustling to the rear of the car, she was lifting up the canvas flap covering the rear when a hand reached out, grabbed her arm, and pulled her into the ambulance—just as the hillside exploded not 20 meters above them.

Adi fell over the back gate. Struggling to rise, she cracked her helmet against one of several shelves on the left side. Each one was heavy with wounded soldiers, some of them crying and moaning.

The man let go of Adi's arm and banged his fist against the side wall. "He's in, Gershom. Go!" He pulled Adi down onto a little stool, as the car backfired and lurched forward. The shriek of artillery filled the air. Through the back flap, Adi saw the road erupt in smoke and flame. The ambulance was pelted by debris as it sped away.

"Put your pack down!" barked the man, his voice low and coarse as a gravel road. Adi complied. She shoved her pack under the cot, keeping her eyes on the doctor, to avoid looking at the broken bodies all around her.

The man was older—fifties maybe—and a doctor, judging by the red cross on his arm band. Stubbled gray hair on a head like a cinder block. He grabbed Adi's hand and pressed it hard against a twisted tourniquet tied around a soldier's neck. It was soaked through with blood.

"Keep the pressure on that," said the doctor. This freed up both his hands to cut the trousers off a soldier's leg. The limb was bent the wrong way at the knee.

"What's your name, boy? What company you with?"

Adi tore her eyes away from the sight of the man's leg and stared at the doctor helplessly, until he looked up from the splint he was applying.

"Not a hard question, son."

Adi gestured to her mouth and shook her head to indicate she couldn't talk. He glared at her for a moment, more artillery exploded to their left.

He jutted his chin at the tourniquet she was pressing on. "You can let go of that." Adi looked down. The soldier had died.

Without a beat, the doctor said, "Grab that roll of bandage there."

Adi was still staring at the dead soldier. She looked up, choking back tears. The doctor gave her a second. She took a deep breath and then nodded. He handed her a pair of scissors, pointed to the soldier on the top cot. "Cut that sleeve away."

Adi stood up steadying herself against the bunk. A fair-haired lad, like a schoolboy playing dress-up, opened his eyes and stared at Adi for a few seconds. She snipped at the cloth and tore the rest of the sleeve away. Skin came off with it. The young man cried once and his head fell to the side.

"He passed out," Doc said. "Easier that way."

The boy's arm was horribly burned, the smell indescribable. She unrolled a length of bandage while trying to keep her stomach from rolling over.

Focus! Basic field dressing. Like Mother used to do. Which reminded Adi of how much she had hated and avoided her mother's work.

Doc covered a soldier's eyes with pads of cotton and wrapped gauze around his head. The man's face and neck were spotted with frightful blisters. When he was done Doc took a flask from his pocket, held it to the soldier's mouth and let him drink. He took a long pull himself, then offered it to Adi. She shook her head and turned to get the scissors.

"All right," he said. "So, who are you then?" The doctor leaned forward, putting his hand into Adi's coat. She lurched back.

"Whoa, kid. Just looking for—"

He reached very deliberately into her left tunic pocket.

"—this."

He held up a little booklet: Paybook was stamped on the cover. He flipped it open and squinted at it by the light from one of the small windows.

"Jean Joseph Goux, of the . . . hmm, 85th Infantry." A hard look passed across the doctor's eyes.

Damn. She should have checked those pockets. Well, it was out there now.

She finished wrapping the bandage and neatly tucked the ends away. She took the scraps of gauze, poured some water from a canteen, and began cleaning cuts on the soldier's face and neck.

• • •

They worked without talking, holding everything down in the narrow space as best they could, while Gershom, cursing and grumbling, wrestled the motorcar along a road that was most likely not smooth even before it was shot to hell by artillery. Finally, Adi folded up a couple of empty sacks and made a pillow for a man who was clearly not going to see the next day. He would likely not be the only one.

"Bad night, last night," said the doctor. "I'd hoped the snow would settle things down. Just goes to show you, I don't know much."

He took a filthy-looking handkerchief from his pocket and swabbed his craggy face. "I know you boys took it hard. I'm happy to see any of you."

"We're getting close, Doc!" Gershom shouted from up front. "Where do you want to go?"

Sure enough, Adi could see signs of life through the slats covering the windows. Cavalry and a group of soldiers and horses pulling cannons.

Doc rubbed his tired eyes with hands that looked more like a farmer's than a surgeon's. He yelled back over the sound of the engine.

"Where do I want to go? I want to go to Florida, America! And sit on one of those beaches in the sun and drink until I don't remember. Why the hell would I know where we're going?! I assume someone is finding us another burned-out house or a barn! Or digging a hole in the earth and calling it an infirmary. Just—take us there, Gershom."

His aggravation bled away, until his face settled back into looking like a worn-out mattress. He sighed and looked over at the young, smooth-faced soldier sitting before him.

"What are you doing in the infantry, Goux?"

Adi shrugged and tried to keep busy with tidying up a bandage.

"Damned waste, is what it is," he said, studying her. "Paybook says you're from Normandy. You don't look like anybody I've ever met from Normandy."

Adi was afraid to look over at him, afraid he was going to notice other things, like her skin being too smooth or her fingers too delicate. In all the excitement she hadn't had time to worry about whether her disguise was fooling anyone. And now she found out she was supposed to be from Normandy.

"Middle Eastern?" said the doctor. "Indian, maybe? I spent a couple years in West Bengal, few years back." Doc tilted his head studying her, as if she were some puzzle that he couldn't decipher. "I guess there's no reason the French army can't have Indian soldiers," he said, scratching his crooked nose. "God knows the Brits brought a few over."

The soldier on the bottom bunk groaned. Doc put the palm of his hand on the man's forehead, checking his temperature.

"I imagine," he said glancing up at Adi, "you want to get back to . . . what's left of the 85th?"

That was exactly what Adi did not want. She was trying to figure out some way to sidestep the question, when—with screeching brakes—they came to an abrupt halt. Adi held on to a couple of the men to keep them on their bunks.

Straight away, the canvas flap lifted and the gate cracked down. There stood Gershom, black smudges for eyes, a mustache like a coal brush, barking orders to several men with stretchers, ready to unload the wounded.

Adi grabbed her pack and wrestled it and herself out of the back of the ambulance. Doc climbed out as well. He looked nearly as unsteady as his patients, leaning against the side of the car for a moment till he got his balance. But immediately, questions commenced regarding the condition of the injured and their designation.

A cocky-looking young colonel started in on Doc about where he'd been and why he'd been gone so long and why he thought it was acceptable to take a vehicle against orders.

Cursing under his breath, Doc pushed past the officer and followed the stretchers down into what looked to be the new infirmary, the root cellar of a nearly flattened barn. Adi was left holding her pack in her arms, around her a beehive of activity. But no one took any notice of a lone soldier from some battalion down the line.

Now what to do? She dropped her pack to the ground and sat down on top of it.

What, if anything, had she solved with this charade? Other than keeping herself from freezing to death and getting murdered. There was that. But what now? Where to go? She had no idea where she was, except in the middle of a war.

A map was what she needed. How far was she from Alorainn? And Coal. She shuddered at the memory.

She dug through the small haversack at her waist and broke off a piece of muddy-gray chocolate from a half-eaten bar. It tasted about as good as it looked, but it was something. Around her, soldiers rushed to and fro: French, British, and Belgium, even Afrikaners and Indians. There were a pair of Scotsman in kilts. They were digging holes in the earth—long zig-zagging trenches, an almost impossible task in this cold ground. Why were they doing that?

Xander and Xavier would know what this all meant. She stifled a moan at the thought.

They've been out there, somewhere, for a year and a half or more! They must have thought she'd given up on them. George, too. And Thomas and Uncle Henri and all those lovely people.

She touched her fingers to her lips. Damn it. George would have come back from Paris and found her gone. Without a word. And now—well, what difference did it make. They would surely have forgotten about her by now.

She loosed the strap on her helmet and let it fall into her lap, a relief to get the thing off. She rubbed her hands across her head, and bits of freshly cut hair fell into Jean Joseph Goux's helmet.

She looked down and saw scratched under the brim, a small heart with an "JJ" and a "P" etched inside. Jean Joseph and . . . Paulette. The name he'd whispered as he died.

This made her feel about as miserable as she figured she could manage.

Poor Paulette. She'll never know what happened to him. Like George. I'll get myself killed out here and he'll never know. I'll just be that strange, cheeky girl that he kissed in the garden. She blew little pieces of hair out of her helmet.

She couldn't talk to anyone. She didn't know anyone. She had five or six francs in her pocket. She didn't know what two of the riddles meant; why "Jeremiah was quite blind" or what the "blood in the bread" might mean! She'd cut off her hair. She wasn't even herself anymore.

Dropping her head into her hands, she felt tears sting her eyes. Stop it! No sitting here crying like a girl. You're not a girl any more.

Someone cleared their throat behind her. Adi looked back over her shoulder.

The doctor was sitting on a pile of sandbags taking a bite from an apple. He had another in his hand. He tossed it over to Adi. She polished it up on her coat-sleeve and took a bite. It was bruised and a long way from the tree. It tasted like a small miracle, nonetheless.

The sun cut through the clouds for a moment as they ate their apples. The old man sat with his mud-caked boots crossed, eating everything but the stem. He played with a little silver medallion on a chain around his neck as he considered the soldier before him.

Chapter 24

Just as Adi had feared, George returned home to La Maison Chinoise to find her gone.

No note, nothing said to Thomas. Augustin was concerned for a moment that the young woman was a figment of his friend's imagination. Maybe an elaborate prank.

However, when it was discovered that Halick was missing as well, and Detective Lendt—taken all together, this formed a sinister picture that was hard to ignore.

George was devastated.

He tried taking it out on Thomas, though Thomas was beating himself up enough for the both of them. When it became clear that he wasn't to blame for Adi's vanishing act, they were left with nothing but speculation. It took half the afternoon to catch Augustin up on the rest of the story: kidnappers, brothers, watches, and riddles. But in the end, they had to admit that they didn't know much more than Belfort, and that they used to throw cats off towers in Ypres.

Thomas found another detective to replace the missing Lendt, but the man's efforts, though diligent, were ultimately fruitless. The days turned to weeks with no clues.

Then it was August 1914.

And as Uncle Henri had predicted: like dominos falling, everyone declared war. No one wanted to be caught on the defensive. Everyone mobilized. And so it began.

By the end of September, Augustin was called up to join his cavalry regiment, which made George feel even more worthless. Despite Thomas's best efforts, George started drinking again. Thomas grew accustomed to collecting his friend from the police at odd hours. Or equally alarming, dragging him away from enlistment centers, where he attempted on several occasions to join up.

It was a wet miserable autumn in Alorainn, as it was all across Europe in 1914, but few complained. However inconvenienced they might have been, the thought of hundreds of thousands of their fathers and sons, brothers and husbands, marching along muddy roads or living in rain-filled trenches, put their trifling discomfort in perspective.

· · ·

The duchess, rather than becoming debilitated by the uncertainty of her only child's fate, instead grew more engaged, first with the running of the household and then with the business of state. Through it all, she maintained that Halick would be returning any day.

To no one's surprise but her own, after years of disinterest as the duke's wife, the duchess realized she had a ferocious appetite for power. Every day she took on more of the duties she had been grooming Halick to assume—after what she envisaged would be George's inevitable disintegration.

As is so often the case in times of great uncertainty, people are more than willing to give up authority to someone who can assure their safety. With the ever-closer war as an excuse, the duchess turned an open household into something resembling an armed camp.

Some members of the family said they didn't care what the woman did as long as she kept the war on the other side of the wall. Aunt Elodie, on the other hand, wondered if she was the only one to notice that the formerly colorful, largely ceremonial, palace guard had been replaced by a group of dark and dangerous-looking thugs.

· · ·

For a time at least, far enough away from the invading armies and front lines, life in much of Europe carried on, as if a war was something that one could be excited about but still ignore, like typhoons in the China Sea.

Bakers still rose before dawn to make bread and children continued to neglect their lessons. In Paris, as in Berlin, women in violaceous gowns and men in hats (quite as tall as last year) attended the opera. People carried on affairs in Saint Petersburg and embezzled from their business partners in London, just as they had before.

Most everyone strived, for as long as they could, to deny the fact, becoming clearer as the months flew past, that this war, the first one they'd seen in a generation, spreading from Europe and Russia to the Middle East, to Africa and India, China and Japan, was not going to be over by Christmas.

Alorainn had no standing army. This didn't keep a good portion of the household from joining up with the French. Cousin Klaus, having people in Bamberg and generally being contrary, wanted to fight for Germany, but was dissuaded. George's uncles Robert, Sébastien, and Henri went off to serve in the French army as officers. This only exacerbated George's feelings of frustration. He stayed drunk for the better part of a year—living up to all of the duchess's hopes for him, driving Thomas near to distraction.

This went on until one morning when George found himself waking up in another cow pasture. Lying there, staring up at the clouds, he came to the conclusion that he'd been going about this all wrong. Taking the weekend to shake off the worst of his hangover, he quietly put his affairs in order. Monday morning, bright and early, he got Samuel to give him a ride on his motorcycle to the train station in Saint Clouet—without a goodbye to anyone. Not even Thomas.

In the city of Lyon, a couple of hours south, a barber cut George's beautiful ash brown curls down to stubble, and he traded in his fine suit for a well-used one and a sensible pair of shoes.

That afternoon, he managed, finally, to find someone unobservant enough to sign him up. It was a year to the day since Adi had disappeared.

Chapter 25

The abbot lifted the box from the brown paper and twine it was wrapped in. A simple cardboard thing, half the length of his hand, banged up on the corners, like a box one might keep recipes in. There was a little metal slot on the front, with a label, reading, H-K. Someone had drawn a line in ink through the letters.

Abbot Berno had to sit down. No matter how many times he opened these boxes, it never failed to make him light-headed. This was the fifth. And in weight, at least, identical to its predecessors. He lifted off the top and removed the layer of cotton batting.

The contents were the same: a dozen gold coins, Spanish, dated 1786, bound together with a pair of red rubber bands. Four cut diamonds, of a carat or two. And, lastly, a pair of emeralds the size of June beetles.

Abbot Berno shook his head in wonder and swabbed his brow with the sleeve of his robe. He coiled the twine and neatly folded the paper.

As always, it was addressed, in a somewhat childish hand, to *Xander & Xavier Dahl c/o Abbot Berno, Gentiana Monastery.*

• • •

"That's because you're an idiot," said Xander.

"Why does that make me an idiot?" replied Xavier.

"Well, it's not just that that makes you an idiot," he said. "Hand me that drill, the little one."

The boys were high up in the scaffolding on either side of Brother Christopher, helping him repair the old library shelves.

Since their disappearance, the boys had grown half a foot, though it hardly seemed they'd added a pound; side by side, they were like a couple of match sticks.

Xavier put aside a worn copy of *Le Morte d'Arthur* and handed over the tool.

"I'm just saying, if it was a few hundred years earlier—we'd be fighting. Wouldn't matter that we were twelve."

"I'm pretty sure we're the same age," said Xander. "And I'm only eleven."

"Quit interrupting. Remember the Children's Crusade in the thirteenth century. All those kids went to fight in the Holy Land."

"No they didn't," said Xander. "Half of them died crossing the Alps, and the other half was sold into slavery when they got to Genoa and the sea didn't part for them."

"Quiet please!" said a voice from below. There were still a few of the brothers and a professor or two, working at the desks despite the construction.

"Is that true?" whispered Xavier.

"Yes," said Xander. "And the father of the German boy, who heard voices and started the whole thing, was hanged by the families of the other children who had followed him. You never pay attention in History."

Brother Christopher blew curlicues of wood shavings off his new shelf.

"Thank you, Xander. There's little enough to be said for the age we live in, but at least we don't let children fight in wars anymore. Least not here."

"Yeah, but bookshelves?" said Xavier. "There's got to be something more important than this we could be doing."

"I'm sure Brother Tobias would love to have you help lay pipe for the new latrines," said Brother Christopher. "These buildings have been perched on the side of this mountain for ages, through more wars than anyone can even remember. The only reason they're still standing is because somebody goes to the trouble to fix the shelves once in awhile."

"I seriously doubt that anyone has ever mended this shelf," said Xavier. "A wonder the whole thing hasn't come crashing down."

A voice from below called out, "Boys. A word, please."

They looked down. The abbot and his assistant were crossing the room through the desks.

Brother Christopher took back the drill.

"All right, boys, try not to—"

But they were already scrambling down the scaffolds like monkeys. They dropped from a considerable height right in front of the abbot, whose birdlike assistant Brother Hilbert burped out a little shriek.

"Will you quit that!" said the abbot. "You're going to break your necks one of these days."

"Sorry, Father Abbot," said Xander.

"Sorry, Father." Xavier kissed his ring.

"I thought you might like to know," said the abbot, studying the boys, "that you've received another package."

"Another one," said Xavier. He looked at his brother.

• • •

Nearly two years earlier, the boys had awakened in a state of great confusion, to find themselves in a strange bed, in a tiny dark cell. They couldn't remember the night before, except pieces of a nightmare they both seemed to have had.

Abbot Berno had been the one to come in and throw open the shutters on the window, letting in the morning light.

He calmed the boys and explained that as far as he had been told, there was a fire in their home. They had been saved by a stranger passing in the night. Though the man tried, he was unable to save the young woman in the back bedroom.

Xavier would not talk for several weeks. Both of the boys often woke in the night, with dreams of fire and shadows and Adi crying. Some of the brothers feared that the shock had been too great and that they would not recover.

But Abbot Berno told them, "Give it time. These boys are stronger than they look."

Sure enough, before the fall turned to winter, kept busy with studying and chores and new friends, the light—most of it, anyway—returned to their eyes.

One couldn't say the same for Halick.

The twins weren't the only boys delivered to the abbey that week.

Brother Andrew found Halick, dumb and vacant-eyed, standing just outside the front gate. He carried no papers, but in the pocket of his rather fine suit was a letter addressed to Abbot Berno.

Seeming to be quite moved by the lad's predicament, Father Abbot insisted that Halick remain at the abbey and not be sent to the home for the mentally defective in Besançon (as several of the professors and non-clerical members of the staff had recommended). The boy talked only occasionally, and then nonsensically, but he was for the most part capable of feeding and caring for himself.

Halick was given a broom and spent his time sweeping the courtyard and the cloisters. The brethren found it touching that most mornings, the young man could be found cleaning up the grounds around the abbot's little house.

• • •

Two weeks after the twins were deposited at the abbey, the first of the packages arrived.

Brother Jacques, returning from a journey early in the morning, found the package near the front gate leaning against the feet of the statue of Saint Alberic. There was a note inside explaining that the contents of the box were to compensate the abbey for the cost incurred in the room and board and education of the twins. They continued to arrive like clockwork, every six months, on or near the eleventh of the month.

This caused much excitement among the brethren, as the contents could cover the annual operating budget of the abbey. The abbot disappointed many when he announced simply that the package would be put aside for the boys, for when they came of age. There was no signature, no return address. No one was ever observed leaving them.

At first the boys had been excited about the parcels and fascinated by the mystery they represented.

Having few facts, they speculated endlessly, coming up with more and more outlandish theories. They had, after all, been raised in British India where they were as likely to hear tales of Father Christmas as they were of the god Shiva wandering the countryside disguised as a beggar.

Xavier was sure the packages were coming from the mysterious stranger who had saved them.

"Immensely wealthy, but wracked with guilt," explained Xavier, "he's trying to make it up to us—for having failed to rescue Adi."

Xander leaned more to theories involving their late grandmother. He suggested that she had only faked her death to avoid having to care for them. She was now living in an Italian castle, sending them riches to assuage her guilt.

Or perhaps, he said, their father had been taken captive by an Indian king. And though he was, so far, unable to escape, he was managing somehow to steal and smuggle out gold and diamonds. This had the added benefit of explaining why the letters they'd written to their father, given to the abbot to send, had not yet elicited a response.

Naturally, they had come up with stories about Adi. That she was alive. That she and their grandmother were both living in that castle—Adi not wanting to have to take care of them either. Xander didn't like this story. He argued that if Adi were alive, she would be looking for them.

But as the war and real life grew more immediate and the months turned to years, they told these stories less and less and the parcels became little more than a melancholy reminder of what they had lost.

Chapter 26

A pistol shot cracked the stillness. Up and down the line, the shriek of whistles. German soldiers, with a roar between rage and terror, poured out from the trenches by the thousands. Up the ladders, heads down against the rain, they were met by the clap and staccato of rifle and machine-gun fire. The air filled with a mist of blood and the sound of bullets piercing bodies.

Christian Schmidt leaned against the side of a ladder and waited his turn.

At twenty-one stone in weight and a good head taller than the men pressed around him, he was a hard target to miss. His sergeant held him back, a hand on his shoulder. You didn't waste a soldier like Christian Schmidt, sending him up in the first wave.

In the nearly two hundred and forty days that he had spent in the trenches at the front, he'd been shot and gassed and filled with more splinters of shrapnel than he could count.

There was a time when he'd been scared to death to climb the ladder, to face the guns. But he didn't think about it much anymore. It wasn't that he felt he was indestructible, it was just that after being tired and hungry and terrified for so long, he didn't really care anymore. He'd given up on winning the war. He'd abandoned hope of returning to his farm, or ever seeing his mother and sisters again. The only thing he believed in anymore was the bullet that would make the noise stop.

His sergeant tapped him on the shoulder. He started up the ladder.

• • •

Adi knew it was a crazy thing to do—for so many reasons. But she'd missed her chance a dozen times. The thought of being covered in blood and muck for another day was more than she could stand.

Transferring wounded to the hospital a few days ago with Gershom, she'd seen light reflecting off the water beneath a bombed-out bridge. It was not too far to the west, and it was well back from no-man's-land.

Three o'clock in the morning now. After five endless days, the shelling had finally moved down the line toward the southeast. Everyone had their head down, huddled in their niches. It was the best chance she was going to get.

One of the things she'd noticed since she'd joined the society of men (among so many things) was that there appeared to be two kinds of men. One did their business in groups, laughing and talking. (Adi tried her best to never see this.) And the other, despite the impossible circumstances, still insisted on at least a modicum of privacy. Adi let everyone know that she was of the latter type. There was a certain measure of mockery to be contended with, but they had grown accustomed to her slipping away at odd hours.

The water under the bridge turned out to be more ditch than stream, stagnant but not yet unwholesome. The earth was torn up as it was everywhere, but not too badly.

With a last look around, she peeled off her tunic and unwound the soiled cloth that bound her breasts. She'd start with the top half.

Lifting the watch from around her neck, it occurred to her that this was the first time she'd had the damned thing off since she'd recovered it from Halick on the cliffside. She looked at it for a moment and then hung it on a branch close at hand.

Falling, falling, head spinning, she swooned. Then she was kneeling again beside the water.

Adi steadied herself, a hand to her forehead. What was this thing doing to her? She shook her head. There was no time to speculate.

Reaching down, she pulled out a bit of soap tucked into the top of her boot and began splashing water on her face. It was nippy in the dark May morning, but she didn't care. Oh, to be clean!

And then . . . a pistol shot echoed across no-man's-land. The shriek of whistles. The roar of a thousand German soldiers.

Grabbing her things, she reached for the watch. If only she could leave the thing hanging there. Snatching the chain off the branch, she dropped it back around her neck and ran.

• • •

It was forty-three years since there had last been a war between the European powers: France versus Germany, in the so-called Franco-Prussian War. Since then, little had altered in the way the military thought about battles, but everything had changed with the machines with which they fought.

The expectations of glorious cavalry charges, the sweep of armies with banners flying and bugles blaring, had, within weeks of the start of the war, crashed to earth. It made no difference how brave the cavalry officer was; he and a hundred like him were but a moment's work for the machine guns.

Artillery and tanks, airplanes, flame throwers, poison gas. Europe had perfected these devices of eradication against the rebellious subjects of their African and Asian colonies, never following the logic to the end, that one day the machines would be turned upon the people who made them.

So this war, with its perfectly matched armies, was to be fought from holes in the ground. Men in trenches faced other men in trenches, across a no-man's-land of shell craters and razor wire.

• • •

In the past four months, Adi had seen the infirmary move a half-dozen times.

There was the root cellar that Adi had started in, a bombed-out chateau, a brothel, a barn. They stayed a fortnight or only a few hours before the shelling got too precise, or the enemy pushed through the line again.

But a week ago, their luck ran out. After the German artillery took down their little schoolhouse, there was nowhere else to go but into the ground, underneath a crooked slab of reinforced concrete, all that was left of one of the old abandoned French fortresses. This was the first time since she'd been with Doc that they'd had to be in the trenches. He hated it. "Mud is no place to be practicing medicine!" he yelled.

• • •

Adi piled in through the low doorway of the infirmary and ran smack into Gershom. The tray of surgical instruments he was carrying crashed to the floor.

"He's here," yelled Gershom.

Doc stuck his head out of the back room and glared at Adi, just as the clangor of machine guns, perched a meter above their heads, began. Clumps of dirt fell from the low ceiling.

"Where the hell have you been, Goux?"

Adi gestured vaguely over her shoulder.

Doc pointed his chin at the forceps and scalpels in the dirt. "Clean that up and clear those tables off!" He smacked Adi on the helmet with his hand. "And don't go off like that, without telling anyone."

A fidgety young captain leaned his head into the room. "Ready, Doc?"

"Ready as we're going to be."

Gathering up the instruments from the ground, Adi dumped them together onto a shelf with tin plates and playing cards. She took a deep breath to steady herself. The air was thick with the smell of cordite and sweat.

• • •

Ten meters before they got to the enemy trenches, the man running alongside Christian Schmidt stopped as if he'd hit a wall.

Without a sound he dropped to his knees and tumbled down into the fetid water at the bottom of a shell crater. A dark stain bloomed on the front of his tunic. Schmidt jumped in after. The other man with him did likewise.

Of the dozen or so soldiers in the group that had climbed up the ladder with Schmidt twenty minutes earlier, there was only this one left, a boy, his mouth slack, his eyes already like a dead man's. Schmidt didn't know him.

They were lying in the shell crater, catching their breath, when the grenade splashed into the water at their feet. Schmidt dropped his rifle and rolled over to the puddle. He fished about in the black water, pulled out the prize, and flung the grenade over his head, back to where it came from.

Taking out his pistol, he listened for the explosion above, then motioned for the boy to follow him.

Before the echo faded, they'd closed the distance and jumped feet-first into the trench. There were three dead soldiers and several more wounded, holding their hands to their heads, deafened by the blast. Schmidt fired at them and pushed the boy along the trench to his left. They almost made it around the zig-zag corner before the bullets caught Schmidt.

• • •

The wounded started pouring into the infirmary as soon as the counterattack began. Every table in the low-ceilinged room was filled as fast as Gershom and his bearers, Lebeau and Cloutain, could get them there.

"Someone hold this man down!" yelled Doc, attempting to stop the blood gushing from the neck of a flailing soldier. Adi dropped a roll of bandage and threw herself across the man's legs.

Over her shoulder, from the passageway, she heard guttural shouts in German. Spinning around, she spotted Lebeau staggering backward into the room, clutching his stomach, followed by a young German soldier, his bayonet slick black.

Behind them was a huge bear of a man, a smoking pistol in his hand, blood covering most of his face. Ducking his head through the low doorway, the German stood up inside, smashing one of the lanterns with his helmet. It crashed to the floor, splattering kerosene fire onto his boots. He looked around the room, confounded at finding himself in an infirmary. For a long second, everyone stopped dead.

Then the stretcher bearer, Cloutain, fired his pistol at the young German soldier. He missed, shooting out another lantern instead. The big man, his boots ablaze, took Cloutain down with a blow to his head.

Adi rolled off the table as the young soldier lurched forward with his bayonet. She grabbed up a metal tray, scattering instruments, and deflected the blade. Brandishing the tray, she stumbled forward and slammed the young man hard underneath the jaw, dropping him to the ground.

The only remaining lamp swung wildly in the middle of the ceiling, as shadows leapt across the room.

Adi spun around to see Doc against the wall, fighting to wrestle the pistol away from the giant. She threw herself at the huge man, pummeling him with tiny fists. He reached around and swatted her to the floor.

The soldier's gun was an inch from Doc's head. Adi snatched up a scalpel from the ground, got up on her knees—and drove it, with both fists, into the man's thigh.

Bellowing, the German smashed Doc against the wall, dropping him, unconscious, to the ground. Reaching over, he seized Adi by the scruff of the neck and banged her head onto the hard dirt floor.

• • •

Christian Schmidt stood up, the room spinning around him. With thick fingers, he tried to clear away the blood pooling in his eyes, but it just kept dripping.

Remembering the gun, heavy in his hand, he held it up, examining it in the pale light. All the dirt caked into its crevices, it was a wonder it still worked. Cocking it, he leaned down and leveled it at the back of Adi's skull.

• • •

In the corner of the room, a long shadow from the lantern flickered and appeared to solidify on the wall, like iron filings on a magnet.

Her forehead pressed to the ground, Adi drifted back into a sort of wakefulness. Out of the corner of her eye, she saw the bottom of a dark coat and black leather boots stepping forward from the darkness. She heard leather soles grinding bits of broken glass—and then, more immediate, the sound of a pistol cock. Adi's heart nearly stopped at the sharp report of a gun going off. Blood splattered across her face. The gunshot reverberated in the little room, as the big German soldier collapsed to the floor next to her, the tiniest wisp of smoke drifting out from a neat hole in his temple.

"Give me your hand."

Dazed and streaked with blood, Adi allowed Coal to help her stand. He leaned her up against the wall, a palm to her chest to steady her. Picking up a rag from the table he dabbed it to his tongue and began to wipe the blood from her face.

Drifting in a little sphere of calm, Adi's eyes opened and looked into Coal's. Tiny flecks of gold floated in the gray of his iris.

There was shouting from outside. Doc groaned and began to stir in the corner.

Adi, her head clearing, looked once more at Coal, then pushed him aside to get to Doc.

She helped him sit up as Gershom and several other soldiers dashed into the infirmary.

When Adi looked over again, Coal, the bloody rag in hand, appeared to be stepping backward into a shadow.

Part 3

Chapter 27

November 4, 1918

"Oww!" said Augustin. "Thomas! Will you stop fussing with it. It's fine!"

"There's blood running down your sleeve," Thomas replied. "I just want to tighten the bandage up a little."

Augustin tried to remove his arm from Thomas's reach, but this was difficult as they were both sitting on the same horse.

"Leave it, Thomas," said George, lifting up in his saddle to look over the ridge ahead. "Won't be more than an hour or so before we reach camp. We'll have a medic check it, soon as we get there."

With the front pushed up north for the first time since the war began, this should have been an easy run for them. They rode through the night, south from Rethel to Reims carrying a report on the dismal state of the railway line.

It wasn't the Germans that caused the trouble for Augustin this time, just a stray coil of barbed wire in the dark. Down went Augustin's horse. A shattered fetlock joint kept the beautiful mare from ever getting to her feet again. An exposed corkscrew picket sliced through Augustin's overcoat into his arm. Before he'd let Thomas look at the wound, Augustin put his hand over the horse's eyes, whispering to the animal for a moment. He put her down with a single shot.

No time to waste, they continued on their way, riding double, alternating hourly.

• • •

Two and a half years had passed.

Soldiering was not what George had envisioned when he finally managed to sign up (under the name Thomas Augustin).

How he managed, in the first few weeks, to avoid being court-marshaled and shot for insubordination was anybody's guess. Following orders was not something that came naturally to him. And to be honest, George simply had no idea how helpless he was in the real world. Without servants. Without Thomas.

But with perseverance, and a certain amount of ridicule from his fellows, he learned to keep his head down and stay out of trouble.

Training camp at Etaples was truly dreadful. But the barracks, the bad food, the early hours, were so odd to George that he managed to view them rather like roughing it on some sort of nightmarish camping trip.

That whimsical notion ended as soon as his company began the long slog north to Verdun, to be thrown into "the furnace," as the endless battle had come to be called. There, in a muddy trench that no amount of rumors prepared him for, the reality came crashing down on his head.

It was a miracle that he survived long enough to be spotted by a sergeant who'd been a groundskeeper at the royal estate. It took a week for word to get to Thomas and Augustin, several more for them to track him down.

Neither of them had laid eyes on George for the better part of a year.

They found him on the morning after the French lost the hills of Le Mort-Homme in the battle of Verdun. He was alive, but you would be forgiven for mistaking him for one of the 30,000-odd soldiers who were now scattered like so much gray and khaki on the barbed wire coiled across the once verdant landscape of northern France.

They sat beside him on a pew in the shell of a chapel serving as a makeshift hospital. George stared at them through the remaining lens of his glasses, as if he wasn't sure who they were. Shaking his head, he laughed to himself a little, before he buried his head against Augustin's chest and wept like a child.

It took them until dinner time (not that there was any dinner) to convince him to leave the trenches. He argued that the other men were counting on him. After attempting to reason with him, they resorted to blackmail; if he didn't stop this nonsense and come away with them, they would tell his fellow infantry mates who he really was.

That didn't work either, so they were forced to resort to the truth, which was clear to anyone not in shock—he had no mates left, almost everyone in his unit had been wiped out the day and night before.

• • •

By the end of 1914, there was nothing left of the telephone and telegraph lines, the railroad tracks, or the roads. They'd all been destroyed by the shelling. The only way for information to travel was by courier: on foot, bicycle, motorcycle, and horseback.

In the trenches, George had experienced this firsthand— insufficient information leading to disaster, thousands of soldiers killed by their own artillery, due to communication breakdowns.

So George proposed a compromise that day. He would drop his disguise as an infantryman, on the condition that he would continue serving as a courier on horseback—a position that he claimed was safer, and that, as a superb horseman, he was better suited for.

Thomas had grown concerned of late about the duchess's behavior. He argued that George's presence was needed in Alorainn. But George refused to return. He didn't care if he was the heir. He was not going to stand by and watch while others fought and died.

Augustin contended that the occupation of courier was only marginally less dangerous than what George had been doing. But recognizing that they weren't going to be able to talk him out of it, he and Thomas finally relented.

They had a condition of their own, however; this crazy plan could go forward only as long as George didn't go it alone.

"I'm a better rider than you're ever going to be," said Augustin. "Hell, Thomas is a better rider."

Once the deal had been struck, they picked up his pack and took him away to recover from his wounds, as much as could be. In a little hotel outside Nancy they waited. Uncle Andre had lunch with General Foch, and called in a few favors. Before a month passed, they had horses and kits sent up from home. No one ever said being royalty didn't have its advantages.

The only remaining hurdle was the constitution of Alorainn.

Fortunately the duchess was surprisingly cooperative. It kept George away from home, which was entirely to her liking.

• • •

As Augustin had predicted, the occupation of messenger was, in its way, as dangerous as the trenches. After two and a half years in the saddle, they'd had more close calls than they cared to remember. It was a miracle that all three of them were still alive.

Augustin was an excellent horseman but that didn't keep him from having his horse shot from beneath him on their second day out. It was only George that kept him from packing up and leaving when he had to put the horse down in the middle of a muddy field.

Being a cousin to George, Augustin had known him since they were both eight. But the first time he had paid him any mind was several years later, at the party to announce George's father's betrothal to Johanna. Augustin and George spent the afternoon smashing all the windows out of an old house on an adjacent property. They were severely punished, and had been partners in crime ever since.

Augustin was, as many men are, in possession of a multitude of acquaintances. But he had few real friends. He could afford to take most things for granted—his family had more money than God. But, though he'd never been exactly sure why George liked him, he never took George's friendship for granted.

If anyone could claim to have known George longer than Augustin, it was Thomas. They'd been together since they were in diapers.

Thomas's mother had been lady in waiting for George's mother, until the duchess's death. It was only natural, when George came of age and Thomas returned from school at the abbey, that Thomas officially become valet to the heir. Naturally, since Thomas had been taking care of George, in one way or another, pretty much his whole life.

As treacherous as that task was in the midst of a war, in some ways it was easier to protect George from enemy soldiers, hunger, and trench foot than from himself. The balancing act between being his friend and being his valet had gotten to be nearly impossible in the few years before the war. More and more of Thomas's day had been spent worrying about whether George had wrapped an automobile around a tree or managed to drink himself to death.

So, in some ways, as horrible as everything was (and the war was horrendous beyond words, the sights they saw, the hardship they experienced) and though they complained endlessly about the mud, the food, the heat, the cold, and the fleas, and talked ceaselessly of the war being over and done, and returning to their previous lives . . . truth be told, though no one ever said it out loud, the three of them wouldn't have missed it.

• • •

One might have thought that the subject of the beautiful brown-skinned girl who had appeared in Alorainn for a few brief moments, nearly four and a half years earlier, would be long spent. Augustin had hardly laid eyes on the young woman.

But, much as it was in the trenches, a day in the life of a courier swung between heart-stopping terror and utter incessant boredom. Though constantly on their guard—trouble could arise in a heartbeat—most of the time they sat in their saddles and watched the landscape pass. And they talked. And of all the topics that arose, the one that appeared with the most regularity was Adi.

• • •

For Augustin, it was largely about the riddles. It would have been hard to devise a better, longer-lasting entertainment for whiling away the hours. They had managed to get another one of them figured out, after Belfort and Ypres. But the last riddle was killing them.

Of course, what really made it so intriguing was the mystery that came along with the young woman herself. It didn't take much time for Augustin to become as invested as his friends.

Thomas would agree, but for him there was more to it than that, more than just a game and a puzzlement. First of all, Thomas felt he'd lost Adi. If he had been paying more attention, doing his job, she wouldn't have disappeared. And because of that carelessness, this woman, whom he considered, in many ways, responsible for the positive changes in George, was lost to them.

There was another reason. Though Thomas had a pretty strong sense by this time in his life that women probably weren't to his taste, the too brief time he'd spent with the girl was the closest he'd ever come to questioning this preference. He'd really liked her, and it was the rare day since she'd gone that he didn't miss her.

For George, it was even more complicated. Nobody's fault, perhaps, but his life was altered the day he met her. He was pretty certain the irresponsibility and the boozed-out oblivion of those years would never return. But neither would the simplicity or the careless joy. In a way that was now impossible to separate, her appearance was forever entangled with a war and the collapse of the world as he knew it.

There was that.

And there were her beautiful hands curled around her face as she slept that first day in the car seat. The light that shone in her eyes when she was excited. The way her lips trembled when she kissed him that night in the orchard.

He knew Thomas felt guilty, that he held himself responsible for her disappearance. But to George's thinking, it was all his fault. His fault for not kissing her again. His fault for acting like a witless schoolboy the next day.

For leaving her there.

For a while, that was how he had looked at it. Bemoaning the loss, blaming himself, certain that Adi, if she thought of him at all, probably thought herself well favored to be away from a charming drunkard.

But now, and more and more—especially when he would wake in those early morning hours, when the desolation would roll in— it would come to him: she hadn't become bored with waiting, or gotten fed up with him and left. Something had happened to her. Something to do with the mystery that twisted tight around her.

This was why, for all these reasons, though any fool would understand that the girl was surely gone and never to be seen again . . . this was why they still pondered that fourth riddle and that point on the map that might tell them where her fabled lost brothers were. And that last riddle, that might, just maybe, lead them to something more.

Chapter 28

Adi walked through the doorway into what remained of the kitchen.

There wasn't much left of the *grande maison*, only the foyer and a few meters of wall, held together by a bramble of ancient rosebush. The rest of the house was a pile of debris, knocked down years before by artillery.

Pulling her greatcoat tight about her against the November chill, Adi sat herself onto one of the chairs that still had most of its seat intact. In the mornings, when it was quiet, she liked to sit at the big wooden table next to the glassless windows and think. She was close enough to the hospital to hear if anyone yelled for her.

Someone was shouting now. But it wasn't from the hospital.

Lifting up in her chair, she could make out soldiers, couriers—three of them on two horses, riding into camp from the east, getting a warm welcome from a group of men by the gate. It was too far away to make out the riders' faces. They must've come down from Bazancourt or Rethel, maybe. That couldn't have been easy.

"Just keep the bandage dry. You'll be fine."

Adi looked over to see Doc helping a soldier up the steps from the basement of the hospital. An American from the west. New Mexico, or that other one? Arizona. He was smiling, his arm no longer in a sling.

"Mer-ci, Doc, and bon voyage," he said. He spotted Adi at the table over at what was left of the kitchen. "You boys keep your heads down up north, hear?" Adi smiled. The soldier gave a wave and made his way back in the direction of the tents.

Doc squinted up at the sky, the light glaring off his dirty glasses. He shuffled over to the *maison*. "The weather might just cooperate for a day or two."

He examined the choice of chairs at the table until he found one acceptable. Lowering himself down, he leaned back against the wall.

• • •

The immovable front had finally moved. For the first time in four and a half years, armies were on the march again.

Not that the Germans had made it easy. Just a few months before, small bands of special forces outfitted with automatic rifles and flame throwers had swept through the lines, reinforced by a moving barrage of artillery. The British 5th Army had nearly broken. For the second time in four years, the Germans had come within a few kilometers of marching down the boulevards of Paris.

But they had neither the men nor the resources to support this tactic for long. The assault collapsed upon itself and the Allies rushed into the breach. The Americans had finally joined the fight. The Austro-Hungarian Empire had surrendered, abandoning its alliance with Germany. Troops were deserting. German cities were dying of starvation and the Spanish flu. Baron von Richthofen, "The Red Baron," had been shot down. They had no hope now of winning the war. They struggled only to better their bargaining position for an armistice that was, now, as inevitable as the sunrise.

This didn't mean much to Doc and Adi. They were presently eighty kilometers from the front, but that didn't keep a steady tide of wounded from pouring in every day. Tomorrow, their rotation in this rear-area hospital was done. It was back to the front.

• • •

Adi looked at Doc for a moment, then reached over and took his glasses from his nose. It was a wonder he could see through them, speckled as they were with spots of dried blood and Lord knows what else. Like the rest of his uniform. Not that hers was much cleaner.

She pulled out her handkerchief, exhaled on the lenses, and began wiping them.

Doc took the opportunity to rub his filthy hands across his face. He turned and looked out the window. From where they were sitting one could see the sky and a distant curve of the Vesle River. Beyond that, a bit of Reims Cathedral rose up through the haze. You could almost make believe that the city wasn't a shell-blasted ruin.

"When I was growing up," said Doc, "some child drowned in that river every year. It's like glass on the surface, but the current was fierce."

She handed him his glasses. Doc put them on, smudging the lenses in the process.

"We used to, my family, used to come here every August when we were kids. About a half-mile up river, where my cousins used to live."

Adi leaned her chin on her hand to listen. It wasn't often that Doc would quit yelling and just talk, rarer still when he might say something about his previous existence. Most of his conversation would lead you to believe he was born an old army medic.

"Right down the way"—he motioned with his hand—"there'd be people in boats, kids swimming, families picnicking." He laughed. "We made sure my mother never heard about all those people drowning—she'd have never let us go in."

This sounded like something she recalled Xavier and Xander telling her. That they'd had the same rule with their mother. Or was it their governess? "Always in trouble," they said. "She never knew the half of it."

At least that's what she thought she remembered.

These days it all seemed but a dream, her life before. The only thing real anymore was the never-ending war and the wounded, Doc and Gershom and the others. She was not a young lady at university, as she had once dreamed. Or even a girl with a beau, engaged or married. She was Jean Joseph Goux.

She watched Doc as he tilted his head back and closed his eyes, letting the pale sun warm him.

Pulling the watch up from inside her coat, she laid it on the table. She hardly felt wobbly anymore to lose contact with it. Probably that strange reaction had just been her imagination anyway.

But it had gotten harder for her to look at the thing, this reminder of her failure. To ruminate on the boys' whereabouts was to invite an almost paralyzing anxiety. She had dwelled upon the mystery until her head ached, till she thought she would go mad. She never got close to an answer. Who was he? Why had he done these things to them? Why had he saved her life? If indeed he had saved her. And been there in the middle of a battle? The further away the memory got, the surer she was that it was a result of having her head banged on the floor.

She slid a fingernail under the lid and pulled it open. The boys stared out at her, their appearance never-changing, no matter how much time passed.

She had no idea what she looked like these days. There weren't a lot of mirrors in trenches—nor in the hospital, for that matter. The wounded didn't need reminding of what they'd lost. Nor did she. It terrified her to think of how little of herself might still be recognizable. Just as well, she thought. That silly girl, off to Paris, to live her life in splendid isolation, discarding her brothers like a pair of shoes she no longer fancied.

She flipped the watch face around. The first three squares on the left were now empty.

It still took too long, but she had gotten better at figuring the time. Thirty-six hundred seconds in an hour, 86,400 in a day, 604,800 in a week. A meager 859,429 seconds was all that was remaining. She watched as they ticked away: 7, 6, 5 . . .

Less than seven days remained. She tried to breathe through the tightness that gripped her chest.

Three of the riddles were deciphered. That was to say, only one more had been added to the Belfort and Ypres that George and Thomas had come up with. The third one was solved a year or so after she became Jean Joseph Goux and started living in holes in the ground.

That one she owed to Gershom Yachov and a soldier from Besançon.

• • •

She'd come back to the infirmary one night from her visit to the latrines. She looked over to see that a couple of stretcher bearers were sitting in the corner, looking guilty. Gershom sat between them holding the watch open in his hand, not looking the slightest bit guilty.

"Your cockamamie watch?" he said. "Who made this? And what do the riddles mean?"

"Give it back, Gershom," Doc rumbled from his chair where he was napping. Adi grabbed the watch back in astonishment and held her hands wide to ask how he'd managed to lift it from her.

Gershom grinned. "I was beginning to think you weren't gonna notice. I've had it since we were on the motorbikes this afternoon."

According to rumor, Gershom Yachov, before he found his way into the army, was something of a *gonif*, which, he explained with a crooked grin, was Yiddish for "thief."

No one knew where he came from. No one was sure he had ever even signed up. He had simply been around one day when Doc needed a driver. He was fearless behind the wheel and brilliant at procuring supplies, so no one questioned why he would be crazy enough to be there when he didn't have to be.

Because of him, the riddles became a regular topic of conversation in the infirmary. At first, most of the men didn't know what they represented, something about this Second Lieutenant Goux's brothers having been kidnapped. Perhaps his sister Adi as well. Didn't matter to them; it passed the time.

At the beginning, the men thought Goux to be a bit of an odd duck, with his not speaking and his peach fuzz cheeks. But there was something about his shy manner and good nature that inclined most of them to look after the lad. Woe be it to you if Doc caught you being mean to the kid. The colonel who muttered about "not having some bloody brown wog bandage me" found himself face-first out in the mud.

His loss. At this point Adi, as anyone who paid attention to these things agreed, had marvelous hands.

It had not started out that way.

Often as not in those first months, when the wounded started pouring in, Adi would have to run from the room, to let her stomach stop turning. Or go and be sick somewhere.

Doc would curse and shout after her, "Goux! Get your ass back in here! It's just a goddamned leg wound!"

She did her best. Dragged herself back in.

Until one day, she realized—staring into the chest cavity of a young British soldier, his heart still pumping—that it wasn't the human body that made her sick, but the violence done to it.

Once she understood this, her attitude shifted. When she saw some part she'd not seen before—a lung, or a kidney, or the valves of the heart—she began to appreciate the opportunity she had stumbled into. She was receiving training that only a handful of women could claim.

There were women in the war, she knew: cooks, nurses, prostitutes—she'd even seen some ladies driving ambulances. And of course women like Edith Cavell, the gallant British nurse, shot by the Germans. But as far as she knew she was the only woman in an infirmary, actually doing surgery at the front. It made her smile to imagine what her mother would say if she could see. Well, the doctor part, at least. God only knows what she would make of Second Lieutenant Goux.

For months Adi had been certain she'd be found out. It was inconceivable that she could keep fooling all these men. They were men! Didn't they know what men look like?!

It didn't hurt that everyone was covered in mud most of the time, bone-tired, staring at their boots. But, as the days turned to months, she began to understand—people saw what they expected to see. They could not imagine a woman dressed as a soldier, holding a scalpel, covered in blood. So they didn't see her.

Of course, it would never have worked if they had heard her voice. That would have been the end of it right there. Thinking back to lunch with George's family and their discussion about all those women in disguise who fought in the American Civil War— she hadn't thought it possible. They must have had low voices.

Once, on leave, in a little town south of Troyes, they had eaten an unforgettable dinner in a restaurant run by one of Doc's old schoolmates. The man and his wife had made a big fuss over Doc and his friends, putting them at the best table in the room, though they were certainly the only diners in the place who were not of high rank.

Adi saw a different side of Doc. He was a Frenchman after all, food his lifeblood. She finally got to experience what real French food was like: smoked ox tongue, partridge, and snails, wonderful wines, strange pâtés, and cheeses. For several hours, the war was pushed aside and Doc, with the assistance of a couple of bottles of extraordinary wine, turned into . . . himself, she guessed.

She did have a real fright, however, when she caught the owner's wife staring at her through the meal in a curious manner. At the end of the evening, the woman leaned in to Adi and whispered, "Bravo, *mademoiselle*."

Adi almost had a heart attack, but no one else appeared to notice.

• • •

One rainy afternoon, when neither side had the will to make the mud worse by shooting at each other, they were sitting around in the infirmary playing poker and talking. At the table with Adi and Doc and Gershom was a man from Besançon with an ungainly bandage wrapped across his nose. A couple of days before, a sniper's bullet had blown the spectacles off his face, taking a small piece of the bridge of his nose with them. Having lost his glasses, he'd been holding his cards at arms length to read them. The infirmary always had a collection of eyeglasses, left by soldiers who no longer required them. Between hands, Adi sorted through them for the man to try on. They finally found a pair that would do. "Bless you," said the soldier. "I was like Jeremiah without his spectacles!"

Doc dealt the next hand and looked to Adi to start, but she was sitting there staring into space.

"What is it?" he asked.

Turning to the man, she pointed to her mouth and made a backwards motion with her finger.

Familiar with her gestures, Gershom asked the man to repeat what he'd said about his friend who lost his spectacles.

"My friend?" said the man, confused. "Oh. Not my friend, I was talking about the prophet Jeremiah."

Adi pulled the watch out of her tunic and opened it up to the third riddle. She slid it across the table to Gershom, signing for him to read.

"Like, I don't know it by heart," said Gershom.

"How will you find . . ." he recited. ". . . now that–Jeremiah's quite blind,

"A cool drink of water for the wanderers' father,

"After forty years of thirst has left him quite cursed

"and unable to step cross the border."

The man looked around the table in bewilderment at the sudden, breathless attention he was recieving.

"I think you'd better tell us, soldier," said Doc, "what you meant by the comment about Jeremaiah?"

Turned out, there was a huge sculpture, a bunch of biblical figures around a hexagonal column, in a monastery down south: Moses, David, Daniel, Zachariah, Isaiah . . . and Jeremiah.

Originally a fountain in the monastery's courtyard, it came to be called the Well of Moses.

Adi tapped her knucles on the table and gestured to her eyes.

"Yeah," said Cloutain, one of the nurses. "What's that got to do with him being blind?"

The soldier from Besançon continued.

The marble figures composing the Well of Moses were quite realistic, with impressive detail. King David had ivory strings on his harp. Mary wore a metal crown. And Jeremiah had little copper glasses perched upon his nose.

During the French Revolution, when the citizens of France were taking out their frustrations on the church, the monastery was destroyed and the sculpture was knocked about. Someone made off with the clever little spectacles. Never to be seen again.

Therefore, rendering "Jeremiah quite blind."

Adi banged on the table again to get the man's attention and tried to sign. Doc helped her out.

"Where?" he barked. "Where is this fountain?"

Utterly confused, the man stammered, "It's—it's in the—city of Dijon."

The infirmary erupted into shouts of "The map! Get the map!"

Doc was ahead of them. Out from the inside breast pocket of his coat, came a folded map.

On his birthday the year before, Doc, who complained endlessly about "never knowing where the hell they were," was presented with a map of France by Gershom. No ordinary map this, but the sort available only to generals and high-ranking officials. They knew better than to ask where he'd managed to find such a thing. When not in use, it was always tucked safely in Doc's pocket.

He spread it open on the tabletop and they all gathered around, Adi in the middle.

Standing out amidst the myriad dotted lines, circles, and scribbles indicating their travels was a thick black ruled line extending from the city of Ypres in Belgium, down to the town of Belfort, near the border of Switzerland. On more than one occasion they had noted the coincidence between this line and the nearly unchanging demarcation of the Western Front.

The man from Besançon stuck his head into the circle and put his finger down upon Dijon. "This means what?" he asked.

One of the interns did his best to explain, making a rather fanciful mishmash of the details. Adi let it be, as did Doc. It was just as well that the men were not too clear on the particulars.

The excitement diminished, however, once the realization hit home that without the fourth city they weren't much better off than they'd been before.

A soldier came in with a mangled hand—caught in the feeder on his machine gun.

Doc folded up the map and bopped Adi on the head with it. "We got three, Goux. We'll get the last."

Everyone got back to the card game, but Adi's heart wasn't in it anymore.

• • •

Adi looked over at Doc. He was studying her and the watch sitting before her on the table. Rubbing his thumb across the silver medallion around his neck, he shook his head and went back to gazing out at the landscape.

Adi looked at the little swallow flying, as always, across the back of the watch. Time flying.

But not for much longer.

In a week, it would all be done. Whatever it was. This game she was supposed to be playing. It was a miracle she was still alive. Were any of them? The boys? George and Thomas? Coal? It had been so long.

"I can't remember," said Doc, "the last time we came here to the river. Don't know why we stopped. Always figured Lisette and I would bring the girls . . ."

Doc drummed his fingers on the table, dropped his chair down, and stood up.

He sniffed and rubbed at the end of his nose.

"Just as well," he said, looking over at Adi. "It's going to be a long long time before anyone has a picnic in this place again."

If Adi had been able, she would have kept him talking. Maybe she'd find out why he wore his wife's medallion around his neck. Find out what happened to Lisette and his daughters.

But maybe it was just as well. They all had their secrets, didn't they?

Doc slapped Adi on the shoulder. "Come on, my talkative friend. We got work to do if we're going to head up to Mézières with the Americans tomorrow. Let's go see if anyone has managed to scrape together something like breakfast in this godforsaken place!"

The Watch's Tale

Tapping his fingernail against the top of the jar, Coal watched over the body. It was taking so long he began to think he'd misjudged the man. It had happened. Not often.

But at last, the creature climbed up out of the man's throat. A fat thing with terrible long legs. It tried to dart away. Coal caught hold of it.

Then he saw the girl.

Eleven or twelve, maybe. Pale with a scarlet slash of lips and eyes too large for her face. He kept an eye on her as she stared unblinking from the end of the hallway. He was going to bolt and put the bug in its jar later, but the girl's expression of calm fascination kept him there until he was done.

A decade later, in a theater in London, Coal looked up in the middle of the third act of *Hamlet* to see the girl staring at him from her box. She had grown into her features and was alarmingly beautiful.

She found him during the interval, standing alone in a shadowed alcove. With her lady's companion waiting at a discreet distance, the young woman approached. She bowed her head, her hands to her breast and declared, "The day you took my uncle, *monsieur*, was the day my life began."

He insisted he'd had nothing to do with the man's death. But he saw in her eyes that there wasn't a thing he could say that was going to dissuade her from her interpretation.

Her uncle had left her with a fortune, some compensation for what he had taken from her in her youth. With it, she purchased a crumbling fortress and a substantial piece of property south of the city of Nancy and built a great estate. No small feat for a young woman in that time. She offered the house to Coal, then and there. He declined.

Not to be deterred, she told him she would have another house built for him in the forest nearby.

"Do I look as if I am in need of a home?" he asked.

With the tips of her fingers, she brushed the hair from her forehead. "I would never presume to know, *monsieur*. Only, if some day you desired to lay your head upon a pillow . . ."

• • •

After years abroad, Coal returned to France. Curious about the young woman, he searched for and found her estate near Nancy.

At the southern end of an orchard of chestnut trees she'd had planted, there was a smaller house. Not too close, but not too far. Peering through the windows, he saw no sign that anyone other than a maid frequented the place. There were fresh roses by the bed. He concluded that someone had been replenishing them for years.

Returning to the estate, he sat in the branches of the tree outside her study and observed the young woman working at her desk. Reading to herself what she had written, she stroked her cheek with her quill feather.

He watched her for hours, until, famished, he knocked on her door.

He had had no more plan than that he might find a meal or stay the night. But before he knew it, a year had passed. And then a second. He took to calling her Viviane, after the witch in the King Arthur legend who enchants Merlin into an endless sleep.

After too many quarrels over his untidiness, he left the estate, but made it only as far as the smaller house. There, she let him be, mostly. He would return from his wanderings to find a painting propped up on the kitchen table or a grand piano in the parlor. And again, for a time, he would be beguiled into staying.

Living in the great house with a pair of servants, she spent her days writing poetry and some indecipherable epic, about a war between the earth and fallen angels living on the dark side of the moon. For several seasons she was enthralled with Indian mysticism, filling her rooms with pictures of Ramakrishna and Sarada Devi and engaging in practices of silence and meditation.

• • •

He tried to stay. But his hunger for solitude finally outweighed his desire to see her eyes, to watch her brush the hair from her forehead the way she did. Over time, Coal learned about her years in the clinic and the fires, and why she had been living alone with her uncle. She was mad, he knew. And, over time, she became more so.

So, out into the world he went, to meddle again in the affairs of men.

• • •

It seemed no time at all.

He found her on a bed of straw, in the room where her sumptuous four-poster used to sail like a great ship. She had, at some point, given the estate over to the Poor Clares or the Carmelites, and appeared to have taken vows herself. But the house was empty now. Why they had left or why she had not gone with them, he'd never know. Old and still beautiful, even in death, she lay in the corner, her wrists cut open, haloed by pools of dried blood.

Back in the little house, perched on the keys of the grand piano, he found a small package wrapped in butcher paper and twine, addressed simply: M. Coal. Inside, scratched on a slip of paper, were a few lines from Hamlet's soliloquy. And there was a pocket watch.

On the inside was a portrait of the two of them. Nested behind that was a poem; a rhyme about hearts sealed forever in a jar. And on the back of the watch was engraved a swallow circled by the words *tempus fugit.*

Rubbing his thumb back and forth across the lid, Coal watched, as far off through the forest of chestnuts, the grand chateau lit the twilight as it burned.

Chapter 29

"You've got to be kidding!" said George. "Aunt Elodie—locked up?"

Uncle Henri looked at them from under his fearsome eyebrows and shook his bare head. He didn't look as if he were joking.

• • •

As soon as George, Thomas, and Augustin had given their report to General Maistre and received the reply, Uncle Henri pulled them outside the command post. Their delight at seeing him was short-lived.

"Nice to see you, too, boys. Now be quiet and listen."

It was one shock after another, Aunt Elodie's detention being but one. There'd been arrests and imprisonment, judges removed, property confiscated.

Henri conceded that much of the news out of Alorainn was rumor, at best second- or third-hand. But the talk was all the same: a perpetual state of martial law. The royal guard transformed into the duchess's private army. There'd even been whispering about hangings.

Now the lads understood why news from home had grown so infrequent and short on specifics. It wasn't simply the war and lost letters.

The one constant in all the accounts was Duchess Johanna. No longer encumbered by the stronger members of the family, she had remade Alorainn in her image.

"It was admirable," said Henri, "that we all went off to do our duty, but we were fools to leave Alorainn in the hands of this madwoman. I'm as much to blame as anyone, ignoring warnings, postponing visits."

"We haven't been back in . . ." George looked at the others. "Well, I haven't been back at all. Not once. Thomas was there briefly, but not in—"

"Almost sixteen months," Thomas said.

"I told you you couldn't trust that daft woman," said Augustin.

"Not what you were saying this morning," said George.

"Well—I never said she wasn't attractive."

"Oh, for God's sakes," said Henri.

"I'm just saying"—Augustin tugged at his bandage—"she was broken to start with, but after Halick disappeared, she's gone over the moon."

"Augustin!" said Uncle Henri, noticing the young man's arm. "You're wounded."

"We're on our way to the infirmary," said George.

"It's nothing," said Augustin. "Just need to change this dressing. I can do it myself."

"He's afraid of the flu," said Thomas.

"He should be," said Uncle Henri. "We've been lucky here so far, but the thing is spreading like wildfire."

"See, I told you," said Augustin.

They passed through a makeshift mess area, tables set up outdoors to take advantage of the sun. Soldiers, medical staff, and wounded, eyes glazed in fatigue, were beginning to straggle in. Augustin looked down at the trays and shook his head in disgust.

"One of the infirmaries," said Henri, "just there." He pointed across to a piece of wall, held up by a briar rose. "Next to that. Down in the basement. I'll meet you there with your furlough orders." He started away. "Oh! And don't leave without your mail. I'm tired of carrying it around."

He stopped again. "Listen. I know you've got to report back to Foch. But when you're done—get home, hear? Quick as you can. But be careful."

• • •

The soldier's head was wrapped in bandages, cotton pads over both his eyes. Coal held the young man's arm, helping him across the patch of rough ground.

"Right," said Coal. "But isn't the—doesn't the mustard gas pool up in the bottom of the craters?"

"Yes, Father, sometimes, when it's cold."

Coal was dressed in an army chaplain's uniform, white clerical collar, a silver cross on his lapel.

"So, you think," said Coal, "that God is punishing you for—?"

"Because I'm a coward, Father. If I hadn't hid in a hole. If I'd kept going with my mates, I wouldn't have—I wouldn't be like this."

"Here, sit." Coal sat the lad down on a crate in the warm sunlight. Dragging over another box, he winced as he took a seat next to the boy. From that vantage point, he could see most of the camp. He patted his pockets for his spectacles. Lately, he could hardly go out in daylight hours without tinted lenses. He'd taken these off an engineer in the wreck of a troop train near the Italian border the previous year.

"So, instead of being blind, you'd be dead like your friends?"

The boy fumbled trying to get a cigarette from the pack. Maybe he was crying. It was hard to tell, the lad's eyes bandaged as they were.

"Give it to me."

Coal tapped a cigarette out the pack, pulled the petrol lighter from his pocket, and lit it. He took a drag and stuck it between the soldier's lips.

"Do you know," said Coal, "why Moses wasn't allowed into the Promised Land? After forty years in the desert?"

"No, Father. Why?"

"No, I'm asking you," said Coal. "I've read it a hundred times and it still doesn't make any sense. God tells him, Moses, to strike the rock with his staff, once, to get water. Moses hits it twice. God gets angry at him."

"But I don't—what's that got to do with . . . ?"

Coal looked past the soldier and saw Adi and the old man coming up out of the mess, trays in hand.

"I don't know. Just that I don't think it pays to lean too much on this whole 'God's will' thing."

"Father?" said the young man, confused.

"You can't say He picks favorites, though, can you? Even if you're Moses.

"What amazes me," said Coal, rolling his shoulder, trying in vain to ease the ache, "is that in the face of all this you can still ask these questions. Whether you're a good man, whether you've done the best you can? How bad would things have to be, before you wouldn't ask these questions, I mean?"

Coal watched as the girl sat herself on a bench, the doctor next to her. She pushed her food around on her tray and stared into space.

"I don't know, Father. Can it get any worse than this?"

"In Hell, maybe." Coal took one of the lad's cigarettes for himself and returned the pack to the boy's pocket.

"I guess that's all Hell is, really. Just the place where no one asks questions anymore."

• • •

Coal sat smoking on his wooden ammo box, leaning to the side occasionally to keep out of the girl's line of sight. He hardly need bother. She wasn't noticing much of anything these days.

Under his breath he cursed. It was inconceivable. The girl—still here, still playing this imbecilic game. Would she not concede, even now? Less than a week. What chance did she have? Wincing, he dug his thumb into his shoulder.

For a time, the wound had appeared to be, if not improving, at least not getting worse. But in the last few months it had festered again, seeping through bandages, ruining his clothes. He could hardly use his right arm anymore. And he was sure that the gash was giving off a foul odor.

It had taken him much too long to recognize the bind he was in. Until the game was done, he couldn't take the watch back. But without the watch, he would . . . ? Well, he was not exactly sure what. He had become convinced of one thing, however: the seconds ticking away were not just the boys', but his as well.

He fiddled with a ring, too small to push past the first knuckle on his little finger. He'd taken it a couple of weeks before from the hand of a girl buried in the rubble of a bombed-out building in Tolmezzo, in northern Italy.

He couldn't identify the stone, couldn't see the color. Another result, he was certain, of being so long separated from his watch. In fits and starts, all his senses had grown dull. It was a wonder he could even walk. And the headaches and the—

"For Christ's sakes," he said out loud. "Stop your whining and do something."

The young man sat up, as if he'd been slapped. "But—I—I—" he stuttered.

"No. I don't mean you," said Coal.

"But—you're right, Father. I'm just feeling sorry for myself. There are men with no arms. No faces."

Coal looked over to see the girl and the old man getting up from their bench. They dropped their trays off and started back.

Coal got to his feet as well. He dropped his cigarette into the mud and pushed at it with the toe of his boot. Taking hold of the young soldier's arm, he pulled him up.

"Come on boy. Can't sit around here all day. There's work to be done."

• • •

Doc and Adi made their way back to the infirmary; there was only so long they could stand seeing soldiers eating Maconochie and milk biscuit sludge.

As she and Doc came down the steps into the infirmary, Thomas was the first one she saw. He was steadying another soldier who was in the process of having the wound on his arm irrigated. They'd heard the man cursing half a block away.

The same instant that she saw Thomas, she heard:

"God sakes, Augustin. Keep this up and you're going to wake the Germans."

"They're eighty kilometers away," said Augustin.

"Yes. That's what I'm saying."

It was George—his hair cut shorter, his face leaner, but looking splendid in uniform.

He turned and looked right at Adi.

But with the morning sun streaming into the basement all he could see were two silhouetted figures coming down the steps.

Adi stood frozen, the weight of years and the strain of impending failure rendering her brain nearly unable to grasp what was before her eyes.

Doc said to the intern cleaning Augustin's wound, "You can't just bandage that! Goux. Show him how to stitch this up."

Before she knew it, Adi was up the stairs and running. Pushing past soldiers, she ran through the tents and fled down into the communications trenches, into what used to be the trenches of the front lines.

Gasping for breath she collapsed onto the firing shelf. A big brown rat grudgingly moved aside, scuttling back into a space between the sandbags. It watched as Adi stood up, sat down, and stood again and then proceeded, her fists clenched, to stomp circles in the mud.

• • •

By the time she got her nerve up to go back, they were gone. As she slunk down the stairs, she gestured to Doc, something about the food making her sick.

Doc wasn't buying it, but he let it pass.

When she found out later that afternoon that George and Thomas and the other man had left the camp, she teetered between disappointment and relief, which only took a moment to turn to despair. It gathered over her like a small dark planet.

It was just her bad luck that there were no Germans across no-man's-land to put her out of her misery. Though she knew she was too much of a coward for that.

She opted instead for a bombed-out house down the road away from the river. She dropped down at the bottom of a ruined staircase, put her fists to her face, and cried till the stars came out.

Chapter 30

Xander and Xavier had been spying on Brother Christopher for several weeks now, which somewhat explained why they were peeking at him from the inside of an armoire in the abbot's office at 1:30 in the morning.

The boys had often thought there was something curious about Brother Christopher.

Men who chose a monastic life, they had noticed, were by nature ofttimes a bit peculiar. There was always something illicit going on in an abbey. Inappropriate reading material. Middle-of-the-night visits to the kitchen. Difficulties with celibacy vows. Graffiti in the latrines. Smoking behind the library.

Brother Christopher, as far as anyone knew, engaged in none of these activities. He was the picture of a proper brother and had been since he'd joined the abbey a short time after the abbot arrived. Always on time, conscientious, hard-working, and modest. Behavior he'd encouraged, with debatable success, in the boys.

Which was why it struck them as noteworthy when it was rumored that Brother Christopher had been spotted of late in odd places at odder hours with strange people. Or so several senior boys had informed them (in barter for Xander's copy of a magazine with an illustration of a naked mermaid on the cover).

It wasn't long before they were playing detective. Xander had protested. He held Brother Christopher in very high regard, knowing he was largely responsible for pulling them through that first dark year after they'd arrived. But with as much concern as curiosity, the boys began shadowing him.

Just when they thought there was nothing to the rumors—precisely at the point when Xander had begun to declare, "I told you so"—they saw Brother Christopher sneaking into the abbot's house in the wee hours.

What were they to do? Confront him? Snitch on him, when Father Abbot returned from his trip? More information was what they needed.

• • •

The first night, the only creature other than themselves that entered the little office was a good-sized rat. He stopped and sniffed up at the crack in the door of the wardrobe where they had hidden before going on his way.

The next night they'd had a trickier time getting out of the boys' dorm unseen. By the time they arrived at the abbot's quarters, someone was already there in the office; it was hard to say whom. They returned to their beds. Hours of lost sleep were not helping their schoolwork.

Third time was the charm. Not long after they had settled themselves in the back of the closet, they heard the door to the house creak open, more quietly than if it were the abbot himself.

Peeking out through the abbot's vestments, the boys watched as Brother Christopher secured the door to the office behind him and then struck a match, lighting a stub of candle from his pocket. He placed it on top of a paperweight and set to work. From the sound of it, he was attempting to pick a lock on one of the drawers in the great desk. Apparently unsatisfied with his tool, he searched about until he found a letter opener. Pushing the chair back he weighed the knife in his hand and stood up. He came straight for the wardrobe and flung open the doors.

"Dammit! I should have known!" whispered Brother Christopher to the two wide-eyed faces staring out from the shadows. "Well, get out of there! You've got to leave. You can't be found here." He grabbed them by their shirtfronts, pulling them from the cabinet.

"But, Brother. What are you doing here?" Xander gestured to the desk. "What are you trying to find?"

"Doesn't matter, the locks are impossible," he hissed. He dragged them to the door. "Now come on."

"Not for Xavier," whispered his brother.

"What?"

"I've already been in the locked ones," said Xavier. "What d'you want in there? It's just papers."

Brother Christopher stopped, calculating furiously.

"How long would it take you?"

"Why are you doing it?"

Brother Christopher pulled at his earlobe. "You're just going to have to trust me." Without waiting for a response he pushed the boys behind the desk and pulled aside a curtain. "How about this trunk? Can you get in there?"

"Probably," said Xavier, looking at the large portmanteau tucked away in the shadows. "But why? Abbot's our friend, too."

"Yes, well, we'll see."

The twins looked at each other, a whole conversation in a glance. Xander nodded and handed Xavier his pocketknife.

"Hold the candle over here." Xavier dropped to his knees and before Brother Christopher had a chance to be amazed, the boy popped the lock open.

Brother Christopher listened for a second. Dead quiet except for their breathing.

"All right," he said, swinging the lid open.

Everything was there in the trunk, except perhaps a toothbrush. The abbot was clearly prepared to travel. Which was odd, as he was already away. Why would he have another trunk?

Brother Christopher removed the sectional trays and compartments, being careful not to disturb the contents. He reached the lower level. Riffling through a layer of decidedly non-clerical attire, he found what he was looking for.

"Now tell me if you think the abbot's your friend." He pushed aside the clothes to reveal two black cloth sacks. Pulling the first bag out he dropped it into Xavier's hands. Remarkably heavy. The boy loosened the strings to see, but they could all hear the sound of the gold coins clinking inside.

"And here's the other."

He tossed the second bag to Xander. Opening it, even in the dim light they could see the emeralds glow like new leaves.

They were speechless.

"Now put them back," whispered Brother Christopher.

"But why would he want to?" muttered Xavier, tears in his eyes.

Brother Christopher hurriedly stacked the last of the items in order and quietly closed the trunk. "I'm sorry, Xav."

"Maybe it's got something to do with his brother coming?" said Xander.

"What!" asked Brother Christopher. "What did you—where did you hear that?"

Xander pointed to a letter on the desk, under the paperweight.

"From the abbot's brother. He says he's coming to visit."

Brother Christopher carefully opened the letter. He scanned it quickly, looked utterly confused, read it again.

Shaking his head he put the letter back in the envelope and tucked it under the glass paperweight.

"That might explain it," he muttered.

"Explain what?" said Xavier.

"I'll tell you later. Put everything back the way it was and get out of here."

• • •

On their way out they nearly collided with Halick who was standing just outside the door.

"Good God, Halick!" whispered Xander. "You nearly gave me a heart attack!"

"Time for bed, buddy," said Xavier. "Come with us, we'll tuck you in."

But Halick just shook his head, picked up his broom and went back to sweeping by the light of the half moon.

The Abbot's Tale

1908

The train came to a halt a half-mile before the station at Saint Roche. The snow had come early, with the leaves still on the trees, bringing down an old linden onto the tracks.

The two men in the first-class car stepped down from the train, continuing their conversation while they stretched and smoked a cigarette. One of the men was in monk's robes.

When it looked as if the train might soon be continuing they stepped into the woods to relieve themselves.

• • •

Nicolas Paul didn't mean to kill the monk.

That is to say, he hadn't planned on such a thing when he found himself sharing a train compartment with the man in a black robe and wooden cross, attire he was all too familiar with, having until recently worn it himself.

They liked each other right off. The brother was excited and apprehensive about his new posting—he was to be made abbot. He was delighted to have someone who would listen to his concerns, someone refreshingly knowledgeable regarding the ebb and flow of life in an abbey.

Nicolas Paul knew he had the kind of face that put people at their ease: eyes as blue as the sea, and a manner that invited confidence. At first, he listened merely to pass the long night on the uncrowded train. But as the French countryside slipped past the black windows, he saw a way to slip the noose that had been drawing close about him for the last six months.

As they pooled their bread and cheese and chocolate to make a late supper, the brother had explained: to chose a successor from outside the abbey was unusual but not unheard of. Near death, the abbot of the Gentiana Abbey had selected his friend and colleague to fill his shoes, assuring his flock that they would grow to admire the brother as much as he had.

"How exciting," said Nicolas Paul, passing what was left of the wine. "Of course, I could see how that would make you nervous. So . . . you've never met anyone at the abbey?"

"Not a soul," said the brother.

• • •

Most of the passengers were asleep when the fallen tree was removed and the train started up again. Only a couple of people had noticed the two men smoking and talking in the cold air. No one saw the two sets of footprints heading into the woods. And no one took note that only one came back to the train.

Chapter 31

Spring 1868

Coal sat in a back pew of the Cathedral of Reims looking up at the morning light illuminating the arched ceiling so far above. If he squinted, he could imagine it was a mile high. The choir and orchestra, a couple of hundred strong, filled the immense space with Beethoven's *Missa Solemnis*. A serendipity. He had been crossing the square on his way to . . . somewhere, and he'd heard the sound of singing. A pair of trumpets as he entered a side door, and then a thundering explosion of voices knocked him back on his heels, nearly stopping his heart.

It was an unlikely pairing, Beethoven and Reims Cathedral, and not one that would be happening in a year or two when the Germans and the French returned to their endless squabbling. Truly, Coal had never been able to understand; these beings who could make wars were also the ones who built this building and wrote this symphony.

"Who knows," he murmured, "what it all means."

• • •

November 6, 1918
Five days left

Tagging along with a dozen or so American soldiers, Doc and Adi marched into what remained of the city of Reims. Gershom hadn't much liked the idea, but Doc said he needed to see the city again. And he liked the Yanks.

Before long they had a couple of children and a few tattered adults marching with them. It never ceased to amaze Adi to see people living in such desolation. So many windows had been blown out by the shelling that in the streets the broken glass came up to their ankles. It made a brittle whispering sound as they walked.

Just after noon they stood in the courtyard, gazing up at the heartbreaking ruin of the cathedral. Tears streaming down his cheeks, Doc stood staring, muttering curses under his breath.

The American colonel next to him raised his hand to shadow his eyes, as a delicate cloud of pink discharged from his chest. A crack of far-off gunfire, and the man fell straight back into the street.

That was how they found out that the reports of the German retreat from the city were incomplete.

The Americans spread out, trying to spot the sniper. Everyone scattered, taking cover wherever they could.

Adi grabbed the children by the hands and ran into the shadow of the cathedral. Doc and a private dragged the colonel in by the straps on his backpack.

Pushing the children behind her, she dropped her pack and pulled out a roll of bandage and tossed it to Doc. He was feeling around inside the wounded man's tunic to judge the extent of the damage. The look on his face told her all she needed to know. He chucked the bandage back to her. Breaking off half of the colonel's ID tag, Doc put it into the hand of a young private. The lad wiped tears away with the back of his hand and put the other half of the tag in his pocket.

Doc dropped down onto a block of stone next to Adi and the children, who were snugged in as close to the wall as they could manage. He took out his handkerchief and loudly blew his nose. He looked over at the children, a boy and a girl.

"Did you know," Doc said to the boy who sat staring at the dead colonel, "most of the kings of France were crowned in this church?"

The child, no more than seven, tried to pay attention to the old man, but the dead soldier and the sound of artillery starting up distracted him. He held the girl's hand, his little sister from the look of her. She was pushing at shards of blue stained glass from the blown-out church windows. They littered the ground like jewels.

Adi looked up behind her at the towering cathedral, or what was left of it. The Germans had been firing on it since the first months of the war. An error in aim, they asserted.

It was, even in this ravaged state, like nothing Adi had ever seen. Everywhere you looked, saints and angels and spires rose to heaven, held steady by huge stone buttresses arcing into the sky.

Gesturing to the little girl, Doc continued, as if they were a family on holiday.

"See the statue over there?" He pointed to the bronze figure on horseback just visible around the front of the church.

"That's Joan of Arc. She and the Dauphin, who was about to be crowned Charles VII, walked right through the front doors of this place. In 1427. Right over there."

"14 . . . 29," stammered the girl.

Doc smiled. "I stand corrected."

The air reverberated with the shriek of an artillery shell passing over the top of the cathedral. A young American soldier muttered to himself, "Six-inch howitzer."

A building half a block to the south exploded.

Doc looked at Adi. "Get the boy!"

The boy's arms tight around her neck, Adi ran across the cobblestones into a side street. Close behind, Doc, carrying the girl low in his arms, was already out of breath and wheezing. Even without his pack, he wasn't going to keep this up for long.

"Over there," said the boy, pointing to a pile of debris at the base of an elegant gray three-story building. Just above the pile of stone was a hole in the wall big enough to step through.

There was a large tarpaulin, hanging loosely over the break just inside the wall. Adi held it up for Doc and the girl. Outside they could hear shouts in German and boots running up the sidewalk.

The boy wriggled free of Adi's arms and slid to the marble floor.

They were in a gallery of a museum, the walls covered with gold-framed paintings, three deep, down from the high ceiling. There were a few paintings on the floor and a few more hanging loose in their frames next to the hole in the wall, but other than that and a thick layer of dust over everything, the place was remarkably intact.

Shouting from outside.

The boy took Adi by the hand and pulled her down toward doors at the other end of the room. The girl tugged on Doc's sleeve, but out of breath, he pushed her to follow Adi.

"Hide the kids," he whispered, pulling his pistol from his holster.

Adi hesitated.

"Goux. Don't argue."

The girl said to her brother, "Not that way, they'll see us."

They ran to a small door directly across the room; clearly, it was not their first time here. Passing through, Adi looked back to see Doc hiding himself under the side of the hanging tarp. The boy pulled the door shut.

A short dark hallway and they came out another door on the other side. Before them a staircase curved up to the second floor.

They charged up. Back through the little door they'd come through—shots fired!

More yelling, running. A boot kicked open the door. The handle broke off and went skittering across the marble floor. It came to a stop at the bottom of the staircase.

In the silence, a young German soldier looked up at Adi and the kids at the top of the stairs.

Adi stared back. The man was holding a pistol but seemed uncertain about shooting. At the children, perhaps? Or maybe it just didn't feel right to him to be killing people in a museum.

The little boy grabbed Adi's sleeve and pulled her into the next gallery.

"No!" The girl shook her head, whispering, "We can't get through that way!"

The boy looked up to Adi as the sound of boots on the marble stairs echoed off the arched ceiling.

Nothing for it. They kept going.

Most of the light in the long gallery was coming through one of the windows. An unexploded shell had smashed through the shutters and glass and embedded itself into the floor. As they ran through the gallery, startled pigeons flew up to the ceiling.

Some of the paintings had been removed from their frames, which leaned lonely against the walls. The floor was cluttered with packing crates. Adi grabbed up a crowbar as they turned the corner into a small gallery at the end. Sure enough, there was no exit. They were trapped.

Motioning for the children to get behind her around the corner, Adi held the crowbar high.

The sound of boots—and then nothing.

She took a quick peek out, sure she was going to be staring into the barrel of a gun. She heard a cough and then another, all the way at the other end of the gallery. She looked out again.

The soldier was sitting on a wooden crate staring at a painting on the wall. He took his helmet off and put it down next to him on the box. Another bout of coughing took him. Putting his pistol back into his holster he removed the cap from his canteen, took a swig. This settled his cough for a moment. Catching his breath, he tilted his head a little and gazed at the landscape.

What in the world? Adi leaned back into the small room. The children stared up at her. She raised her shoulders and shook her head. What were they to do now?

She looked up at the painting in front of her and considered the alternatives.

Was the soldier trying to trick them? It seemed bizarre. Did he think they'd gotten away? Wouldn't he at least . . .

Distracted, Adi looked up again at the painting.

People being burned at the stake. Lots of them. She glanced down at the title on the frame.

Strasbourg Massacre 14 February 1349. She stared.

It didn't come up very often, the question of whether Adi was allowed to laugh out loud. There'd been precious few occurrences these last years. The children stared open-mouthed at the young soldier, hopping up and down, a hand over his mouth, trying to restrain his laughter.

Adi didn't need to look at the riddle. The last riddle. She knew it like she knew her name. Well, better than that; she wasn't sure about her name sometimes.

"Not a word of it true and none of it new,
a morality play that caused some dismay,
because of the smells from the poisonous wells,
and the blood in the bread
from the children was bled
kindled an auto da fe
on Valentine's day."

Everything that had been discussed about the fourth riddle—it all came together.

Burning at the stake was what "auto da fe" came to mean during the Catholic Inquisition. Jews became the victims of this treatment because of the cretinous superstitions that they poisoned wells and baked bread containing the blood of Christian children. But no one—no one passing through the infirmary, at any rate—knew about this "Massacre."

The 14th of February—Valentine's Day!

In Strasbourg, France!

She had to go.

Taking the children by the hand, she walked out into the large room.

The soldier turned his head and looked over at them. Closer now, Adi could see how terribly gaunt he appeared. He took a crumpled pack of cigarettes from his pants pocket. In passible French, he asked Adi, "Have you got matches, *mein herr*?"

Adi shook her head.

"Ah, well," he said, putting the pack back in his pocket. "*So es geht.*"

Yes, so it goes.

They walked past the young man, but he began to cough again and scarcely seemed to notice.

• • •

In the middle of the gallery where they'd come in, Doc sat on a round high-backed sofa, his dusty horizon-blue uniform distinct against the red velvet.

A few feet away, beside a pedestal supporting a sculpture of a man on a horse, a German soldier lay dead upon the floor.

Adi scanned the room. If there were others, they were gone now. She motioned for the children to follow close behind her.

Doc had taken off his silver medallion and chain and was pouring it absently from hand to hand. There was blood on his fingertips, and between his feet, blood dripping on the marble floor.

Adi sat next to him and carefully pulled aside the front of his greatcoat.

He allowed her to examine him for a moment. When it was clear to both of them that there was no stopping the flow of blood, he held her hands tightly for a moment, then sat back.

She wiped her tears.

Shivering, Doc pulled his coat tight up around him. "I'm sorry," he said. His breath was short and his face had grown pale and worn.

"I should never . . . have let you stay. All this time."

He took his glasses off and tried to straighten out the frames a little. He put them back upon his nose.

"I kept thinking the war had to end. Or at least, we'd find some safer place."

He started coughing. He wiped at his mouth; his teeth were slick with blood. "Or, we'd just figure out that last damned riddle, and go."

Adi remembered and held her hands up.

"What?" he said, raising his shaggy eyebrows.

• • •

The bullet had gone right through the map in Doc's pocket, torn through it as surely as it had his chest.

"Damn," he muttered, wincing as they pulled the precious map from his coat. Adi opened it up on his lap. The children gathered around. "Could be worse," he said. There wasn't much blood on it and the black rimmed bullet holes were mostly through Germany.

Adi tapped her finger on the city of Strasbourg. He squinted down at the map. "You sure?"

Adi nodded, trying to think of some way to explain.

"Doesn't matter," he said, his eyelids fluttering. "As long as you know."

Trying to trace his finger from the city of Dijon across the map to Strasbourg, his hand shook badly, so Adi did it for him.

There wasn't much there at the intersection of the two lines just south of a town called Epinal.

"What does that say?" Doc squinted hard and read the small type there in the mountains. "Ah," he said. "Gentiana Abbey. That's good."

His head fell back, just as it did when he dozed off in his chair. Adi watched him, as she had so many times in the past few years. After a second, Doc opened his eyes again and reached out his hand. "Here, take this." He dropped the silver medallion and chain into her palm and squeezed her hands tightly when she tried to protest.

"No, no. Lisette would have wanted you to have it," he said, closing his eyes. "Never made sense for me to be wearing it, anyway. Saint Margaret . . ." he whispered as he died, "she is, after all . . . the patron saint of young women."

Part 4

Chapter 32

November 6–9, 1918

Clear of the museum, Adi and the children crept carefully back to the cathedral square.

The artillery had been silenced and the Yanks, across from the church, had half a dozen German soldiers lined up against the wrought-iron fence. Adi looked at the men, in their makeshift uniforms, wondering if one of them had shot Doc. But, pale and emaciated as they were, it seemed a miracle that they were standing at all. A couple of them were nothing more than children and one of them was surely much too old to be shivering at gunpoint in an icy drizzle. Brushing tears from her cheeks Adi shook her head and led the children away.

A playmate led to a cousin, and then to a grateful uncle. The big man hugged Adi so hard she thought her chest would break. The little girl threw her arms about Adi's legs and held tight but the boy became suddenly shy. Adi shook his hand formally but then pulled him to her.

She hitched a ride back to camp, hanging on to the side of a rundown supply truck. But just as they were turning away from the river Vesle, Adi saw the first of a long line of vehicles coming north from the camp. Banging on the side of the truck to slow it down, she hopped off.

It wasn't long before she spotted a truck with a red cross. There was Gershom peering over the steering wheel, Cloutain and Lebeau at his side. She waved her arms above her head. Even as he was pulling the truck onto the shoulder, Gershom took one look at Adi's face and he knew.

She explained to them as best she could what had happened. Gave them the half of Doc's ID tag and a slip of paper from the Americans telling them where they could find the body.

It was an awful thing to see the light go out of Gershom's eyes, though she imagined hers looked like that as well. Pulling him aside she signed that she was leaving—that she had solved the last riddle.

"Ah," said Gershom, with a sad smile. "Did he know?" Adi nodded. "So, it's good," he said. "He died happy."

He offered to go with Adi, said he didn't want to be there anymore without Doc. She considered it, terrified of going it alone.

But, someone had to go take care of Doc. And in the end they both knew he wouldn't like it if both of them abandoned the infirmary.

She kissed Gershom on the cheek and left him weeping, his head against the side of the truck.

• • •

Many times Doc and Adi had gone over the dangers and complications of traveling. If she was caught by the wrong people, it wouldn't matter that the war was coming to an end. She would be seen as a deserter. And hundreds of men over the last four and a half years had died before a firing squad to make the point. She, of course, would be at a particular disadvantage, not even having the ability to fabricate some story. There were many soldiers on the move, however; as long as she could blend in, she should be safe enough.

As she stood on the roadside, waiting to hitch a ride, she took out the map. Her map now. She tried not to look at the rust colored stain across it. Tracing out possible routes to arrive at the abbey, she shook her head and marveled at how close it was to where she'd started. The abbey was less than thirty kilometers from Alorainn.

• • •

A Daimler truck carrying a broken anti-aircraft gun heading south had taken her as far as Châlons-sur-Marne. She slogged through the rain for the rest of the afternoon and then slept, curled up under an abandoned pigeon coop. That was day one.

Next morning, in a pouring rain, about to climb into the back of a truck full of soldiers, she recognized the coughing and the fevered complexions of Spanish flu. There was nothing to be done for them. She waved them on.

Before long, she ended up in the back of a covered horse-drawn cart with a mother and her children. The woman gave Adi her baby to hold and then promptly fell asleep on the pile of hay. Adi didn't mind the baby; he babbled and cooed and snuggled his little head against her chest. But the cart moved so slowly, she could have made better time on foot. It did make her feel safer though, appearing to be with a family as she headed farther away from the front.

So far, so good. Maybe it was the red cross on her arm, maybe her honest face. Perhaps it was just too much trouble to be suspicious of a soldier unable to speak. That was day two.

• • •

On day three she found a bicycle.

She'd slept the night in a bed after slogging all day through the mud and cold drizzle. Sheets and a lovely quilt and a child's lamp on the bedside table—it was heavenly. The back half of the house was missing, sheared clean away by artillery, but still and all, she got a decent night's sleep for a change.

From the back of the house in the morning mist, she heard the sound of birdsong.

High in the branches of an apple tree a bluebird sang, perched upon the handlebars of a bicycle, no doubt relocated by the blast. The bird, late to be this far north in November, was jewel-like against the gray sky. It tweeted once more and was off.

It took Adi a while to figure how to get the bike down, sure that it would be too damaged to ride.

The tires were a bit low but otherwise it was in good working order. It even had a little basket in the front to tie her things onto.

This was more like it. Not as fast as a truck, perhaps, but more reliable and better at getting along the cratered roads. Most of all, she was in charge.

• • •

On day four, just past noon, she rode through a deserted little town. Montiers-le- . . . something, read the still-remaining piece of the sign. Other than shelling the place, the Germans had left most of it intact.

As she pedaled through the square, she saw what appeared to be a smartly dressed man without a head in the back of a bombed-out shop. She circled around for another look.

A mannequin stood in the rubble of a men's clothing store. She stared at it for a moment, and then leaned her bike up against what was left of the doorway.

• • •

The statue of the beautiful boy riding a dolphin had long ago been blasted to bits. The pieces of marble lay under water in the fountain in the center of the town square. The week's rains had filled it to the brim.

She put her stack of new clothes down on the pavement: a white shirt, trousers, a suit vest, and an overcoat.

There were bees on the label of her beautiful new bar of soap. She looked at it for a moment, then unwrapped it and placed it on the edge of the fountain. With a last look around, she began to peel off her uniform, piece by piece, until she stood there shivering, naked as a baby.

In she went.

The water was so cold it couldn't have hurt more to have a layer of skin removed. That was about right, considering how long it had been since she'd had anything like a proper bath.

Gasping for breath, she washed and scrubbed her skin and scalp till her fingers ached. When she couldn't stand the cold for another second, she leapt out and dried herself with the tablecloth she'd found in the cafe.

While she was buttoning her excellent new vest, she glanced down at the filthy pile of uniform she'd cast off. Like a chrysalis it lay, still retaining her form. The memento of her last three years. Goodbye and thank you, *Monsieur* Goux.

Picking up the watch, she put it—the yoke—back around her neck.

She found a rucksack and transferred only as much of her kit as she thought she'd need. The pockets of her new vest would do for most of her smaller medical gear. Clamp and folding scalpel here, stitching needle and gauze there. There'd be no more lugging about gas masks or extra pairs of boots.

She did keep her beautiful little "Ruby" M1914 pistol. She'd never once had to use it. But she didn't need anyone to tell her it was a dangerous world out there. She buckled her holster under her overcoat.

Standing in the sunshine, she saw her reflection in what was left of a shop window and took what felt like the first deep breath she's had in years. She felt so light. She was so light—she imagined she might lift right off the ground.

Climbing back onto her bike at the edge of town, she saw the whole valley stretched out before her. Down the hill she went as if she were flying.

• • •

Coal stood in the shade of the laurel tree on the arching stone bridge, and thought about crow's feet.

That was one of the names for the little multi-pronged metal spikes he had ruining the pockets of his overcoat. They were called caltrops, or cheval traps, or crowsfeet, which they resembled. They'd been around for centuries, good for stopping soldiers, horses, camels, vehicles, what have you. The question was whether or not he would be throwing the nasty little spikes onto the downward slope of the bridge, where they would be hard to avoid.

It was a cockeyed thing to do—cheating, pretty much. And he never cheated.

"Well, hardly ever," he said, wincing at the sunlight glaring off the water beneath the bridge. He dug around until he found his tinted lenses and put them on.

"Hasn't she cheated? Without her little helpers, she'd have ended up in a ditch somewhere, a long time ago."

There was one fewer of those helpers now. This made Coal's head ache a little less.

Delicately, he removed the caltrops from his pockets, placing them on the moss-covered side of the bridge. It was almost impossible to get them out without pricking his fingertips. There was nothing left in the pocket but a pack of Portuguese cigarettes and a couple of gold coins.

"Chances are," he said, tossing the spikes onto the bridge one after another, "on a bicycle, she'll not even hit one of them."

• • •

George and the lads nearly made it to headquarters without incident.

Crossing the river Meuse, only a half-dozen kilometers from the camp, they ran across enemy soldiers—deserters, probably. Or remnants of the eastern front.

They thought they'd gotten clear, until Augustin's mare stumbled.

The bullet missed the front edge of the saddle and Augustin's leg, passing into the animal's chest. She dropped gently to her knees and lay down as if she were sleeping.

They made it back—again, on two horses, Augustin cursing the whole way.

After they'd given their final report, Augustin checked to make sure he had his billfold and, without another word, hopped a truck into the city of Soissons.

Three hours later he was back, pulling up in the most rundown, beat-up, bullet-shot automobile any of them had ever seen. He wouldn't say how much he'd paid for this prize, but they could tell from the look on his face that it had been a fortune.

He didn't care—said he'd have paid twice that to not ever have to be responsible for another horse.

Thomas suggested that they get a good night's sleep and start fresh in the morning for Alorainn. They argued the point for a moment and then started throwing their things into the back seat.

They submitted their furlough papers, collected all the odds and ends that had been accumulating at headquarters, grabbed all the rations they could get their hands on—and they were on the road.

• • •

They headed south all night and half the morning, before they turned east. Then the car broke down.

It took the rest of the day merely to find someone who could work on a valveless automobile and most of the next to find spark plugs for it.

They sat about the mechanic's yard, talking and playing bocce ball with the man's sons.

Deciding to use the nearly inedible dry rations as prizes, Thomas dug about through the pile of clutter that had ended up on the floor of the back seat.

"Hello!" he said, holding up a little leather satchel. "Where did this come from?"

Augustin leaned in.

"Our mail! That's what Henri was going on about. It must have gotten thrown in with all our other rubbish."

As they feasted on a sublime cassoulet made by the mechanic's wife, they went through the bag.

There was a stack for Augustin, a few for Thomas. But most of the letters were for George. Aunts and uncles and cousins, appealing to him, the tone becoming more and more urgent, to return and soon. Every page was an arrow to his heart.

Augustin emptied the satchel, pulling out the last small letter from the bottom of the sack. It was addressed to Thomas.

"And what have we here?" said Augustin. "Nice handwriting. And not from Alorainn. Could it be . . . ?"

George stopped reading for a second, snatched the letter and tossed it to Thomas.

• • •

By the time the mechanic's wife brought out the glazed apple tart, George and Augustin were thoroughly despondent. Thomas had a different expression.

"*Monsieur,*" said the wife to the young man, "are you unwell?"

The rest of the table turned his way. Thomas did look as if he'd swallowed his tongue.

"Um," he said and closed his mouth, looking hard at the letter.

"You okay?" George asked.

"Uh, huh," Thomas managed.

"Out with it Thomas Hast," said Augustin. "We've got enough bad news."

"I think," Thomas said, faintly, "I found Xander and Xavier."

"What!" said George. "You figured out the riddle?"

"Not exactly."

Chapter 33

Before she hit the ground, Adi had been having a wonderful day-dream as she pedaled along the country road. Sparkling silver platters, spread across the library table, all those years ago. A meal she dreamed of often, and bitterly regretted not finishing. The onion bhaji, the tikka massala, the alu gobhi, all the dishes steaming in the afternoon sun. Instead of being alone, though, she was there with George and Thomas and the boys, all tucking in and laughing.

The caltrop slashed her front tire like butter, jamming right through the metal rim of the wheel. The bike went down. Adi hit the ground with a shriek as another of the spikes sliced into her shoulder.

She lay there afraid to move, afraid the pain could be worse, though at the moment that seemed unlikely. The culprits, ugly little tetrahedron-shaped bundles of spikes, were right before her eyes, on the downward side of the bridge.

She was always signing to wounded soldiers—breathe. She understood more than ever why that was so difficult.

When her head stopped spinning, she lifted herself up, careful not to roll onto other spikes on the ground.

It could have been worse. She'd landed, for the most part, in the track of some vehicle—a truck, from the size of the tread—that had come through before her and swept up many of the caltrops. Sure enough, she saw the trail swerve from that point; a gash ran along the side of the stone bridge, showed where the truck had hit.

She looked down. The damned thing was jutting out of her arm. Only her coat and shirt sleeve had kept it from making it all the way to the bone. She leaned over and picked up one of the others from the ground. The spikes had no barbs, thank God. She had seen ones that did, like horrible fishhooks; there was no way to get them out without tearing the flesh.

She took hold of the thing, about the size of a small plum, and with one sure movement, pulled it from her arm. The point was slick with blood. At least it wasn't rusty.

She slid out of her coat and rolled her sleeve up, took her brand-new handkerchief from her pocket and held it tight against the puncture, cursing the evil scoundrel that threw the things down.

• • •

She cleaned the wound in the stream and bandaged her arm, saying a prayer against tetanus. After clearing the rest of the spikes from the bridge, she looked to her bicycle.

The front tire was shredded.

She looked up the road. The tires of that truck would have been damaged. Where did it go?

Just over the hill, she saw the roofs of a couple of houses. She decided to push the bicycle at least that far before she gave up on it. She wrenched the last caltrop out of the wheel and put it with the others beneath a rock. She pulled her overcoat back on, placed her rucksack in the basket, and started rolling the bike toward the village.

• • •

Even before she'd come around the curve, she heard the men squabbling. She spotted what could be a garage.

Through the open gate, she saw a couple of men under the hood of a truck. It looked as if a wheel had been removed from the front passenger side.

Discretion was in order. She might not much like the people driving this truck, who hadn't even bothered to pick up the rest of the caltrops on the bridge. The godawful ache in her arm wasn't helping her disposition, and the blood had come through the bandage and ruined her beautiful new shirtsleeve.

Leaning the bicycle against a fence post, she took her pistol out of her holster, checking, as Doc had taught her, to make sure there was a bullet in the chamber.

Running across the street, she stole up alongside a high wall. A few feet from the gate, she heard the argument resumed. Something about the inferiority of French automobiles.

She took a quick peek around the corner.

A couple of men were standing around a rabbit cage, smoking and talking. A couple of others worked on the wheel.

It seemed normal enough.

Or maybe not.

Next to the rabbits, Adi spotted an old woman, looking like someone's grandmother. She was tied to a chair with a gag in her mouth.

A scrape of gravel behind her! Something dropped over her head, she couldn't move her arms. She was shoved from behind.

In through the gate she went, tripping on the cobblestones, down onto her backside. A tire around her midsection.

She looked up to see a black man towering above her.

He leaned down and snatched Adi's pistol from her hand. It was like a child's toy in his.

"This is why I couldn't be takin' my nap?" he said. "'Cause you thought midgets'd be sneaking up on us?"

More men of various sizes and colors sauntered over to have a look. They appeared to have been either French or American soldiers, but were all in the process of whittling away their uniforms.

"Well, what have we here?" said a handsome Yank with blonde slicked-back hair.

"Don't know, Freddie," said a man with a narrow face and doleful eyes. "This place's not as empty as you thought."

"I guess not, Joe." Freddie squatted down to get a better look at their prisoner. "This one's sure not from these parts."

Yet another American—this one with a face like a ferret—smirked up at the big black man. "Look, Thibodaux, it's your little brother." He broke up laughing. Everyone ignored him. Freddie looked at the blood trickling down Adi's arm.

"Looks like you had a little trouble, son. What you up to here?"

Adi shook her head and struggled to get free of the tire.

"We don't have time for this," said another Frenchman, still wearing most of his uniform. He looked down at Adi with eyes like a wolf. "Do him, and let's get back on the road."

"We're not going anywhere, Nantes, 'til you finish patching the tire," said Freddie. He nodded to Thibodaux.

With no more effort than lifting a cat, the big man picked Adi up and stood her on the ground. The tire dropped to her feet.

"Yes, yes," said Nantes, pushing Adi aside. He took the tire and turned back to his repair table. The other men did likewise.

Freddie sat back on his haunches, studying their guest. "Huh," he mused.

Joe looked over at him. "You thinking what I'm thinking?"

"Depends on what you're thinking," Freddie said.

"I'm thinking that that boy is small."

Freddie stood up, a couple of heads taller than Adi. "Then, I guess, we're thinking the same thing. You better tell the Frenchies we're going back to plan one."

Joe blew out his cheeks. "Nantes ain't gonna be too happy 'bout that."

"Yeah, well, what is he ever happy about? I'm not so good at climbing walls, and I don't think he is neither—despite his blather."

He looked down at Adi. "You don't talk a lot, do you, son?"

• • •

Adi was furious.

She had her coat. All the rest was left behind.

She sat on the hard front seat of the truck, wedged snugly in between Freddie and Thibodaux, Joe behind the wheel. The suspension was shot, but it didn't seem to discourage the man from barreling down the back roads as fast as the old army vehicle could go. She could only imagine how bad it was for the seven men in the back under the canvas. "The Frenchies," as they were referred to, though they appeared to include a Russian and the shifty-looking American they called Ferret.

How could she have been so foolish? Going in there, with that little pistol. She'd never even fired it at anyone! She was lucky to be alive.

She wasn't sure why, though. Something to do with where they were heading. A robbery, from the sound of it. A tiny window to be squeezed through, maybe?

The good news was that—so far—they appeared to be heading, at least roughly, in the right direction, and that whatever they had in mind, it was going to happen tonight.

She tilted her head a little toward the mud splattered windscreen. She could make out Orion's Belt low in the sky.

"Damnedest thing, ain't it?" said the big man on her right with a low rumble. "How they got a whole 'nother sky over here."

Adi glanced at him and nodded. After all this time, though, it was hard to remember how exactly it was different.

Freddie took out a little flask, handed it around. To be amiable, Adi took a small sip. It tasted like gasoline.

"That boy Nantes's wired pretty tight, ain't he?" said Thibodaux, loud enough to get over the sound of the engine but not enough to be heard by anyone in the back.

"Yeah, for a minute there," said Joe, "looked like he was gonna shoot the old lady."

"Yeah," replied Freddie. "It did, didn't it."

"I guess he got his reasons for being sore at the *mademoiselles*, right now," said Thibodaux. "But that lady was nice. No call to be scaring her that way."

Adi wondered which other *mademoiselle* he was referring to.

"She'll be okay," said Freddie, patting the big man on the leg. "I doubt being tied up in a chair for an hour was the worst thing that happened to her the last four years."

At least these guys didn't want to kill an old lady. Adi sighed; there was only so much comfort she could take in the idea that not all the men she was with were murderers.

Zooming through an intersection, the headlights on the truck flashed for an instant on a sign. Had it said Gentiana Abbey? She banged her boot on the floorboard.

Freddie looked over.

"We just got us a little business to take care of," he said, "and then you can get back to yours."

She sat in the dark, squeezed tight between the men, hoping to God this might be true. But there was no way of knowing if he meant what he said. And any way you figured it, the Americans were three against the seven men in the back. She seriously doubted if they would be so agreeable when the time came.

Through the grimy windscreen Adi saw a mountain ridge etched against the night sky, like a row of teeth, with one great fang rising in the center.

Adi knew where they were heading.

Chapter 34

After pulling the truck off the road, the men, with Adi in tow, marched a quarter-mile through forest and fields. Not a word from the men, other than Freddie and Nantes quarreling in harsh whispers at the back of the line.

Their breath visible in the cold, they watched from the dark woods as a guard made his rounds before the massive walls of La Maison Chinois. Though she had never seen the royal estate from this direction, there was no doubt where they were.

They watched the guard in his tall boots and grim black uniform pass before the huge stone wall. The only guards Adi remembered seeing were ones with big colorful feathered hats that stood by the front door sometimes. The guard passed by.

"We've got an hour," whispered Freddie.

• • •

Adi looked up through the ornate ironwork of the gate into the garden. The only sound was the splash of water from the fountains. A half moon, rising up over the trees, made shadow shapes of the acres of sculptures and topiary.

It was just as she remembered it.

Almost.

"What are you waiting for?" Nantes hissed to Freddie. "Get on with it then. Show him."

The men turned and stared at Adi. Ferret snickered. She could make out his rotted teeth in the moonlight.

Freddie stood next to her, head pressed up against the bars of the gate. He put an arm around her neck, staring at the landscape, like they had all the time in the world.

"Nice, ain't it?" he said. "Used to be somebody's castle. Which I guess explains—this." He slapped a hand against the massive stone wall. "Secure gates on the front and on the north side. The back side's right up against the mountain. And this wall, twenty-five, thirty feet high, around the rest of it. Which," he glanced over to Nantes, "some people think you can throw a rope over."

Adi looked up. It seemed to go up forever.

"Anyway, there's no unguarded entrance, 'cept for this." He nodded to the garden gate.

Adi pulled at the heavy iron bars. Rusted and ivy covered. Solid as a rock and cold as ice.

"It's fastened from the inside," he said. "But only with a sliding bolt. Nantes's brother was a footman in the house, before the duchess had him hanged. It opens. Or so he told Nantes."

"And he better not be making it up," Joe said under his breath.

Adi looked over at Freddie, puzzled.

"What's this got to do with you?" he said with a grin. "Step this way, little buddy."

He took Adi by her coat sleeve and pulled her through the circle of men, down a couple of meters to the right. Adi winced and rubbed her shoulder with her hand. It ached with a dull throb. If she hadn't seen the point on the spike, she would think it was still deep in her arm.

At the base of the wall, amidst the weeds, Adi saw water pouring from a mossy drainpipe into a shallow ditch; a runoff for one of the fountains, maybe. It was no more than eighteen or twenty inches wide. She stared at the pouring water for a few seconds.

Oh, no!

Adi took a step back, shaking her head, adamantly.

"I told you he wasn't going to like it," said Joe, looking down at the pipe. "I sure as hell wouldn't want to go up in there."

"Now, now," said Freddie. "I'm sure it's not as bad as it . . . looks. Anyway. He's going. Nobody else here fittin' in that thing."

• • •

Freezing water filled her pants legs as she lowered herself down onto her knees in the ditch.

Thibodaux held on to her overcoat. There wasn't much point in keeping it on. It might be warmer, but it would weigh her down and broaden her shoulders. And she'd definitely want something dry to put on when this was over. Assuming, of course . . .

"Hurry up," hissed Nantes. "We're running out of time."

Adi took a last glance at the pistol barrels pointed at her, and slid into the pipe on her stomach, gasping as the runoff soaked the front of her shirt and vest.

"Hold it," said Joe. He slipped something into her back pants pocket. "This might come in handy." She had no time to wonder what it might be before a couple of the men grabbed her boots and gave her a shove. After that she was on her own.

The slippery algae from the runoff made it easier to slide herself forward up the slight incline, but when her boots hit it, she got no traction at all. The trick was to push against the dry sides of the pipe, though that was easier said than done. After a couple of minutes, the muscles in her legs were screaming. She had to stop till the burning let up.

A gun barrel tapped impatiently at the bottom of the pipe. She continued.

• • •

It was pitch black, not the slightest difference if her eyes were open or shut. She began to panic, her imagination running away. Strange scraping sounds. Creeping just behind her. What was that? Something slithering up the pipe? Touching her leg? Her face. Spider's silk over her eyes. The occupant skittering across her scalp! Was it going down her shirt collar!? She shook her head, couldn't reach back. The pipe was growing narrower. She was sure of it! She would be stuck, unable to go back?! She was lying in her coffin!

Stop, stop, stop!

She lay still. Took a breath. Another.

Just a bug, dammit. Just a pipe. You've been in worse than this.

She imagined Doc and Gershom there. They'd laugh. Gershom would say something funny in Yiddish.

More tapping from the bottom of the pipe.

Yes, yes. She took a deep breath. I'm going.

• • •

It was hard to tell how long it took, maybe twenty minutes. Maybe twice that. The tapping and hissing from below faded away into the sound of water splashing ahead. She'd lost all her body heat and was shaking uncontrollably.

Water fell across her hands and arms as her fingers touched a wall—a ninety-degree turn upward in the pipe. She tilted her head as best she could and peered up into the splash of frigid water. Three feet above, there was a flicker of cold moonlight.

For a few dreadful seconds, it seemed she wouldn't be able to bend enough to make the turn. Her damaged shoulder seized as she scraped against the stone; she wriggled upward. The overflow from the fountain poured down on her like icicles. She made it up onto her knees.

Oh, dear Lord! There was an ornate metal lattice between her and freedom. Clutching at the solid metal, she looked out, the moon reflecting off the surface of the water. She was going to freeze to death right here!

Then it came to her. *What have I got in my pocket?*

Squeezing her arm behind she carefully pulled the thing out. A screwdriver with a black wooden handle.

At least someone had been thinking about what might be at the end of the pipe.

It wasn't the perfect tool. The screw-heads were on the other side of the grate. But it was something. Something to get leverage with. Her fingers ached so much from the cold, she could hardly grip the thing. Commanding her hand to obey, she jammed the head into a sliver of an opening and leaned hard into it.

The screwdriver snapped.

With a splash and a clink, the metal shaft fell into the dark water. *Merde!*

But—another tiny noise. One of the screws plopped into the water in the fountain. She'd bent the grille. Was it enough? She wrapped her fist around the wooden handle and began hammering away.

• • •

The third screw broke, the grate twisted aside—and she dropped forward into the water. It closed over her, sucking the air from her lungs. Shaking and sputtering, she climbed up over the side of the fountain.

For all the time it took, she was not nearly as far up from the garden gate as she would have imagined. She could see gun barrels—one of them, the Russian's rifle—pointing at her through the bars. It would be ill-advised to make that kind of noise with the guards this close, but she didn't put it past them.

Didn't matter. She was going to freeze to death in these wet clothes. Wiping the water off her hair and face, she scrambled down to the gate. She had to get that coat on.

"Good work, son," whispered Freddie. "Now one more thing." He pointed his pistol in to the bolt on the side of the gate.

Adi dug around through the ivy till she found it. She would have to lift it up and then slide it free.

She wondered how long it had been since the brother had reputedly thrown this bolt. Couldn't have been that recent from the look of it, if at all.

She took hold of the metal bar and yanked upwards.

Nothing. She tried again—the cold cut into her fingers like a blade.

"*Monsieur,*" growled Nantes. "If you do not open this gate, I will shoot you, and the crows will have your eyes for their breakfast."

"That's very colorful, Nantes," said Freddie. "Now, shut up.

"What am I thinking?" muttered Freddie. He turned to Joe. "Oil can!"

"Right," said Joe, digging around in his duffel bag for a moment. Out came a little gray can. Followed by a good-sized wooden mallet.

Adi applied the oil to the hinges and Joe handed in the hammer.

The Frenchmen with the black-rimmed glasses ran up. "Guard. About a minute."

Even with a rag over it, the mallet was making more noise than they wanted.

Once, twice, three times.

"Come on, come on!" hissed Nantes.

With all her might . . . Adi threw the bolt.

Chapter 35

November 10, 1918

The thieves fell through the opening, Freddie shoving them to one side or another. He pushed the gate to. No time to slide the bolt.

Footsteps approached. They held their breath. The Frenchmen had their knives ready, the huge Russian, a cudgel in his hands. Adi was shaking so badly from the cold she was afraid the sound of her teeth chattering would give them away. Thibodaux reached over and took the mallet from her hand. The footfalls stopped outside the gate.

Freddie, barely hidden by the bars and the ivy, braced the portal and held a finger up to the big man with his hammer.

In the shadow of the alcove, the piss splashed onto Freddie's boots. It seemed to take the guard forever to empty his bladder and nearly as long to get over the coughing fit that came after. The man was not well. Thibodaux lowered his mallet.

Done coughing, the guard buttoned his fly and with a groan continued on his rounds.

Adi reached up and pulled her coat off of Thibodaux's shoulder. With aching gratitude she slipped into it.

Now what?

It was Saturday night, Sunday morning. She had only a little more than twenty-four hours left to get to the boys, before the stroke of six on Monday morning.

As far as she could make out, it wouldn't take long to drive to the abbey from here, an hour or two, if the roads weren't too bad. But without even a bicycle, it would be—she did a quick calculation—maybe a day and a half to walk. And that's if she left now and didn't stop. And didn't sleep. Or eat. Not good enough.

But none of this mattered if she couldn't get clear of these men.

Nantes was whispering instructions to Renard—a lanky man, missing a good piece of his bottom lip—and then to the others. Ferret looked over his shoulder at Adi and flashed a rotted smile.

Now that she had served her purpose, there was no telling what they might do. If it was up to Nantes, she'd be dead already, Adi was certain of that. She looked at the three Americans; she couldn't help thinking that they were coming to the same conclusion about their odds. Joe raised an eyebrow to Freddie. Freddie considered the situation for a second, shook his head ruefully, and shut the gate behind them.

A hand landed on Adi's shoulder.

"You looking a little cold, son," said Thibodaux. "Why don't we get in that house, where you can warm up some?" Joe took Adi by the other arm and they started walking her fast toward the house. Nantes looked over suspiciously.

"Well, come on," Freddie said, with a grin. "We ain't getting any younger standing here." Nantes smiled coldly. A small gesture to his men. They slid knives back in their scabbards.

• • •

The shadow figures rushed across the lawn to the manor. For the first time, Adi got a clear view of the house. It was almost entirely dark. It was late, but she never remembered it looking so deserted. Where was everyone? It didn't matter. There was no way to go now but through the house.

With the butt of his pistol, Renard smashed a window pane on the library door. Adi could have told them that it was never locked. Or at least never used to be. But she was done being helpful.

One of the Frenchmen took a stack of cloth sacks out of his bag and handed one to each man as he entered. As Adi stepped through, Nantes shook his head. "Not him."

The men entered the library and headed down to the far end where the largest cabinets were. Nantes posted the Russian at the garden door and Ferret at the door leading to the hallway. They were sullen at not being allowed to loot, but knew better than to argue with Nantes.

She walked into the room, water still dripping from her onto the marble floor; her boots squeaked a little with each step. Clutching her coat tight around her, she wandered over to her favorite table, still in its place.

The silver inkwell was there, and the beautiful millefiori glass paperweight. A stack of books sat before her chair, as if she had only been gone for a moment.

This room, in this house, where she spent her last moments before the world changed. The lovely, odd family, so kind to her. Now here she was, returning in the company of thieves.

Golden rings, cameos and pearls, an ivory satyr, a twelfth-century Virgin and child—one after another they were dropped into sacks. Napoleon's sword came off the wall in its scabbard and joined a violin and a pair of Turkish silver daggers. A ruby-studded crown, ancient coins, silver candlesticks, and golden goblets. Nantes's brother had clearly scouted the place. They knew what they were doing.

In a fury, she watched as one of the men used his knife to hack an exquisite Spanish still-life from its frame.

Enough! This had to stop.

She looked over to Ferret standing between her and the hallway. He was muttering to himself, scraping under his fingernails with the point of his knife.

Where were the Americans? She scanned the dark room. There, near the big globe in the corner, huddled together in discourse.

Freddie glanced over to her. She held his gaze for a few seconds and then she pointed to the garden doors.

He tilted his head, warily, and then whispered something to the other two. Adi picked up the paperweight from the table and headed for the hallway doors.

"Nantes," whispered Ferret. The Frenchman looked up from his work. *"Bordel de merde!"* he hissed. "Get him! Before he brings the guard down on us!" The Frenchmen dropped their sacks and pulled knives.

Adi threw her shoulder hard against a tall Louis XV secrétaire, a spherical brass astrolabe on top. Renard made a diving lunge, too late. The brass exploded on the floor like a crash of cymbals, pieces rolling and spinning everywhere.

Across the room, Joe sputtered, wide-eyed.

Freddie grabbed him and Thibodaux by the sleeves. "Time to go, boys!"

Thibodaux looked up from the statuette of a golden lion in his hand over to the other side of the room. "We can't leave the little guy," he said.

"He's made his bed, pal. We're getting, while the getting's good."

Watching as the Frenchies closed in on Adi across the room, the big man pulled back his arm and hurled the lion in a perfect arc. The crack of bone as it hit Ferret solid in the chest was followed by the sound of the lion clanging like a gunshot on the marble floor.

"We're in it now," said Joe.

He walked up to the Russian standing before the garden door, casually tossed his duffel bag to the man and then dropped him with a single blow to the head.

"Guess I wasn't cut out to be a rich man," he said, rubbing his hand, taking a last look at the room. He followed the other two out the door.

Adi saw her chance. Grabbing a cart bearing a silver tea service, she hurtled it across the floor at the men, the pieces chimed like bells as they hit the marble. Jumping over Ferret, whose hands still clutched his chest, she pulled the door open. But as she stepped through, she was grabbed by the arm. Renard lunged, his blade slicing through her overcoat—missing her ribs by a hairbreadth.

Adi spun around and caught the man hard in the nose with the millefiori paperweight in her fist. Down he went in front of the others. She slammed the heavy door shut in their faces. She could hear Nantes cursing as they fought to get the door open.

Down the corridor she flew, white curtains ghostly in the moonlight. Was there no one in the house?

She reached the grand staircase. If she could make it down, perhaps she could lose them in the servants' quarters. But, too slow. Before she'd reached the first landing, the thieves had caught up with her.

Nantes spun her around and cuffed her hard across the face. "Let's see how much noise you can make now?" he hissed. Hoisting her by the front of her coat, he put the point of his knife beneath her chin.

Vibrating like a hummingbird, a gunshot blew past Adi's ear, caroming off the marble bannister. And another. The Frenchmen with the black glasses jerked and fell.

She looked over her shoulder. It wasn't the thieves shooting, but the royal guard. She banged her knee into Nantes's abdomen. Hitting the stairs, she dove for cover behind a statue along the curved railing.

Realizing their mistake too late, the thieves were caught between two groups of guards, above and below.

Arms over her head, Adi crouched low as shots flew around her. The barrage lit up the staircase. A couple of the men broke through the guards at the top of the stairs, crashed through a high window, into the gardens below. The rest died as they might have on the fields of Verdun, in a hail of bullets.

• • •

When the smoke cleared and Adi opened her eyes, she was circled by burnished black boots. She looked up to see gun barrels and cruel faces.

"What shall we do with him, Your Highness?" asked the commander.

Carrying a silver candle holder, a figure in a dark robe, adorned with golden arabesque, descended the stairs.

Stepping lightly past the bodies, Duchess Johanna, her voice languid with sleep and narcotic, said, "Stand him up."

Speaking to the terrier tucked into the crook of her arm, she said, "Let's get a look at our thief, shall we, Bouton?" Unhappy with the turmoil, the dog fidgeted until his mistress put him down.

Adi was hoisted to her feet. The duchess held the light up and stared at the face before her.

"Why he's nothing but a . . . boy." She hesitated, her brow furrowing. Her eyelids fluttered, heavy with the effort of grasping what was before her.

In a haunted voice that only Adi could hear, she whispered, "I know this face."

The duchess choked back a cry. Adi's eyes went wide with alarm. Oh God! She knows me!

"Everything all right, Your Highness?" asked the commander.

Behind the duchess's violet-tinged irises, emotion struggled with reason. Clearly, not for the first time.

But in a moment, the ice had reformed, the storm dissipated, replaced by a look that could almost be mistaken for serenity.

The duchess reached her hand out and pulled at the girl's cropped hair. Staring in wonder she examined the slight fullness in the front of the coat.

"Good work, commander," said the duchess, not taking her eyes off the girl. Carelessly, she traced her fingertips along Adi's downy cheek. The commander inclined his head.

"Now. Would you explain how these . . . men, are in my house?"

Before he could answer, one of the guards was seized by a bout of coughing. Adi snuck a glance. All the signs were there—the sweat-dampened forehead, the bluish tinge to the skin. Looking back to the commander, she saw he was in much the same condition.

"It appears they might have entered through the garden gate, Your Grace."

"Such high walls," said the duchess. "So many guards. And still we're not safe."

The dog yapped.

"Bouton! Get away from there!"

The dog was sniffing at the stream of blood trickling down the marble stairs from where Nantes lay. The duchess leaned down and scooped up the animal.

"What should we do with him, ma'am?" asked the commander.

Without another look at Adi, the duchess drew up the hem of her robe and started back up the stairs.

"He has stolen from us. Hang him."

Chapter 36

Thomas read his letter at the mechanic's table.

Turned out, his friend Mark was now Brother Mark. He'd stayed on at the abbey after he and Thomas were done with school. Recently taken vows, he apologized for not having written of late.

Thomas skipped over news of friends, the departure of one of their favorite non-clerical professors.

"But then"—Thomas looked up at George and Augustin—"near the end, there's a bit of gossip about two students. Twins, who, Mark says, are the talk of the abbey for receiving packages of great value from their patron. Their names," said Thomas, "are Xander and Xavier."

The men sat speechless.

George took the letter, read the line over and over, looking for some flaw in the sense of it. He scanned the date of the letter. Seven months ago. Would they still be there? Why not? Could be.

• • •

Adi was dragged downstairs and thrown unceremoniously into a crowded cell. She found herself a sliver of space against a stone column. Between the days without rest, nothing to eat, and nearly freezing to death, she was done in. She fell immediately into a dead sleep.

She woke briefly to notice she was covered with a scrap of blanket. She looked up to see an older woman sitting beside her, an aunt, whose name Adi couldn't recall. The woman smiled and patted her on the head till she drifted off again.

Hours later, the moon bright through a barred window, Adi sat up from where she'd been sleeping, back to back with the woman. Aunt Anais. Now she remembered.

Oh no! The moon was up. That meant she'd slept all day.

She climbed to her feet, a little unsteady. Looking around her in the pale light, she saw she was in the middle of three adjoining cells. All manner of people were there, even children and the elderly, crowded together in cold, comfortless spaces. Many appeared to have been there for some time.

Most of the family and the servants were here. She recognized faces everywhere she looked. Pretty remarkable, considering how different the context was. Their beautiful clothes served them poorly in this prison cell.

Adi had always known the duchess was unhinged, but this was past believing. What could the woman hope to accomplish? It was not as if she had jailed a couple of people to await trial. She had gone all-in on this madness.

The latrine, a dark niche in the back, was unpleasant, but heaven knows she'd seen worse in the trenches.

As she tiptoed back through the sleeping crowd, a group of men sitting around a square of light from one of the lanterns motioned her over.

She recognized a couple of cousins. Emile, maybe? And an uncle. But the other one . . . ? It took her a few seconds. It was Cook! A little older and a lot thinner.

He had always been on her list of regrets. She'd disappeared without ever letting him know how much she appreciated what ended up being her last meal before the war.

Cook looked up at her and said, "We can't place you, lad. How do you find yourself here in the guest quarters?"

When she indicated that she was unable to speak, Adi saw a look of confusion pass behind his eyes, fleeting memories, not quite adding up. He scratched his head a little and then grimaced. She noticed a good-sized gash across his forearm darkening his shirtsleeve. She motioned for him to put his arm forward into the lantern light.

It was a nasty gouge across the extensor carpi muscle, the meaty part of the forearm. A little more and it would have been severed. It was becoming infected. She sniffed it. Not good, but not too bad.

Adi motioned for the men to give her a little room and removed her medical gear from her vest pockets. The best of it had been left in her rucksack with her bicycle. But she had the basics. It would have to do. Cutting away the shirt sleeve she tweezed out as much of the debris as she could see.

To the men, she signed drinking from a bottle.

They shook their heads.

"Hold on," said Cousin Emile. He stepped over several people in the dark, there was a little shriek, and he was back with a silver flask. "Aunt Tudie," he said with a grin. "She keeps it tucked in her corset."

It smelled like vodka. Adi used a few drops to sterilize her curved needle and silk thread and then she poured some into the cut. Cook gritted his teeth. She motioned for him to take a swig.

By the time she had him sewed up and had bandaged the wound with a piece of a dress hem, word had spread. Many had not come here easily and the guards had not been gentle.

She fashioned a splint for a footman with a broken fibula (using poor Aunt Tudie's corset). She bandaged a missing fingernail on a young boy's hand. Right through the bars of the cell next to them, she lanced a contusion on a woman's forehead.

While they were waiting for Cousin Emile to round up some more "antiseptic," Cook studied Adi with frank curiosity.

"Hey Doc?" he asked. "By any chance, you got a sister?"

Adi smiled sadly at her new title and shook her head.

• • •

After Augustin's motorcar had broken down a couple more times, it became clear that they were going to have to split up. There were two places to be, no time to spare, and they had a motor that was held together by not much more than George's belt. Despite George's indignation over the implication that he was incapable of doing anything by himself, it was decided that it made the most sense for Thomas to get dropped off at the crossroads to the abbey. George and Augustin would continue to Alorainn.

Hard to say whether it was George's distracted cheekiness or Augustin's self-righteous grandiloquence that got them into more trouble with the guards when they tried to drive in through the front gates of La Maison Chinoise at midnight, in the muddy, broken-down automobile. If ever they'd needed Thomas and his prudence, it was now. But he was not there to mediate.

The royal guard was, understandably, on edge the night after the thieves had broken in. The man who had stopped to do his business outside the garden gate had been locked up in a dark hole with no food nor water. The rest of the guard had been reprimanded, and their pay docked. These men neither knew nor cared about "The Family" or "royal heirs." They had George and Augustin out of the car and face-down on the pavement before they could reach for their holsters.

"This is . . . surprising," said Augustin, wincing at the gravel pressing into his cheek.

"Maybe we need to start paying more attention when Uncle Henri's talking," said George.

• • •

Everyone in the three cells who wasn't already awake was awakened by the yelling and commotion coming down the stairs.

"Oh, no," murmured a governess. "Not again."

"Who's left?" said Cook.

Someone with a view of the stairway whispered, "A couple of soldiers, I think."

Adi looked out through the bars, astounded. It was as if they were following her. She reminded herself, it was George's house, after all.

Uncle Léon croaked. "Is that you, George?"

George put a finger to his lips and shook his head, ever so slightly.

He turned on the jailer, a disturbingly large and unattractive man, and exclaimed, "You dimwitted simpleton! You're not putting me in the back cell! Do you have any idea who I am! I will only be in the front cell!"

The guard had actually been about to unlock the front cell. He stopped and growled, "You'll go where I put you, pretty boy!"

He proceeded to unlock the back cell and shoved them into the crowded space. "You're done giving orders here, boy!" Returning the key ring to his belt, the guard walked back to the end of the hall. With a satisfied snort, he hung up the lantern and deposited himself in his chair.

"What was that all about?" said Augustin, picking himself up from the floor.

"You'll remember in a minute," George said.

Aunt Elodie threw herself upon the boys. "Georgie! Augustin!" she whispered excitedly. "I knew you'd come!"

"Sorry it took so long, Elodie," said George, seeing the state his delicate aunt was in. He looked around him. It was a dismal sight. They all looked tired and hungry and bedraggled.

Everyone gathered to the bars of their cells, as close as they could get to the boys. In the middle cell, Adi peered out from behind Cook.

Samuel, the chauffeur, leaned in and shook George's hand.

"How goes it, my lord?" he asked, heartily.

"The world still spins, Sam. Just a bit wobbly right now. Don't worry, we'll fix it."

Adi looked at George, grasping hands and embracing everyone who could reach him. He looked nearly as bad as the people locked up, unkempt, bruised, and dusty. But, though he was in the same fix they were, he had that irresistible smile on his face, not the slightest bit anxious or afraid. People were touching him like a good luck charm.

He was certainly older, she observed. In his face, around the eyes. Not a boy any more.

She looked down at her clothing. Maybe it was time to say the same for herself. A crack opened in the storm-cloud hanging over her head. Could it be, out of nowhere, she had one more chance?

Taking the watch out of her pocket, she opened it up: 28,044 seconds. She calculated: less than eight hours to get to the boys. Might as well throw in with the people who were smiling and laughing.

She pushed her way to the front of the crowd. George was only a few feet into the next cell, but encircled by admirers.

Adi reached through the bars and tapped a little girl, no more than five or six, on the shoulder. She handed her the watch and pointed to George. He was whispering something to Augustin, gesturing over to where the jailer was sitting. Augustin nodded, then noticed the child attempting to squeeze through the crowd. He leaned over, scooped her up and handed her to George.

"And what's your name?" said George, addressing the little girl.

Not to be diverted from her task, the girl held out her hand.

To say that George froze would be to put it mildly. He was a statue.

Adi could all but see the workings of his mind as he tried to solve this riddle.

Augustin, speaking to the head gardener, noticed the silence and glanced over at the object in the girl's hand. He took one look at the golden thing that he'd never laid eyes upon, but knew so well.

"Holy Mother Mary!" he said.

Chapter 37

"That man, he said to give you this."

The child placed the watch into George's hand and pointed to Adi standing on the other side of the bars.

The crowd parted. Everyone stared. From behind her, Adi heard Cook finally put the pieces together, muttering, "Well, I'll be fried in fat."

George was speechless. Looking from the watch to Adi and then back again, he opened his mouth and shut it. Countless questions collided in his head. He settled on the immediate.

"Do you know about the abbey?" he asked.

It was Adi's turn to be astounded. How could this be? She would hardly have imagined he would remember her, much less—

She nodded—yes, yes!

"And you know, there is little time left?"

She nodded again and held up eight fingers.

"Eight . . . hours," said George. "Yes. That's about right."

Augustin stepped forward. "Six A.M. November 11th!" he said and bowed. "Augustin Canclaux. Pleasure to make your acquaintance, *mademoiselle*. I mean that! I can't tell you how exciting this is."

"Sorry to interrupt," whispered Samuel. He gestured down the corridor to the jailer. If the man wasn't asleep, he was doing a pretty good impression of it.

George held his hand up to Adi.

"Just—just a minute," he said.

To her bewilderment, George stepped over to the front of his cell, hopped up on a ledge and reached his hand through the bars. High up on the outside of the last column, he felt about for a little part of the elaborate design at the top, a small stone elephant. He tugged at it, till it slid out from the pillar. Then he gave it a turn.

The door to the cell clicked open.

George put his hands up, halting the shout that was about to burst from the crowd. He stepped down, pointing to Augustin and Samuel. "You're with me."

• • •

In a family of eccentrics, it was generally understood that George's great-grandfather took the prize. If family lore was to be trusted, he never wore the same pair of trousers twice and he had a miniature horse, with whom he took tea.

But most notably, he was responsible for the expansion of the original buildings of the royal estate, which, unknown to all but a few, included a labyrinth of hidden passageways and escape routes honeycombing the palace. Having lived through the carnage of the French Revolution, he declared that that would never be his family's fate.

On George's tenth birthday, his father initiated him into the hidden secrets of the house. This information was not always treated with perfect reverence by the lad. His uncanny ability to disappear from a room was regarded by many in the household as nearly supernatural.

• • •

Fifteen minutes after the cell door popped open, the only person locked up was the jailer, bound and gagged, his eyes practically bugging out of their sockets in infuriation.

Because this wasn't the only card George had up his sleeve. In addition to the secret latch that opened the cell door, there was a hidden passageway out of the dungeon itself. This led straight into the caverns under La Maison Chinois, emerging not far downriver in the barn at the back of the head gardener's cottage.

Except for George, Adi, Augustin, and Samuel, everyone— aunts, uncles, valets, chambermaids, young children, and old men and women—had now passed through the doorway to safety.

Cook, the last to go in, had picked Adi up and hugged her so hard she practically fainted. Now, only the dust, disturbed on the ground in front of the wall, gave any evidence of their passage.

Getting the exodus up and moving had kept them too busy for talking. With the final instructions given and the door closed behind them, George turned at last to Adi. That was when they heard the coughing from the top of the stairs.

• • •

No banister on the ancient stone steps. Duchess Johanna kept her eyes on her elegant shoes, tip-tapping unsteadily as she descended from one pool of lantern light to the next. In a greatcoat the color of blood, fashioned tight about her waspish waist, with epaulets and high Prussian collar, she cut an unmistakably military figure. The effect was much diminished, however, by a wracking cough that stopped her in her tracks as she worked her way down the stairs.

Catching her breath, a half-dozen steps from the bottom, the duchess finally looked up.

To Adi's eyes at least, the woman appeared to be no more perturbed by the developments before her than she might at discovering an inappropriately seated dinner guest. Sweat trickling upon her brow, the fever and cough were clear signs of full-blown influenza. But the look in her dark-rimmed eyes suggested other more insidious ills.

Johanna turned slowly from the empty cells and the bound jailer, to the four figures at the bottom of the stairs. As her eyes skipped from face to face, her placid façade began to tear.

Removing her gloves, she stood looking toward them, pulling at the fingertips with her teeth one after another.

Augustin whispered, "Why doesn't she get the guard?"

"Do you think she could?" George replied, as the woman managed to make the final step down.

Augustin moved Adi behind them.

"Hello, Johanna," said George.

"Well, George, what a surprise," said the duchess.

"Yes, I'd imagine it is."

"And Augustin. You're looking well. Your name came up recently. I can't recall . . . something Tudie said."

"Was that before or after you put her in the dungeon?" asked Augustin.

Johanna smiled vaguely and tilted her head a little to see behind the men.

"And the young woman. I knew you'd be here," she said to Adi. "In your imaginative little costume." She tried a laugh but suffered another coughing fit instead.

When she recovered, she said, "Forgive me. I seem to have caught a bit of a cold."

Augustin held up the jailer's key ring on his finger.

"I suppose so," said George. "Safest thing for now." Samuel nodded. He and Augustin advanced toward the duchess.

Holding her hand up to make them wait, she coughed a few more times into her fist. Then pulling a pistol from her coat pocket, she fired and struck Augustin in the thigh.

Augustin spun around with a howl and fell back into George's arms. They both went down. Samuel moved to cover them.

"You're making me nervous, Samuel," she said, motioning with her pistol. Glowering at her, he sat down next to George.

Adi dropped to her knees next to Augustin, who was moaning and cursing and struggling to get to his feet. George held on to him.

"Stay down, Gus."

Adi tore open the khaki around the bullet hole and examined the wound, as best she could in the feeble light.

Though there was substantial bleeding, the bullet hadn't hit the bone, nor the femoral artery—that was most important. And it seemed to have passed through cleanly, though she wouldn't be able to tell for sure until she examined him properly.

Adi looked up to see the duchess pointing her gun with dreamy fascination at each of them, one after another. "If I can shoot them," she murmured, her eyes following the bit of smoke rising from the gun barrel, "does that mean they're not a figment of my imagination?"

Adi unbuckled Augustin's belt, pulled it free, and wrapped it around his thigh. Taking a bit of gauze from a vest pocket, she placed it over the wound and cinched the leather tight.

That would have to do for the time being.

Augustin winced and squeezed the girl's hand.

"It's okay," he said with a dreadful grimace of a smile. "Happens to me all the time."

Looking to George, he said, "You didn't tell me she could dress a wound."

"Who knew?"

A squeak from the jailer distracted the duchess. She looked over. He struggled against his bindings.

"God, he's an ugly man," she said to no one in particular. Raising her pistol, she fired twice randomly in the direction of the cell. The bullets went wide, but the jailer tumbled his chair over in a panic, shouting into his gag.

Cheeks dangerously flushed, Johanna undid the buttons on her coat. Steam rose into the cold air from the nightgown she wore beneath.

She began to pull things from her inside coat pockets: papers, spectacles, bits of jewelry. She let them all drop to the floor. Finally, she found a little aquamarine tinted bottle. With her teeth she pulled the glass stopper and spit it to the floor. She pointed her gun at Adi.

"Goddammit. Why is it . . . the only person I want to talk to . . . can't speak!" She coughed as though she might crack open her narrow chest. "On your feet, little one!" she rasped.

She took a swig from her bottle, and watched as the girl got up.

Adi exchanged a look with George, as if to say, how much longer are we going to let this woman call the tune?

George gave a little nod.

The duchess grabbed Adi by the arm and pushed her up against a stone column a few feet away.

"All right. We'll do this your way." With arms shaking, holding the pistol in both hands, she pressed it to Adi's forehead. "Yes or no questions. Do you know where my son is?" she said quietly.

Adi shook her head as best she could with the barrel pressed against her.

"Do you know what happened to him?"

Adi shook her head again.

"Did you leave this house with my son?"

Adi nodded.

"Were you . . . involved with him?"

Adi couldn't prevent an expression of repugnance at the notion.

"My son, not good enough for you?" said the duchess, seeing the look in the girl's eyes. "As if you would ever be so fortunate— you repulsive little—My son was—" A fit of coughing took her.

From behind, George reached out and removed the gun from Johanna's hand. She tried to grab it back, hitting and scratching at him. He held her for a moment, but she tore away with what little strength she had left and stumbled for the stairs.

Samuel moved to go after her, but George shook his head. "Let her go."

• • •

In April of 1917, America finally joined its allies, Britain, France, and Russia, in the war. But along with the more than two million troops came a new player in the drama.

The best guess was that the virus came from an American army base in Kansas. A nuisance when it first appeared in the spring of 1918, by August of that year, through mysterious transformation, it had become more deadly than any disease in the history of mankind.

For the sake of morale, the major players in the war censored news of the epidemic. Spain, being neutral in the war, was not so inclined. This gave the world the impression that the contagion was worse there. Hence, it came to be known as the Spanish flu.

The pandemic was all over by the following spring, but not before it killed more people than the Black Death in the Middle Ages, estimates ranging from twenty to one hundred million people. From Boston Harbor to the Fiji Islands, from tiny villages to the largest of cities, there was nowhere on earth not affected.

And that was certainly true of the battlefields and trenches of the war. Soldiers, their immune systems already weakened by malnutrition and fatigue, their lungs damaged by mustard gas, crowded together in barracks and ships and holes in the ground; they were particularly susceptible. More of them would fall to influenza than would die in combat.

• • •

By the time George, Samuel, and Adi managed to get Augustin to the top of the stairs, they found the duchess crumpled in the door-way leading to the courtyard. The fever, like the madness, having done with her, had fled, leaving her cold and dead as a stone.

The royal guard had done likewise. The virus had run through the barracks like a wildfire. Faced with an adversary that could not be battered or imprisoned, the men that had not died outright stole what they could quickly lay hands on, and fled into the night.

George and his friends discovered a desolate courtyard, an empty house, and an abandoned front gate, all quiet as a tomb.

Ironically, the only good thing the miserable woman had done was to imprison the family deep underground, safe from the fever burning above.

• • •

George and his friends managed to get Augustin squared away in Samuel's quarters next to the garage. With a bed, a proper bandage, and an injection of morphine salvaged from the plundered office of the house physician, he was losing consciousness quickly. He kept repeating, "No time, no time, get her to the abbey." He waved his hand vaguely in Adi's direction. She nodded in agreement.

"As soon as you shut up and go to sleep," replied George, tucking him in. He turned back to Samuel. "What do you mean the cars don't run?" said George. "None of them?"

Samuel began to remove debris from atop his makeshift desk, trying to be orderly about it. "Oh, to hell with it," he said, and swept everything onto the floor.

George and Adi were too exhausted and rattled at three-thirty in the morning to comprehend what he might be doing.

"A couple of weeks ago," continued Samuel, "when we started getting news that the war might actually be ending, she," he nodded to the courtyard, "really began to lose it. Thought everyone was against her, which was definitely true. That was when she started putting the old ladies and children in the cells. The gates were locked, and she had the guards take away all of the estate's vehicles. Everything! You couldn't find a bicycle. The few horses we had left—well, the thugs took them, every one."

Samuel saw the look in Adi's eyes, as she took in this latest calamity.

"But," he said, raising a finger. "As my father used to say, 'there's more than one way to kill a cat than choke it to death with cream.' Though, somehow, when I say it, it doesn't sound so good."

George cleared his throat.

"Just this, Your Grace," he said, sliding the top of the desk to the floor, revealing a large gray tarp-covered shape that had been holding up the back side of the table. He took hold of the cloth, and "Voilà!"

There was Samuel's 1913 700cc Flying Merkel motorcycle—as bright and shiny and orange as a slice of a ripe cantaloupe.

Chapter 38

At first Thomas thought the sound was the echoing of his own footsteps on the country road. He stopped to listen. The footsteps ceased but, it seemed, not exactly at the same time as his.

Except for hunting owls and a scurrying hedgehog, Thomas had had the way to himself since George and Augustin had dropped him at the crossroad. The half moon followed him up and down for a time, before it was overtaken by billowing black clouds.

There was the sound again. Unmistakable this time, even with the wind picking up. As he was coming up the hill, he looked behind him down into the darkness and could just make out a shape, black against black.

"Good morning, friend," called the shadow.

"And to you," replied Thomas. He unsnapped his holster.

"Didn't mean to startle you."

"I am surprised to find anyone on the road at this hour." Thomas waited, his hand upon his pistol, as the shadow caught up. He gave the man a minute as he was clearly short of breath.

"The abbey?" inquired Thomas.

"Yes," said Coal. After a moment, they continued on together.

"I suppose," said Coal, "the abbey's about the only place one would be heading on this road."

Thomas glanced over, but in the darkness he could discern almost nothing.

"You could be taking sheep to pasture in Dupre," said Thomas. "Except, of course, you have no sheep. And it is three o'clock in the morning."

"It is that," agreed Coal.

Coming around the bend, they could make out the abbey silhouetted on top of the cliff. Not too much farther.

"I wonder . . ." said Coal, stopping to catch his breath again. "You seem an honest man,"

Thomas stopped. "Are you all right, sir?"

"Yes, fine, thank you," said Coal, though he didn't sound at all well. "I wonder . . . as you are on your way to the abbey, if you might do me a great kindness?" Coal reached into his pocket and removed a small package, tied up in paper and twine. About the size of his hand. "I'm delivering this to the abbot. If it wouldn't be too much trouble . . . ?"

"I'd be happy to," said Thomas.

"If you don't want to wake them, I've left parcels before, to the right of the front gate, in the niche at the feet of Saint Alberic."

"I know the spot. I may be seeing the abbot, I could deliver it to him."

"Even better," said Coal. "Well then, I'll be off. Good morning to you."

Thomas continued on his way. From the top of the next rise, when the drizzle began to fall, he looked back, but there was no sign of the man.

• • •

Samuel's motorcycle was about as far from the French army motorbikes she had ridden as a falcon was from a duck.

But there was a problem. This was a racing bike. It was built for speed. There was no seat behind for a passenger. No side car.

Out in the drive, Adi stood next to the bike up on its kickstand, the orange paint gray in the moonlight. It was more elegant than the ones she'd ridden, but the works looked much the same. Where was the oil dripper, though, she wondered.

George and Samuel stepped into the garage, going on about ways they might affix something to the frame for a second seat.

There was no time for this. By a miracle, they were free from the prison, the duchess and the guards all swept away before them. She was not taking it for granted.

She opened up the watch. *Merde!* Two hours and forty minutes! She shut the watch and looked at the motorcycle.

She knew the quickest way to win this argument.

Leaning down, she turned the gas on and twisted the throttle forward. Throwing a leg over, she started pedaling. She closed the exhaust valve, and with a bang, fired up the engine.

George's and Samuel's heads shot around the doorway.

They watched her adjust the carburetor.

"I'm going to get to the point, eventually," George said as they walked over to the bike, "where I'm not surprised anymore."

"Yeah, maybe," said Samuel.

• • •

Xander woke up and wiped the drool from his forearm.

For as long as he'd been at the abbey there had been the joke about Brother Andrew falling asleep at his post in the gatehouse.

"Hard to imagine a place more likely to put you to sleep than this box," thought Xander.

It had been his bright idea to coerce (all right, blackmail) Brother Andrew into letting them man the gate for a few days. What better way to be the first to witness the arrival of the abbot's brother.

If indeed the abbot actually had a brother. It was clear from the look in Brother Christopher's eyes every time the subject came up that there was something about this brother he wasn't telling them.

It then occurred to Xander, "Something woke me up."

He listened for a moment. What was that?

Turning the wick down on his little lantern, to better see out into the dark, he leaned forward and peered through the one tiny window in the guard cubicle. He heard a footstep—

A face filled the window. Xander yelled and smacked himself in the head with his hand.

"Oh!" said Thomas. "So sorry. I wasn't sure if anyone was in there, I tried knocking on the, um—Are you all right?"

"Yes," said Xander, rubbing his temple. "Just scared myself."

"Not your fault I've shown up at this ungodly hour."

"Are you Abbot's brother?" Xander blurted out. "Damn," he whispered. "Supposed to let Brother Christopher ask."

"What?" replied Thomas. "No, but I do have business with the abbot. And I do have"—Thomas slid the parcel out of his coat pocket and held it up to the opening—"a package to deliver. Though I know an hour before morning prayers is a terrible time to be waking him up."

Xander's eyes got big as saucers. He grabbed the lamp to see the parcel more clearly.

Thomas peeked in through the little window at the young man raising the wick back up on his lamp.

That can't be, he thought. Granted, I haven't seen a picture of the boys in four and a half years and they would be that much older. Not to mention, whichever one he might be—he couldn't possibly be the first person I run into here! But, I'll be damned if that's not—"Xander? Or Xavier?" asked Thomas.

"Yes. Xander," he replied. "Do I know you, sir?" Xander was even more surprised when the man before him began to laugh, slapping the ledge on the window.

"No, you don't know me, Xander," said Thomas. "But I know you. Or, at least, I know of you. From your—from Adi."

Xander stared. "Did you just say Adi?"

"I did."

"She died a long time ago."

"Well, Xander," said Thomas, trying to put this delicately. "It's hard to say if anyone is alive after this war, and I haven't seen her in several years, but I know for certain she was alive and well and searching for you, after you were told she'd died."

Xander furrowed his brow and chewed on a fingernail. "I have to . . . you should . . . Don't go anywhere." With that, he was through the little door behind him and gone.

"Well," said Thomas, wiping the drizzle from his forehead, "I guess I'm waiting here."

• • •

There was another problem with the motorcycle.

"I was afraid of that." Samuel switched off his flashlight. He tapped a fingernail on the little gauge. "A quarter tank. At most."

Adi reached for the kill switch on the handle bar. Samuel stopped her. "It'll take more to start it again than you're gonna save." He handed her a leather flyer's helmet and goggles and gloves. They were all large, but they would do.

"We can't siphon some gas out of . . . something?" said George.

"I'm telling you, they took everything." Samuel tapped the flashlight against the tank. "It might be enough."

"It might not," said George adjusting her goggles around her helmet. "Then where's she going to be?"

"Closer than she is now."

George looked into her eyes. "You won't let me go for you."

Adi shook her head.

"Listen, the Madelins . . . downriver. They still have horses, I'm sure . . ." He looked over to Samuel, who looked doubtful.

"All right. Damn it. Go then." He stepped away from the bike, and then immediately stepped back.

"It's just—the thing is, Adi—you're not so good at being somewhere when you say you're gonna be."

Adi pulled the goggles down over her eyes and pushed the bike forward off its kickstand. It started to stall until she adjusted the throttle.

"How the hell do you know how to ride a motorcycle?" George said.

She looked up at him through her lenses. Grabbing the front of his coat she pulled him over and kissed him on the mouth. He kissed her back.

She took a deep breath, straightened her googles once more, and off she went.

• • •

"He what?"

Brother Christopher was up and stepping into his sandals before Xander could answer. They were out the door and running down the corridor as fast as they could, trying not to make too much of a racket.

"He said," whispered Xander, running to keep up, "he thought Adi might still be alive. And he said, he had business with the abbot."

"That's what he said?"

"Yes. And—he's got one of the packages."

Brother Christopher skidded to a halt. "What?"

"I saw the address and everything."

Brother Christopher shook his head, assessing this new information.

"Go wake your brother. Meet at the rendezvous."

• • •

Abbot Berno was awake. He'd hardly slept a wink. He was lying on his cot thinking about porridge. How, if everything went as planned, he would never have to see another bowl of it. Never have to hear another dirging canticle, sung by discordant old men.

And, he thought, rubbing his eyes with the palms of his hands, never again will I have to hear the sound of my son sweeping outside my window.

• • •

Halick. The abbot didn't know him when he first arrived—why would he? He'd never laid eyes on the boy.

But in the small window of time before the war shut down the news, he'd heard the rumors that the son of the duchess of Alorainn had gone missing. He came upon a photograph of the royal family shortly after and he understood. The young man he'd found standing outside the gates of the abbey was his own child.

So many questions. Why had Halick gone missing? What had happened to his mind? And most mysterious and important— why had he been left at the abbot's doorstep?

The day after he appeared, Abbot Berno had packed his trunk, ready to get the hell out of there. Then the first of the boys' packages arrived and changed everything.

• • •

Twenty-three years earlier, Johanna's father, a professor of literature at Leiden University, had been pleased to have this charming young seminary student as his secretary. Nicolas Paul was hardworking and bright, and the professor paid him next to nothing. And being as the lad was practically a man of the cloth, the professor didn't have to be concerned for his daughter, whom he had certainly noticed was ripening into a great beauty.

Several months later, however, when Johanna began to show, she was sent away, "to look after an ailing aunt in Gloucester." And for the first time—but certainly not the last—Nicolas Paul would pack his trunk and relocate.

It was during his time at a Spanish monastery in Cantabria that he heard about Johanna's advantageous marriage into the Royal Family of Alorainn. How she had managed that, he could hardly guess.

Years later, after a few more aliases and many more stories to tell, he found himself in this latest incarnation as abbot of the Gentiana Abbey. It was not lost on him that he and Johanna had ended up living only miles apart.

He'd fantasized about visiting her, but had never acted upon the impulse. Though they might have plenty to talk about after all this time, it would be to no one's advantage.

• • •

When the brothers from the abbey met him at the train station for the first time, he felt like an actor stepping onto the stage. He actually threw up from panic right before the train pulled in.

He needn't have worried. He was brilliant. There were a few close calls, the odd slip. But he always talked his way around it.

Really, it was a shame he didn't enjoy it more. He wasn't a bad abbot, better than some of his predecessors. It was chiefly administration. Keep them busy and stop the brothers and the non-clerical staff from squabbling.

And didn't they all just love it when he did the upright Christian thing—taking in the poor orphaned twins, for instance. It was enough to make him believe in God. How else to explain this bounty being delivered unto him. After all, the packages did come marked *Care of Abbot Berno.*

"God knows I certainly didn't plan on this charade taking so long," he muttered. "Those damned boys, and the waiting. The waiting for that one more package!

"I won't be cursing them much longer. The first decent meal and expensive bottle of wine I lay hands on, I will raise a glass to them. And their mysterious benefactor.

"Or"—he laughed—"I'll be spending the rest of my life in prison. It all depends on the next few hours."

Which is why he'd had poor Brother Hilbert waiting all night in the shadows for the past three nights, to see who might appear at the gates.

Of course he knew about Brother Christopher and the boys and their late-night meanderings. They were amateurs, after all. What he didn't know for sure was, why?

"Isn't it always the simplest explanation, though?" he said

Brother Christopher was planning to make off with the loot. It was obvious. Maybe he was cutting the boys in? Probably not. Doesn't matter. "Everything is safe. Safe in my trunk. In the boot of the car. All ready to go."

Tucking his hands behind his head, the abbot listened to the rain beginning to come down. The sound of sweeping stopped briefly but then resumed.

"When does that boy ever sleep?"

What did concern the abbot, spoiling his sleep for weeks now, was that letter.

On the train, all those years ago, there had been no mention of a brother, though that was hardly conclusive. All of his quiet inquiries since had revealed an impressive number of sisters, but no proof of a living brother.

But Abbot Berno, or Nicolas Paul, or whatever he would be calling himself tomorrow, knew all about the lies and half-truths told in families. After his family found out about the woman and the child and the disintegration of his oh-so-promising career in the bishopric, he imagined that all mention of him had ceased, as surely as if he had died at birth.

It didn't matter. The real abbot's real brother. Or a fabricated one. It amounted to the same thing. Someone who could expose him.

A tap on the door.

"Father Abbot," whispered Brother Hilbert poking his head in, out of breath. "There's a man. A soldier. At the gate. He's got a package."

Chapter 39

"Where are you, Xander?"

Standing as close under the meager overhang as he could manage, Thomas shivered and watched his breath rise up through the now heavy rain.

"Where are you—and what happens now?"

As much as George, Thomas, and Augustin had discussed Adi's mad predicament over the years, they'd never had enough information to know what might happen to the twins if the time ran out. When it got to be 6:01 A.M. on November 11th, 1918.

"It's not as if they're going to simply—poof!—disappear," said Augustin. They all agreed with that.

But sometimes, Thomas wasn't so sure. Though school at the abbey had pretty much beaten it out of him, he was raised a good Catholic boy. Magical thinking was part of the package: walking on water, raising the dead, saints carrying their heads around in their hands. There was always a lot of weird business going on.

"I guess it would be too much to hope," said Thomas, "that Adi might show up. Wouldn't that be wonderful."

He heard a little rattle behind him and turned to see an eye peering through the peephole in the gate.

"Xander?" said Thomas. "Is that you?"

The gate opened with a creak, light shimmering through the rain. There stood a brother, one Thomas didn't recognize.

The man held the lantern up to get a better look. "I'm Brother Christopher," he said.

"And I am Thomas Hast. I do apologize for the hour."

"And I beg your pardon for keeping you standing out in this. Come in. I understand you have a package for Father Abbot?"

Thomas considered handing it over, but then thought better of it.

"Of course," said Brother Christopher, seeing him hesitate. "If you'll come with me I'll take you to his quarters." He opened the gate wide.

• • •

It had been several years since Thomas had lived in the abbey but it took no time at all for him to see that they weren't going anywhere near the abbot's little house.

"Could have moved," thought Thomas.

But as they passed through the cloisters and the back garden, down the stairs to the old chapel, that possibility became highly unlikely.

"I'm pretty certain he's not sleeping in here," thought Thomas, looking up at the crumbling stone façade. Brother Christopher let them in and got the door shut just ahead of a powerful gale. The lantern nearly blew out as he shut the great wooden door behind them. Brother Christopher was going on about the fire that had burned a good deal of the structure back when the place was a nunnery.

The scaffolding on both walls of the long narrow chapel creaked and rattled from the wind flapping through the oilcloths in the unfinished windows above them. As they passed down the center aisle, the circle of light from their lantern lit the remnants of grotesque medieval faces on the frescoed walls.

"Excuse me, Brother," Thomas said, "These paintings—might I have the lantern for a moment?"

With reluctance Brother Christopher handed it over. Thomas placed the lamp upon a creaking shelf.

And then without warning, he grabbed the front of the brother's robe and slammed him against one of the scaffold supports. The lantern rocked on the ledge, sending crazy shadows slashing across the walls. From under the brother's cassock, a tiny derringer clattered to the floor.

Thomas kicked it away and had his own out and pointed before the man could blink twice.

"Sorry, Brother," said Thomas, as the door blew open at the end of the room. "But there's a few too many odd things going on here. Start by telling me where you're taking me and why you thought you needed a gun to do it?"

"You don't understand," Brother Christopher said. "I was trying to—"

Footsteps in the shadows, a hammer cocked right behind Thomas's head. He looked back to see Brother Hilbert holding a pistol.

"Trying to, what, Brother?" said Abbot Berno, stepping into the light.

• • •

Having a reasonably good idea of how to start the engine, Adi had persuaded George and Samuel (and herself) that she knew what the hell she was doing on this machine.

She made it out of the carport—and out of their sight—before she went off the cobblestones into the garden. Barely avoiding a fountain, she kept the bike from stalling and made it back up onto the drive just before the gates. She nearly killed herself a half dozen more times in the first mile. All she could think about was how much of her precious fuel she was burning.

It got better. The brakes on the thing seemed next to useless. And the wind, weaseling its way into any tiny opening in her coat, cut like a knife. But once she figured out how to work the throttle, she realized she was hurtling along like a rocket, sweeping away the miles.

Ahead on the right—There! The sign for Gentiana Abbey. Five kilometers! She could do this!

That's when the mist turned to rain and Samuel's beautiful orange motorcycle drank its last drop of petrol.

• • •

The abbot directed Brother Hilbert to take Thomas's pistol.

"Let's see who we have here," said the abbot. Taking Thomas's pistol from Brother Hilbert, he turned Thomas toward the light.

"I'll be damned—it's—what was it? Thomas Hast! I never forget a name. And look at you. All grown up. You're looking well, Thomas. How've you been?"

"A bit confused at the moment, Father Abbot."

"Yes," said the abbot, his smile fading. "These are confusing times." He wiped some of the rain from his head. "I understand you have a package for me?"

Thomas took the package from his pocket. He'd never actually looked at the address. He tilted it toward the lamp.

"It's for Xander and Xavier?" he said, staring down at it, incredulous.

"Why is this news to you?" said the abbot. He snatched the package from Thomas's hands and dropped it into the pocket of his robe.

Just then, carried on the wind, there came the sound of people shouting. Abbot Berno cocked his head to listen but it was too faint to make out.

"Doesn't matter," he said. "Time for you all to be gone."

"Father Abbot?" said Brother Hilbert timorously. "Shouldn't we wake the brethren and tell them—?"

"Tell them what?" said the abbot, turning his gun on the man.

Brother Hilbert emitted a little shriek.

But it wasn't because of the gun.

The upside-down face of Xavier materialized from the darkness, followed in a flash by the crack of a cricket bat to the side of the abbot's head.

Down he went, dropping the pistol. He clutched his head in pain. Brother Christopher snatched the gun from Brother Hilbert, provoking another squawk from him. Xavier flipped over and dropped from the scaffolding to the floor, followed immediately by Xander.

"Good job, boys!" said Brother Christopher, picking up the abbot's gun.

"Is this the man?" asked Xavier, pointing to Thomas. "You know Adi?"

"We'll get to that," said Brother Christopher. "Help Father Abbot to his feet. Though maybe we should start calling him by his real name, Nicolas Paul."

Xavier leaned over to help the big man up. In that instant it occurred to Thomas that the derringer was unaccounted for.

"Call me whatever you like, Brother," said the abbot. Derringer in hand, he grabbed Xavier and held the gun to his ear. "Ah, ah!" he said to Thomas and Brother Christopher. "Your guns. Down there." He pointed his chin to the far end of the hall.

"That derringer's only got one bullet," said Brother Christopher, still holding his gun on the abbot.

"It will be a comfort, then, that you have another twin to replace this one," said the abbot, tapping the barrel on Xavier's head.

Thomas and Brother Christopher looked to one another and Xavier. No one could argue with the abbot's logic. They tossed the pistols away.

"Walk me to the door, Xavier," said the abbot. They moved away up the aisle but then stopped. The abbot looked back at Brother Christopher.

"How did you know?"

"Seven years ago," said Brother Christopher. "When you were met by the monks at the train station. You didn't know I was there, looking on. I hadn't seen my older brother in years. I was going to surprise him. Imagine my . . . bewilderment, at seeing you introduce yourself."

"I'll be damned," said the abbot.

"No doubt," said Brother Christopher.

Holding tight to Xavier's collar, Abbot Berno marched the lad along till they reached the door, wide open, rain blowing in with the tempest.

"Listen," Thomas said.

They could make out the shouting now.

"Fire! Abbot's house, on fire!"

• • •

The abbot slammed the doors behind them and casting about, pointed at a piece of lumber on a pile of rubble to the right of the entrance. Xavier hesitated.

"Don't cross me, boy," he said, his customary avuncular tone gone.

Xavier picked up the board. The abbot grabbed it from him and jammed it into the door handles.

"Now come on," he barked.

Up the stairs they ran, the abbot pushing Xavier whenever he slowed.

As they came out from the cloisters, brothers were staggering out of the dormitory, rubbing their eyes, pulling on robes.

A brother turned and spotted them. "Father Abbot!" he yelled.

The abbot wrapped his finger around the trigger of the tiny derringer hidden just beneath his sleeve.

"Thank God, Father! You're all right! We thought—" He ran off shouting, "Abbot's safe! He's not inside!"

Coming around the library, they saw bright flames pouring from the back of the abbot's little two-room house. Several of the brothers were attempting to organize a bucket brigade from the well in the courtyard.

"Perfect," muttered the abbot. "I'll get to the car. And away I'll go."

Several more brothers came running up to them. Xavier broke away from the abbot and ran, circling back to the chapel. Short of firing at the boy, there was nothing the abbot could do to stop him. "Doesn't matter," he said, pocketing the derringer.

Standing with his back to the great yew tree in the center of the courtyard, the abbot took one last look at his home of seven years and heard an unfamiliar voice.

"It's not in the car."

He turned to find Halick, broom in hand, shadowed by the branches of the great tree.

"What?" said the abbot.

"Your trunk," said Halick, quietly. "It's not in the boot anymore." He closed his eyes and turned his face to the rain. "I put it back safe. In the closet."

Nicolas Paul stared at his son, searching for some sign of misunderstanding, some indication that his defective brain was getting the words wrong. The boy lowered his head, tears of rain running down his cheeks. He turned to his father and smiled.

• • •

They came around past the library: Thomas, Brother Christopher, and the boys. Xander spotted the abbot first amidst the chaos. "There!" he shouted.

The abbot had thrown open the door of the little house, and was standing looking in at the smoke and flame. Halick, dancing wildly about, laughed and brandished his broom at any of the brothers who got too close. Finally with a hoot, he threw the broom high into the air. Shoving his father into the house before him, he followed and slammed shut the door.

• • •

Coal listened to the screams. Everyone around him, crying and shouting.

You should be crying. You have no idea what trouble will come from this. There'll be no Halick with a pistol. No assassinated prime minister. Or was it to have been the queen? The pictures grew fainter in his mind. The war would not happen the way it was supposed to.

How many times he'd tried to explain to Dr. Bleuler: to keep the balloon from bursting, you've got to keep letting a little air out.

"And what is this 'air' that's filling the balloon?" asked the doctor.

"Human . . . malevolence, maybe? What do I know?" said Coal. "I'm only the piano player."

Flames poured from the windows. Years of plans and improvisation up in smoke. All three of them gone. The duchess. And now the abbot and Halick. All done.

Nothing to even put in a jar. Just ashes.

And you're surprised? Coal said to himself. The way you've behaved. The way you've always behaved. You and your never ceasing carelessness? He stuck his hands deep in the frayed pockets of his coat, jangling the last of the gold coins.

His last minutes were ticking away. The girl had not, would not, could not, get here in time.

"To hell with it," he said. "Ashes. Better that way." He pulled up his collar and turned to leave. Then stopped.

A few feet away, Xander and Xavier, one of them with an arm around the other's shoulder, were staring at the flames. The courtyard was chaos and confusion, professors and brothers and students were working to form a bucket line from the well.

"Boys?" said Coal. They didn't hear over the noise. "Xander! Xavier!" he called.

They turned and saw him there. "Yes, Professor Coal?"

"Come with me. I need your help."

Chapter 40

She tried to get the engine to fire up again. But short of turning the rain to petrol, she knew it wasn't going to happen. Wheeling the bike off the road, she leaned it against a stone wall and clicked off the headlight. The woods returned to a drizzly gray.

She left the goggles on the handlebars, but kept the helmet and gloves for warmth.

She ran.

Nearly an hour later, all uphill now, Adi stood in the middle of the road, leaning on her knees, fighting to catch a breath, trying to ignore how long it had been since she had had anything to eat.

Twenty-four minutes left. No matter how fast she ran, she wasn't going to make it before six. She clicked the watch shut, rain dripping from the brim of her flyer's helmet. She'd seen the towers of the abbey and the smoke rising over the treetops. She took a breath and kept going.

• • •

"What do you mean you can't find them?" said Thomas. "They— they were just here."

Brother Christopher, surprised at Thomas's degree of panic, said, "Don't worry. They're around somewhere."

Thomas passed the bucket along the line. He'd meant to not take his eyes off the boys, but with all the goings on, he'd lost track of them.

The urgency to put out the fire had turned to spiritless labor. There was no one coming out of that house alive. The rain was doing more now to quench the flames than the one or two buckets at a time.

"Do me a favor, Brother," said Thomas. "Could we go and find them? I'll explain later, but I need to know they're all right."

"Of course. We're not doing much good here."

Making a wide circle around the fire, Brother Christopher called to a group of boys staring blankly at the flames. "Paul? Taddy? Anybody seen the twins?"

A younger boy in the back said, "I saw them, Brother. A few minutes ago, at the front gate. With Professor Coal."

"Good work, René," said Brother Christopher. "Would you boys go put some coats on before you freeze to death out here." They nodded, but didn't take their eyes off the fire.

"Coal?" said Thomas. "The—history teacher?"

"You remember him?"

"I think. Wasn't here long before I graduated. Never had him."

"Odd man," said Brother Christopher. "Good teacher, though. He talks about Napoleon, you feel like he was right there. He's been gone a lot. Off to serve, don't know where. Got wounded. Doesn't talk about it. You know."

They got to the front gate. No Xander and Xavier. No Professor Coal either. There were, however, a score of students and brothers gathered around the statue of Saint Alberic.

• • •

Adi saw it as she stumbled around the curve. A spark on the far side of the road, a golden fairy light in the mud, charming her away from the real world. There's no time for this. She could hardly put one foot in front of the next.

But—there was no time anyway. Eighteen minutes left.

She trudged across the road, and leaned over to see.

It was four and a half years since she'd laid eyes on a coin like this. 1786. But even in the dim light she knew what it was. Her mind, tired as it had ever been, calculated the odds of this coin being here independent of Coal.

She couldn't know that at that same moment, a half hour up the hill, Thomas and Brother Christopher and a group of students were all staring down at the same gold coins in a circle (with a ring of emeralds and diamonds next to them) scattered around the marble feet of Saint Alberic—Halick's final act before soldering his soul for eternity to the man who had been his father.

Not that Halick had anything to do with the coin at Adi's feet. The material in Coal's pocket had just finally lost the battle with the caltrops.

What's it doing over here? thought Adi, rubbing the coin with her thumb. Assuming he dropped it on his way to the abbey—wouldn't it be—?

Then she spied the footprints, lots of them, scuffling through the mud, heading off the road. Not to the abbey, but from.

Looking through the woods, a twinkling through the trees, Adi saw the silhouette of the house and gave up fighting her intuition. Dropping the coin in her pocket, she headed for the light.

Chapter 41

The ground, littered with seasons of rotted chestnut shells, slowed her down. The trees were overgrown now, and run wild. But they'd been planted in rows, an orchard once.

It was a fine-looking house, even in the dawn, but it had fallen on hard times. Through a gate she stepped into the yard piled high with leaves and fallen branches.

The front door was boarded over. Another door under an eave to the left was nailed shut.

The seconds were ticking. She should have stayed on the road.

She stepped back a few feet and looked up to the roof. Traces of smoke were coming from a small chimney on the far side. Even as she watched, the amount of smoke increased, turning from gray to black. She caught a light through a slit between the curtains.

She continued around the house. Only windows on the left side, either shuttered or curtained or with glass too filthy to see through.

Around the back, a little porch swamped in leaves. Clambering up the steps, she tried the door. Locked. There were narrow windows on either side, as grimy and impenetrable as the others.

No time for good manners. If it's someone else's house, she'll apologize.

Stepping back on her right foot she slammed her boot heel through the panes. Glass and rotten wood gave way. Reaching her hand in, she felt about for the lock, threw it, and pushed the door open. She listened. Just the sounds that houses make.

A small entry hall. Three doors. Left, right, and straight ahead. The smell of smoke, stronger now.

The door on the left was not locked. But it was only a shallow closet with a mop in a bucket.

No such luck on the second door. In addition to a keyhole lock, there were two more great iron padlocks. Leaning down she peered through the keyhole. Dimly illuminated by moldy skylights, she could make out a hallway stretching off into darkness, doors running the length on either side. Strangely, the hallway had the appearance of being too long to fit within the house.

A bump, the sound of creaking floorboards through the door to her right. Smoke was trickling out along the top. No time to search for another way in, she sized up the door. Paint peeling, worn wood, a rusted old mortise lock.

She slammed her shoulder hard into it and nearly swooned from the pain. Wrong shoulder. Leaning her head against the door to recover, she thought to turn the knob.

It wasn't locked.

She nudged the door open. Acrid smoke whorled around her, blocking the top of the narrow corridor. She ducked down and made her way through the debris piled up along the walls on either side: books, figurines, clocks, birdcages, piles of shoes, and stacks of dirty dishes. She took a peek around the corner at the end of the passageway.

Much of the furniture in the drawing room had been pushed aside to accommodate a huge piano. Like the rest of the room, it was covered with rubbish.

She almost missed the boys, dumped in a heap onto the chaise longue along with a pile of shirts and socks. She ran to them, the canopy of smoke just above her head now. Besides the smoke, there was a sweet chemical odor of—chloroform! Tipped over on the floor, a bottle and a handkerchief. She shoved the cork in the bottle and pulled the pile of shirts down on the spill.

She pulled off her helmet and gloves and reached out to touch the boys' cheeks. One of them groaned. Alive, but there was no time to examine them further. From the next room—the source of the smoke—came the crackling of a fire and the sound of a kettle coming to boil.

Adi ran low across the room and stuck her head into the kitchen.

In the far corner, rising out of a pile of broken furniture and what appeared to be the contents of a man's clothes closet, the flames were a breath away from reaching the curtains covering the windows.

And there, past the table and chairs, on the floor next to the stove, sat Coal. He slouched against the wall, ripping pages out of a magazine, crumpling and tossing them into the fire.

Seeing something out of the corner of his eye, Coal turned and froze, looking as if he'd seen a ghost. The kettle screamed.

Pushing past him, Adi caught hold of the curtains and tore them loose from the rods, out of the path of the flames. She snatched the kettle from the stove, got as close as she could to the flames and poured.

It wasn't enough.

Tossing the kettle aside with a clang and a clatter, she started plucking dishes out of the sink, crashing them to the floor, until she found a pot, full of fetid water. She pulled it out and threw it on the flames. But the fire still grew.

This wasn't working! Could she drag the boys out of the house? Was there time? Did she have the strength?

Just then, behind her.

"Sir! Stand clear!" A hand grabbed her shoulder. Pulled her back. One of her brothers, looking a bit groggy, tottered across the kitchen and dumped a full bucket of water onto the flames. With a great *whoosh!* the fire surrendered.

"Not a bad thing, a leaky ceiling!" said one of the boys, banging on the empty pail.

The other one didn't respond. He stood stock-still staring at Adi.

She threw the window latch and pushed the casement open. A blast of cold November air blew into the room, fluttering magazine pages, scattering the smoke. Now, both of the boys stared.

"Xander," said Xavier. "He—Thomas was right! It's—"

From out of the smoke and shadow, eyes blazing, Coal rose up before them, higher and higher until he seemed to scrape the ceiling.

Adi moved between him and the boys.

But, just as quickly, with a cough and a groan, the man fell into his chair at the kitchen table. From under a crow's wing of black hair he stared up at them, his eyes bruised and runny, a sickly stain darkening the shoulder of his coat.

Muttering to himself, he dug around in the dishes on the table until he found his cigarettes and lighter.

Adi pulled the watch from around her neck and opened it.

Seconds remained. Twenty-four, twenty-three, twenty-two . . . She held it out to the man.

A cigarette hanging from his lips, Coal looked at the watch, clicking his lighter to no effect.

Adi snatched the lighter and the pack of smokes and tossed the lot into the sink. Leaning over, she swept everything away: the books, the cups and dishes crashed to the floor. The boys stared wide-eyed as she slammed the watch down on the empty table. A saucer gyrated on the floor in accelerating circles until, finally it stopped.

Coal looked up at the girl, watching her as she listened to the house moan and creak through the walls, as if these indignities were the last it could bear. There was a popping and cracking sound like marbles bouncing on a wooden floor.

"Don't you know, Adi Dahl," said Coal, nodding his head toward the pile of wet wood filling the corner. "I always have a backup plan."

It took a second. With a gasp of comprehension, Adi grabbed the boys and shoved them toward the open window.

With the tip of his last cigarette, Coal spun the watch around on the table.

"'Tis a consummation,'" he said, with a cough, "'devoutly to be wished. To die, to sleep—To sleep—perchance to dream.'"

He looked over at Adi, the last out the window. Glass began to explode in the back of the house.

"But . . . not just yet," he said and picked up the watch.

Chapter 42

When Xavier told the story, he always claimed he saw sparks flash as Coal's hand touched the watch. Xander said it might have had something to do with the ceiling collapsing. The last thing Adi remembered was flying backward out of the kitchen window.

• • •

They pulled her to safety and watched through the trees as the house burned, like a torch blazing in the dark. Even the chimneys seemed on fire. Wet branches of chestnut trees hissed and steamed in a circle around it, nearly covering the sound of glass popping and cracking in the heat.

• • •

When Adi woke she was on a horse. A dapple gray, stippled across the neck with black spots, like ink flung against a wall.

The dawn was ambling along behind the trees, the sun in no more of a rush to rise this day than on any other day.

Walking ahead of them, a few yards up the road, Adi saw Thomas and a man in a brother's robe. Between them were the boys, even from behind beautiful and tall.

• • •

There were arms crossed in front of her, holding the reins. Adi looked up and saw George's face. She was leaning against his chest, his coat swaddled around her. She looked at him as if it were the first time she'd seen him. Though she thought that seemed to be the case every time she had.

"You . . . found a horse," said Adi in a voice so light and fine, you wouldn't guess it had been tucked away all this time.

George smiled and shook his head and wrapped his arms tight around her. Laying her head back on his shoulder, Adi closed her eyes. She slept and dreamed of blue sky through wisteria.

Epilogue

In the forest of Compiègne, a couple of hours north of Paris, the soldiers on guard duty came to attention as the door at the end of the train car cracked open. A ray of warm light leaked out into the gray morning. A crow circled and landed on a branch at the edge of the clearing.

The Germans came out of the train first, followed by the French and the British. They paused on the coach steps for a photographer to document the event. With no farewell, the Allies went for a walk in the woods.

The Germans stood around the train car, saying nothing. One of them tried to light a cigarette but broke down, his shoulders heaving. His colleagues looked away to give him a moment. When he recovered, they walked back to their train car on the second line.

● ● ●

Done.

Coal sat on the ground and leaned his head against the tree, not caring about the drizzle or the wet leaves soaking through his suit. It was a relief to not have his shoulder hurt any more, but it hardly mattered. He was a candle guttering out. As the doors on the train cars shut one after another, he closed his eyes. "Just for a moment."

In the morning showers, he didn't hear the train engines start up and pull away, one to the north, one to the south. Nor did he meditate on the reception that each would receive arriving at its destination.

• • •

It was cold in northern France during the winter of 1918. There was snow in December, the rivers froze for a time in January. But the spring came and with it a spray of feverfew and toothwort and yellow foxglove, until the volunteer pines in a circle around him got full enough to steal the light.

The clothes he wore fell apart after a few years to be replaced by moss and lichen and creeping vines. Mushrooms and toadstools: milkcaps, pinkgills, pale brittle stems, and jelly fungi grew wherever soil filled the hollows. In the fall, the watch resting in the palm of his hand was often circled by a fairy ring of tiny yellow mushrooms. If it inconvenienced him to have starlings nest beneath his neck for consecutive springs, it didn't show. They quit coming when a skulk of foxes moved into the neighborhood and began to eat the eggs. Though this didn't bother the doves who, except in the dead of winter, cooed every morning under the eves.

• • •

One day, many years after the Great War (twenty-two years, or 681,523,055 seconds to be precise), a boy came to see what the commotion was about at the park near the little train car museum not far from his home.

Through the trees he saw that someone had knocked down a wall of the museum and dragged the train coach out into the square. There were automobiles and reporters and cameras and row upon row of shiny German soldiers standing at attention. In the middle of it all was a German officer, his smile nearly hidden beneath his toothbrush moustache. He stepped up into the train car, followed a moment later by a forlorn French general.

Trying to better his view, the boy stumbled and fell into the brush. Looking up, he saw some sort of statue. Nothing like the big statue of the French general standing on the far side of the park. This was a seated man, covered in branches and leaves, tucked right in with the trees.

There was a glint of gold in the palm of its hand, maybe just tiny yellow mushrooms. The boy tried to scrape it loose from the moss and dirt. Fingers closed around his tiny hand. With a yelp, he fell back on the ground. The statue's eyes opened.

The boy cried most of the way home.

By the time he returned, in the company of his older brothers, the crowd in the park was gone. The only ones left were men with huge hammers, smashing the French monuments. They were even hauling away the train car.

Whatever the boy had seen in the wood was gone as well. There was now only a hollow in the weeds, swarming with grubs and beetles, blanched for want of sun. By the time the boy's brothers, in their boots, had inspected the thicket, any trace of the footprints that had walked away were gone.

Acknowledgments

Several years back I spent a week at Esalen talking fairy tales with Brother David Steindl-Rast. *Silent* is the tree that's grown from the seed, Brother.

Many thanks to the wonderful people at Merit Press, Meredith O'Hayre, Frank Rivera, and my oh-so-invaluable copyeditor, Suzanne Goraj—and most especially my editor, Jacquelyn Mitchard, a great writer, who, as I'd always hoped an editor might do, found my book wandering in the woods and brought it home.

Thank you to all my dear friends who listened and read: Jack and Roberta Forem, Carolyn Yost and Larry Barber, Tinker Lindsay, Peter Chelsom, John Albanis, Fred Joyal, Jaci Sisson, Jackie Jaffee, Suzy Hertzberg, Michael Sigman, Selby Anderson, Carol Kline, and Scott Colglazier (who was there that week with Brother David).

Many thanks to the UCLA Extension Writers' Program that introduced me to the redoubtable Laurel van der Linde. Thank you, Laurel.

Thank you to Lin Oliver and Stephen Mooser and all of the people at the Society of Children's Book Writers and Illustrators (SCBWI).

Thanks to my mom and dad for their unwavering love and support. And to my brother Lance, who can do a heck of a shoulder stand in full lotus—but probably shouldn't.

And endless gratitude to my brilliant writer's group: Kristen Baum, Manisha Patel, Janine Pibal, Margaret Tellez, Mary Lynne Raske, and our glorious leader, Sheila Sobel. I guess you could write a book without a group, but I sure wouldn't want to have to.

To my brother Christopher. Working on the book with you is a pretty good picture of what heaven might be like. Thanks, brother.

Finally, to my beautiful Judith, I could not have done it without you.

About the Author

David Mellon has been painting pictures and drawing storyboards for TV and film for thirty-five years. He lives in Los Angeles with his wife Judith. This is his first novel.